RAMAGE

& The Dido

Other Titles by Dudley Pope published by McBooks Press

For a complete list of nautical and military fiction
published by McBooks Press, please see pages 285-287.

RAMAGE

& The Dido

by

DUDLEY POPE

THE LORD RAMAGE NOVELS, NO.18

MCBOOKS PRESS, INC.
ITHACA, NEW YORK

T 98102

F Pope

Published by McBooks Press 2002
Copyright © 1989 by Dudley Pope
First published in the United Kingdom by
The Alison Press/Martin Secker & Warburg Ltd., 1989

Cover painting by Paul Wright.

Library of Congress Cataloging-in-Publication Data

Pope, Dudley.
  Ramage & the Dido / by Dudley Pope.
      p. cm. — (The Lord Ramage novels ; no. 18)
  Originally published as Ramage and the Dido.
  ISBN 1-59013-024-3 (alk. paper)
  1. Ramage, Nicholas (Fictitious character)—Fiction. 2. Great Britain—History, Naval—19th century—Fiction. 3. Napoleonic Wars, 1800-1815—Fiction. 4. Ship captains—Fiction. 5. Women slaves—Fiction. 6. Martinique—Fiction. I. Title.
  PR6066.O5 R257 2002
  823'.914—dc21

                                        2002010209

Distributed to the trade by National Book Network, Inc., 15200 NBN Way, Blue Ridge Summit, PA 17214 800-462-6420

Additional copies of this book may be ordered from any bookstore or directly from McBooks Press, Inc., ID Booth Building, 520 North Meadow St., Ithaca, NY 14850. Please include $4.00 postage and handling with mail orders. New York State residents must add sales tax to total remittance (books & shipping). All McBooks Press publications can also be ordered by calling toll-free 1-888-BOOKS11 (1-888-266-5711). Please call to request a free catalog.

Visit the McBooks Press website at www.mcbooks.com.

Printed in the United States of America

9 8 7 6 5 4 3 2

To Jane Clare Victoria
With much love

A U T H O R ' S   N O T E

I HAVE TAKEN a liberty with one historical fact. A French frigate carrying the first mango plants from Mauritius to Martinique was captured by the British frigate *Flora*, Captain Marshall, one of Rodney's squadron, in 1782 and taken to Jamaica.

DUDLEY POPE
French West Indies

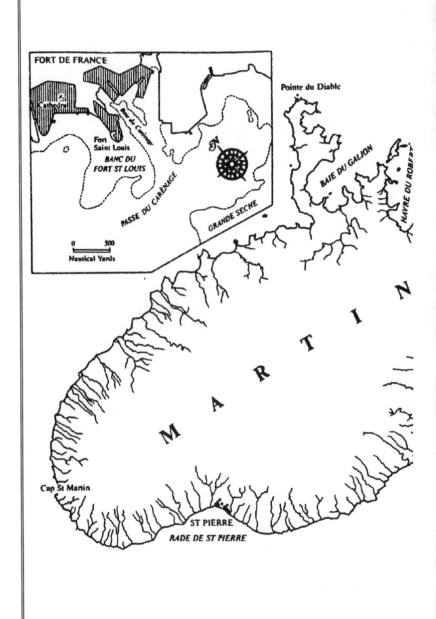

FORT DE FRANCE

Cathedral

Fort
Saint Louis
BANC DU
FORT ST LOUIS

Banc du Carénage

PASSE DU CARÉNAGE

GRANDE SECHE

0   500
Nautical Yards

Pointe du Diable

BAIE DU GALION

HAVRE DU ROBERT

M A R T I N

Cap St Martin

ST PIERRE
RADE DE ST PIERRE

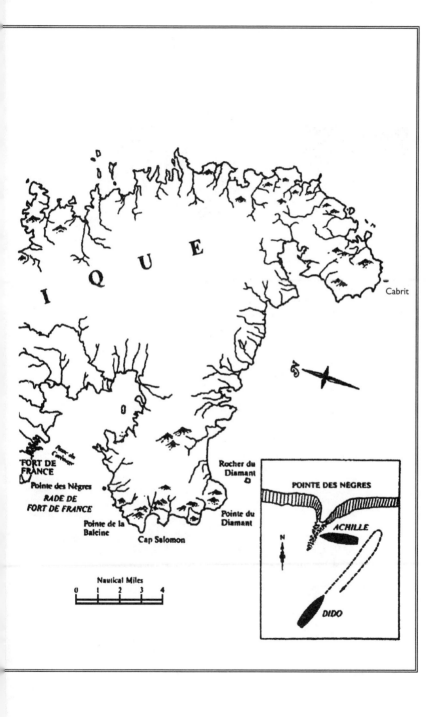

I Q U E

Cabrit

FORT DE
FRANCE

Pointe des Nègres

RADE DE
FORT DE FRANCE

Pointe de la
Baleine

Cap Salomon

Rocher du
Diamant

Pointe du
Diamant

Nautical Miles

0   1   2   3   4

POINTE DES NEGRES

ACHILLE

N

DIDO

CHAPTER ONE

RAMAGE folded the *Morning Post* and sat back comfortably. There was very little news in the paper, and he passed it to Sarah, who was an avid newspaper reader and had already finished *The Times* and sniffed at the lack of anything of interest.

He had another five days' leave; time enough to go down to Aldington and have a look at the Kent countryside, apart from reassuring himself that all was well with the house, although Sarah had been staying there most of the time he was away in the Mediterranean, only coming up to London in a hurry when she heard that he had arrived back in Portsmouth.

His parents' home in Palace Street was a serviceable halfway house for both of them. It was also conveniently near the Admiralty and even nearer the House of Lords, so that his father, the Earl of Blazey, could attend debates whenever he wished.

Ramage was vaguely aware of a horse pulling up outside the front door, although the sound of passing horses clopping their way along Palace Street was nothing out of the ordinary, but a few minutes later the old butler, Hanson, appeared at the door, his spectacles sliding down his nose as usual.

"An Admiralty messenger, my lord: he has a letter for you and needs you to sign a receipt."

Ramage nodded and went to the front door, signing the proffered receipt book and taking the letter. It felt strange, heavy and stiff, as though the paper with its heavy seal enclosed a sheet of parchment. He shrugged his shoulders as he walked back to the breakfast room to rejoin Sarah, who looked up inquiringly.

"Probably fresh orders," he said and, noting the alarmed look on Sarah's face, added: "I doubt if they're urgent; Their Lordships know I haven't had much leave in the past few years."

Sarah walked over to the desk and came back with a paper-knife. "Break the seal and put a stop to the suspense," she said. "I couldn't bear it if you have to go away again so soon."

Ramage was reluctant to hurry: the sheer weight of the packet did not bode well. Routine letters were not written in parchment, and this packet crackled when he squeezed it. He took the paper-knife and pried open the outer seal, and the folded paper opened by itself to reveal a parchment commission inside. He recognized it immediately—but a commission? What was happening to the *Calypso* frigate, which he had commanded for the past few years? She was even now waiting for him down at Portsmouth, under the temporary command of her first lieutenant, James Aitken.

But there was no mistaking the document: there was the Admiralty Office seal at the top left-hand corner, red wax with white paper on top; the blue stamp duty seal below it, with "11 shillings and 10 pence" and a crown; and three signatures beneath the verbiage in the middle. Yes, it was a commission right enough, but sending him where, and in what ship?

He began reading, starting with the first few lines at the top. "By the Commission for Executing the Office of Lord High Admiral of the United Kingdom of Great Britain and Ireland, &c."

Then came the main section of the commission: "By virtue of the Power and Authority to us given, We do hereby appoint you Captain of his Majesty's ship the *Dido*, willing and requiring you forthwith to go on board and take upon you the charge and command of captain in her accordingly: strictly Charging and Commanding all the Officers and Company of the said ship to behave themselves jointly and severally in their respective employments . . . Hereof nor you nor any of you may fail as you will answer to the Contrary at your Peril . . ."

It ended with "By command of Their Lordships" and the signature of Evan Nepean, the secretary to the Board, on the left, and the signatures of three Board members on the right.

The *Dido?* But wasn't she a 74? He had a fleeting picture in his mind of seeing her in Gibraltar some time ago. Command of a 74!

"Why are you grinning?" Sarah asked quietly, obviously fearing the worst.

"I think I've just been given command of a 74," he said. "Let me find a copy of *Steel's List* and check the name."

His father's copy of *Steel's Original and Correct List of the Royal Navy* was on the desk, a thin grey-covered volume. He flipped through the pages until he came to the one headed "A Complete List of the Royal Navy," where all the ships, from the 112-gun *Salvador del Mundo* to hired armed cutters and luggers, were named alphabetically. Yes, there was the *Dido,* at present in Portsmouth and built in 1798. She had been paid off, and obviously he would have to commission her.

He felt a sudden nostalgia for the *Calypso.* And what was going to happen to all the officers and men with whom he had sailed for so long? He would be lost without the old master, Southwick, who had served with him since he had been given his first command as a callow lieutenant in the Mediterranean so many years ago. And the Scot, Aitken, who had once refused a command to continue serving with him. And "Blower" Martin, the junior lieutenant with his flute. And seamen like Jackson, Stafford, and Rossi. Thinking of them took the shine off the new appointment.

"This is a big promotion," Sarah said. "Your father will be

pleased. Getting command of a second rate at your age . . ."

"Third rate," Ramage corrected. "It'll be a few more years before I get the chance of a second rate."

Sarah shrugged her shoulders. "I never did understand 'rates,'" she admitted.

"It's just a matter of the number of guns a ship carries. A first rate has 100 guns or more, a second rate between 98 and 90, a third rate from 80 to 64. . . . The *Calypso* is a fifth rate with 32 guns, and last of all comes a sixth rate, between 30 and 20 guns."

Again Sarah looked puzzled. "I know this is a dreadful thing for the wife of a post captain to admit, but the number of guns does not mean very much. How big is the ship? How many men does she carry?"

"Well, 74s vary slightly—the later ones are larger—but the *Dido* is probably about one hundred and seventy feet long on the gun-deck, has a ship's company of about six hundred, and is around one thousand seven hundred tons—more when she is provisioned for six months, of course. Now can you picture her better?"

"Not really. Will I be allowed on board to visit you?"

"Of course. You'll have to come down to Portsmouth—but there'll be plenty of time: I've got to commission the ship."

At that moment Ramage's father came into the room and wished them both a cheerful good morning. Almost immediately he saw the commission lying on the table, along with a copy of *Steel's List,* and recognizing both he looked questioningly at his son. "You've heard from the Admiralty?"

"Yes, Their Lordships have given me a new ship."

"Oh. You'll be sorry to leave the *Calypso*—she's become a second home!"

"Yes—but they've given me a 74."

"Ha, at last Their Lordships have woken up to your worth!

It was probably that last cruise in the Mediterranean that did it. After all, they gave you a whole *Gazette* to yourself for winkling out those Saracens. What ship?"

"The *Dido*. I have to commission her at Portsmouth."

"*Dido?* She's only seven or eight years old—I remember her being launched at Bursledon. Well, having to commission her is as good a way as any of getting to know your way round a two-decker. You'll be at the mercy of your first lieutenant and master—d'you know who they'll be?"

Ramage shook his head. "All I have at the moment is the commission. I found out she was at Portsmouth from Steel. I don't know whether commissioning just means assembling the ship's company and provisioning, or getting the masts in and rigging her."

The earl smoothed down his white hair and held out his hand. "Well, whatever it is, congratulations. It won't be long before they give you a second rate. Then you'll get your flag!"

Ramage shook his hand and both men sat down again. The earl looked round at Sarah. "Well, my dear, so it is good-bye to frigates. What's it feel like now, being married to a man who is going to command a ship of the line?"

"He'll miss all the men on board the *Calypso*," Sarah said. "It seems a pity that the captain has to start all over again when he changes ships."

"Yes, it is a big change," the earl agreed. "Six hundred or so men instead of a couple of hundred. A really big ship to handle."

Sarah held up her hands apologetically. "Nicholas has just explained to me what a 'rate' is. But tell me, what is the difference between a frigate and a ship of the line, apart from its size and the number of men?"

"Its job, mainly," the earl said. "A frigate is a scout—it acts as the admiral's eyes when working with a fleet, or it does all those jobs that Nicholas has been doing for the past few years. But a ship of the line is just that—a ship that forms part of the line of battle when the fleet is in action. At Trafalgar, the frigates were supposed to stay out of the fight and repeat signals—the classic task for a frigate in battle, not getting involved in the shooting. Nicholas, of course, had to break the rules and get himself into the action, but normally the line of battle will be formed with ships of 74 guns or more. There are still a few 64s around, but they are being replaced because they are not powerful enough to stand in the line of battle."

"So if Nicholas had been given the *Dido* in time, he could have been in the line of battle at Trafalgar?" Sarah asked.

"Yes. Being him, he made up for it with the *Calypso*, but if there is another Trafalgar and Nicholas is part of the fleet concerned, yes, he will be in the line of battle."

"It sounds a dangerous job."

The earl laughed. "No, on the contrary. A captain stands much more chance of being killed in a frigate action than the captain of a ship of the line in a battle like Trafalgar. Just think of the numbers—on board a frigate he is one of a couple of hundred; in a ship of the line he is one of six hundred or so."

"Lord Nelson was killed," Sarah pointed out.

"Yes," the earl agreed soberly, "but he would insist on wearing all his orders and decorations. He was an obvious target for French sharpshooters. Captain Hardy, who was walking the deck with him, was not scratched."

"But Nicholas has been wounded so many times: it doesn't seem fair!"

Ramage said lightly: "The important thing is that I've survived!"

"Does being given a ship of the line mean you won't be away for such long periods?" Sarah asked.

"Probably. Ships of the line are usually attached to fleets, and fleets are not usually at sea for such long periods. Unless I get put on the blockade of Brest—blockade work usually means being at sea for a long time. Still, we don't keep such a close blockade now . . ."

Hanson came into the room again and said apologetically: "There's another messenger from the Admiralty, sir: it is a question of you signing the man's receipt book."

Impatiently Ramage got up from the table and went to the front door. He came back with the letter, picked up the paper-knife and slid it under the seal. "Their Lordships are keeping the clerks busy this morning," he commented. "They'd save on messengers if they wrote letters at the same time as they wrote commissions."

"Well, what does it say?" demanded Sarah. "They may have changed their minds about giving you the *Dido*."

Ramage unfolded the sheet of paper and began to read. Sarah was watching his face and was surprised to see a look of pleasure. The trouble was, she knew, that at the moment Nicholas was more absorbed in his new command than in the fact that his leave was likely to be cut short.

"I've never heard of that before," Ramage commented, passing the letter to his father. He turned to Sarah and shook his head disbelievingly.

"I'm not saying good-bye to the Calypsos after all. She is going to be paid off in Portsmouth before a thorough refit, and orders are being sent to Aitken to take all the officers and ship's company to the *Dido*. Nepean says that Their Lordships have decided that in recognition of their past services, the commission, warrant, and petty officers are transferred to the *Dido* without change in rank. So Aitken is my first lieutenant and I have Southwick as master!"

"Does that mean you still have Jackson and Stafford and Rossi, and the Frenchmen?"

"All of them," Ramage said jubilantly. Then his face fell. "It means I still have that damned gunner, too. Well, this time I am going to the Board of Ordnance to have him replaced. We could get by when he was responsible for only 32 guns, but now we shall have 74, plus 8 or a dozen carronades, and that is too many for that fool!"

"Eight or a dozen carronades? I don't understand," Sarah said. "I thought you said you have 74 guns."

"I have," Ramage explained patiently, "but carronades are extra. For some reason I've never understood, carronades aren't included in the total number of guns a ship carries. It doesn't matter if she's a frigate or a first rate. Carronades are a sort of bonus."

Sarah shrugged her shoulders. "It doesn't make sense—after all, a gun is a gun—it can kill people, even if it is a carronade."

"I agree, darling, but even Father can't explain the quirks of the Admiralty. Anyway, the main thing is that I've got my Calypsos."

"Their Lordships are being very kind to you," the earl said, folding the letter. "I hope you realize that they're granting you an extreme favour. I've never heard of a similar case."

"Nicholas deserves it," Sarah said defensively. "He's been in so many actions, and he's only just been given a 74."

"Whoa," Ramage exclaimed with a grin, "I am still very young to get a 74. You talk as if I'm an old man. I think I am still younger than Lord Nelson was when he was given his first third rate. Anyway, she was a 64, the *Agamemnon*."

"I don't care," Sarah said obstinately, "you're only getting what you've long deserved. And it's only right that you take the Calypsos with you."

"He still has to find another four hundred or so men," the earl pointed out. "I don't know what the *Dido*'s complement is, but he only has 225 men in the *Calypso*, and the *Dido* will be nearer 625. You're going to have a lot of pressed men to lick into shape!"

"Yes," Ramage agreed, "but it's always easier when you have a nucleus of good men to start with."

"Remember Falstaff's words," the earl reminded him. "Although they were pressed for the army, remember that he had 'revolted tapsters, and ostlers trade-fall'n; the cankers of a calm world and a long peace.' Remember, too, that he said that 'A mad fellow met me on the way, and told me I had unloaded all the gibbets, and press'd the dead bodies . . .'"

Ramage laughed because the quotation, from *Henry IV,* was one of his favourites. "Still, when they hear how much my fellows have made from prize-money, I expect I'll get a few volunteers."

The earl nodded in agreement. "Mind you, you probably won't get as much with a 74 as you did with a frigate. By the way, that master of yours—Southwick, isn't it?—should be a wealthy man by now. He's been with you ever since you got your first command, the *Kathleen* cutter."

"Yes, he could retire and be comfortably off. I mentioned it to him once and got a very short answer—he's happy at sea with me. Interesting to guess what he might have done if he had not been transferred to the *Dido.*"

"Retired, I expect. A man like him doesn't want to start having to learn new tricks with a fresh captain—not after so many years with you. Anyway, he must be well into his sixties by now."

"About sixty-five, but he runs around like a young boy."

"How's young Paolo, by the way?"

"You wouldn't recognize him, he's grown so much. More like a junior lieutenant than a young midshipman. He was very excited to have his aunt on board when we came back from Naples."

"From what Gianna said, most of the ship's company were very excited at seeing her. The marchesa was certainly popular!"

"You and Mother don't mind her staying here?"

"Of course not. Anyway, she prefers it when we are down at St Kew—I think the Cornish landscape reminds her of Volterra—Tuscany, anyway. She has plenty of friends now—and I hope she's enjoying her visit to Shropshire at the moment."

Sarah looked at the letter and the commission lying on the table. The important thing neither mentioned was dates. "When do you have to go to Portsmouth?" she asked Ramage.

He felt himself torn two ways: he wanted to be with her, and he wanted to be down at Portsmouth, looking over his new command, like a child with a new toy. The Admiralty letter said nothing about when he should be at Portsmouth, nor did the commission, but it was always understood that "forthwith" was implied.

"I should go down tomorrow. But you'll come with me? There's a comfortable inn near the dockyard—and you know all the Calypsos. You'll find it interesting to see a ship of the line being commissioned."

"She won't if all you have to do is provision and water her!" the earl said unexpectedly. "Just sitting in her room doing embroidery . . ."

"I think I'll start packing," Sarah said. "Just in case you take a long time getting the *Dido* ready. There must be some sort of social life in Portsmouth."

"Oh yes, the whole place positively quivers," the earl said ironically. "What with tea with the port admiral's wife, and a call on the mayor, and giving Aitken and Southwick tea as the gracious wife of the captain, you won't have a minute to call your own."

"You make it sound very exciting. Especially tea with the mayor."

"Well, there's usually a ball or two to liven things up. Make Nicholas take you—I know what a devil he is for dodging them if he can. By the way, take the carriage—the coachman's new and a fool, but Nicholas knows the Portsmouth road."

The carriage left Palace Street two days later, starting off just as dawn was breaking. Ramage and Sarah crossed the Thames at Lambeth Bridge and found little other traffic: there were burly draymen delivering barrels to ale houses and bakers with delicious-smelling newly baked loaves, but otherwise the streets were almost deserted. After some eight miles they reached the edge of Richmond Park, and for the next two miles skirted it on the right before reaching Kingston. They had covered eighteen miles and the sun was climbing higher by the time they passed Lord Clive's estate at Claremont and drove on to Guildford, thirty miles from Palace Street. It was a fine sunny day; Ramage could see few clouds through the carriage window.

"We're going to have a dusty ride," he commented to Sarah.

"It's always either dusty or muddy," she commented. "One day it will be perfect—a day we're not travelling!"

They reached Guildford just before ten o'clock, and Ramage saw a post-chaise coming up to London pull in to change horses. Jessop, the coachman, announced that Guildford was as far as he knew, and Ramage directed him on to Godalming, which they reached in twenty minutes and went on to pass the Devil's Punch Bowl. Once through the hills, they could make better time, and it was just two o'clock when they reached Petersfield and Ramage decided they would stop for a meal and a wash: dust seemed to get through every crack and crevice, and there was no question of driving with the window open. The inside of the carriage smelled musty and, with the dust, made them sneeze occasionally.

While they were waiting for the meal to be served at The

Bell, and Jessop was attending to the horses, Sarah said: "Your father has a comfortable carriage: it is one of the best sprung I have ever travelled in."

"He likes his comfort," Ramage said. "It's a long ride when they go down to Cornwall, and for the last third of the way to St Kew the road is awful. This Portsmouth road is bad enough. To think the telegraph takes only fifteen minutes or so."

"The telegraph?" Sarah asked. "Remind me how it works."

"Well, it's like people standing on hills and waving to each other. The Admiralty has built signal towers all the way from the roof of the Admiralty building to Portsmouth—and it is being extended to Plymouth. There are men with telescopes in all the towers, and as soon as a message starts being signalled from one tower it is passed on to the next."

"What are the signals—flags?"

"No, on each tower is a semaphore—like a man's arms. Different positions mean different letters of the alphabet. So unless it is foggy or dark, a message can be passed just as quickly as the signalman can handle it."

"But surely there are a lot of routine messages—more than the telegraph can send."

"Goodness me, yes. But every evening, at set times, messengers leave the Admiralty on horseback, bound for the various ports—Plymouth, Portsmouth, Sheerness, Harwich, Yarmouth, and so on. It is a regular service, so that the various port admirals know when to expect their mail. And, of course, the messengers bring back the routine correspondence to the Admiralty."

Sarah seemed satisfied with the answer, but then she asked: "Tell me about Aitken. Does his transfer to the *Dido* mean a promotion?"

"Yes, indeed. He will still be first lieutenant, so he's been promoted from the first lieutenant of a frigate to a ship of the line. The same for the other lieutenants. And I shall have another one, too, a fifth lieutenant. And—if I want that many— up to twenty-four midshipmen."

"Do you?"

"No, I'll settle for ten or a dozen, but Orsini will be made a master's mate, so that, in effect, he'll be the senior one. Gianna's nephew has had a good run for his money, being the only midshipman in the *Calypso*."

"You mean you could have had more?"

"Oh yes, several more. But one was enough. Midshipmen get into mischief."

Knowing Ramage's view on parsons, she laughed when she said: "Do you have to have a chaplain now?"

"Yes," Ramage said gloomily. "I got away with it in the *Calypso* because a frigate doesn't have to carry one unless he applies, and I took care none ever did. Still, with a ship's company of some six hundred men, perhaps a chaplain will be useful."

After a comfortable lunch, and a report from Jessop that fresh horses would not be available that day, Ramage, still feeling dazed from the drumming of the carriage wheels, decided they would stay the night at The Bell.

"We're in no great hurry," he told Sarah. "After so many months at sea, it's a pleasant change to be surrounded by trees and green fields, and to hear the birds singing."

"It's even better at Aldington," Sarah said wistfully. "I was hoping we would be able to go there for a few days. You've seen little enough of your inheritance. Just a few days since your uncle died and the will was read."

"Well, you've been there, so that's some consolation."

"Are we in Hampshire now, or still in Surrey? Anyway, it doesn't compare with Kent," Sarah said firmly.

"Tell me, how do you get on with Raven?"

"Splendidly. He must be the perfect manservant. More than that, of course, since he acts as gamekeeper, coachman, gardener, and general handyman, as well as waiting at the table. I'm in good hands."

Ramage nodded. "I imagined so. He looks a bit frightening with that scar across his face, but he must have learned a lot from those smugglers."

"There's still plenty of smuggling going on across Romney Marsh—Raven says the packhorses are out a couple of times a week."

"Good for them," Ramage said. "I've always been on the side of the smugglers—I like to think of the ladies getting their French lace and the squire his brandy!"

"It ill becomes the new captain of a ship of the line to say something like that," Sarah said with mock severity.

"Most post captains are sympathetic towards the smugglers: don't forget, the Customs and Excise are chasing us the moment our ships arrive in a British port. Take on a butt of Madeira if you happen to call at that island and the devils will be charging you duty if you want to land it and take it home. A yard of lace for the lady? Well now, sir, there's duty to pay on that. You've no idea what a close watch the revenue men keep on the Navy. I think they regard us as only slightly less villainous than the smugglers."

"All this talk of villainy is making me feel restless," Sarah said. "Let me put on a coat and hat and we'll take a walk."

They made an early start next morning, after their horses were fully rested, and out on the Portsmouth road Ramage began reading off the distances from London as they passed milestones. After Horndean they drove for a mile through Bere Forest before emerging to find the Portsdown Hills in front of them. They were soon over the hills and running down to Cosham, skirting Portsmouth Harbour as they drove through Hilsea and Kingston, ships' masts and spars lining the horizon, before turning right at the Common and heading for the town centre.

Sarah immediately noticed all the masts of the ships anchored close in and in the dockyard itself. The next thing that caught her attention was the way the town bustled: men who were obviously seamen were rolling casks, pushing carts laden with coils of rope, and dragging wooden sledges, on which were piled a variety of things Sarah did not recognize. And there were the women, standing on corners, walking along the streets with an emphatic swing of the hips, or arm in arm with sailors presumably on leave. Whores, she suddenly realized, cheeks rouged and their clothes brightly coloured. And all, Sarah noted, looking happy. Was it a professional attitude or did they enjoy their work?

"Where are we going to stay?"

"The George," Ramage said. "There are only three inns of any consequence—the Blue Posts, used by midshipmen and the like, the Star and Garter, where lieutenants stay, and The George, used by post captains and flag-officers."

"And ship widows."

"Ship widows?" Ramage asked, puzzled. "What are they?"

"The poor wives left alone while their husbands spend all their time on board their new ships. Like children with fresh toys."

Ramage made a face. "Yes, I'm afraid you'll be a ship widow some of the time, but you'll be able to visit her."

"As soon as possible: apart from seeing the ship, I'm looking forward to meeting all my old friends, especially Southwick, Jackson, and Stafford, and Rossi, of course. And my Frenchmen. I haven't seen them since we escaped from Brest."

"That's a long time ago: why, you're an old married woman now!"

"Our adventurous honeymoon aged me! How many young women find themselves caught in the enemy's country when war is declared?"

"Well, it was an exciting time. Adds zest to life."

Sarah smiled tolerantly. "Zest? Well, counting the circumstances under which I met you along with the Brest escapade, I think I have had enough zest to last me the rest of my life. I'm quite happy to end my days as a staid old married woman!"

By now the carriage had drawn up outside The George and the coach boys—in fact two old men, probably Navy pensioners—were letting down the steps of the carriage with a bang while the innkeeper, probably warned that a carriage had arrived with a crest painted on each door, was standing ready to greet his guests.

Fifteen minutes later, waiting in their room as porters carried in their two trunks, Ramage said: "Now I'm here in Portsmouth, I must report at once to the port admiral. From now on I am not a free man: I am at the beck and call of admirals, and admirals are notorious for having whims."

"Worse than wives?"

"I haven't much experience of wives, but I should guess much worse."

CHAPTER TWO

VICE-ADMIRAL Edward Rossiter, the port admiral at Portsmouth, was a stocky, red-faced man with silver-grey hair who looked more like a prosperous landowner than a sailor, although Ramage knew he had a reputation for being a fine seaman who could handle a ship with the ease of a jockey managing a pliant horse.

He shook hands with Ramage and said: "You're a lucky man to get the *Dido:* she handles well and we have just given her a good refit. But no one is going to thank you for bringing us the *Calypso:* she's just about worn out."

Ramage shrugged his shoulders diffidently. "I'm afraid she has seen some hard service in the last few years."

"Have you commanded her long?"

"Several years, sir; since I captured her from the French in the West Indies."

"That explains it. The master shipwright tells me she has a large number of repaired shot-holes, but the repairs were not all made at the same time."

"By no means, sir. The last lot were done in the Mediterranean, and the West Indies before that. The ship hasn't been in a dockyard since she was fitted out after we captured her, and that fitting out was done at English Harbour, Antigua, which was—and probably still is—a nest of thieves, where it is hard to refit a bum-boat."

Rossiter laughed and said, "Yes, I know about English Harbour. Well, things are a little better here. There's still some work to be done on the *Dido,* but your first lieutenant is busy. He has a copy of the *Port Orders,* and I've no complaints so far: his daily reports come in on time. He tells me he was with you in the *Calypso.* He's new to 74s."

Ramage nodded. "As you probably know, sir, the Admiralty turned over all the Calypsos to the *Dido,* so I have a good nucleus to start with: almost all the men have been with me since long before I commanded the *Calypso.*"

"You're a lucky fellow. But you have to find another three or four hundred men . . ."

"Yes," said Ramage soberly, "and train them."

"Did you bring your wife down with you?" the admiral asked, fully aware that few of his captains were titled and married to the daughter of a marquis and, in Ramage's case, the son of an earl who had been a famous admiral. Captain Lord Ramage, the admiral guessed, was the source of much influence at the Admiralty. In that, Rossiter was in fact wrong: Ramage's only influence at the Admiralty arose as a result of many despatches describing his operations and which had been thought worthy of printing in the *London Gazette,* and there were more and more stories about his exploits in the *Naval Chronicle,* an aptly titled magazine describing the activities of the Navy.

"Yes," Ramage told the admiral, "she is staying at The George." And, realizing this was a good opportunity of making the point to the admiral, he added: "I had been in the Mediterranean for some time, and the Admiralty had just given me three weeks' leave. The orders for the *Dido* came after only five days . . ."

"Well, it's going to take you two or three weeks to get the *Dido* ready for sea, so you'll be able to see something of her."

"This is the first time I've fitted out a 74," Ramage said. "Has she got her masts in?"

The admiral shuffled through some papers on his desk. "Ah, yes, here's yesterday's report. Masts are in, and your first lieutenant is setting up the standing rigging. Yards are on the dock waiting, along with the guns. Oh yes, she's lying alongside the Camber, so you will not need to use a boat, and your wife will be able to visit you."

"I have permission to sleep on shore, sir?" Ramage asked, knowing it was needed under the regulations.

"Yes, while the ship is alongside. After that, I'm afraid not. My apologies to her Ladyship, but I'm bound by the rules of the port."

"She will understand. Well, I'd better get on board and read myself in," Ramage said. "I hope some convoys are due in—I'll need to send out some press-gangs."

"You're lucky: a West Indian convoy is due any day, and another from the Cape of Good Hope. You should find some prime seamen." The admiral smiled. "You are also lucky that some of the ships in port are well supplied with men; only the *Dido* is so much below her complement, so you'll have first choice."

The Camber was only a few hundred yards from the port admiral's house and Ramage decided to walk over, approaching the *Dido* slowly. The dockyard was busy, with men trotting along wheeling handcarts, or being marched from one place to another. Another group of men pulled a cart on which were piled rolled up sails; yet another had several coils of rope. Ramage soon tired of saluting, but he realized there were few post captains walking around the place in uniform with sword.

And there was the *Dido*. She seemed enormous, black-hulled with a double yellow strake above and below the gun-deck. Her masts towered up, the impression of height exaggerated because the yards were not crossed, but lying on the ground, waiting to be swayed up. And rows of guns nestling on their carriages—the great 32-pounders, twenty-eight of them, and thirty 24-pounders, sixteen 12-pounders, and, like crouching bulldogs, eight 12-pounder carronades, the squatness exaggerated by the length of the barrels of the other guns.

Ramage climbed on board to be met by a startled Kenton, who had not seen him walking across the dockyard towards the ship. He gave Ramage a hasty salute while sending off Orsini to find the first lieutenant.

"We didn't know when to expect you, sir," he said apologetically. "I did not see your carriage."

"Don't worry," Ramage said reassuringly, "I walked over from the port admiral's house. It gave me a chance to look at the ship."

Kenton grinned happily. "A bit different from the *Calypso*, sir! Takes some getting used to."

Ramage looked affectionately at the small, red-haired and heavily freckled youth. "Well, Kenton, what does it feel like to be second lieutenant of a ship of the line?"

"Wonderful, sir. And I have to thank you. Shifting all of us from the *Calypso* to here was a big surprise, and we owe the promotion to you; Their Lordships would never have done it but for you."

Ramage waved a hand diffidently. "Well, it's up to you now."

At that moment both Aitken and Southwick arrived simultaneously at the entry port and there was a flurry of salutes and greetings. As soon as they were over, Ramage said: "Mr Aitken, muster the ship's company aft on the quarterdeck: I had better read myself in."

Until he read his commission aloud to the officers and ship's company, he was not officially in command of the ship, and at the moment the parchment was sitting snugly in his pocket.

Within a minute or two the shrill calls of the bosun's mates, followed by the bellowed orders to muster aft, were echoing through the ship, and Southwick was standing beside him, saying in a low voice: "Bit o' a surprise, sir, shifting us all from the *Calypso*!"

"Not unwelcome, I trust?"

The old master grinned, taking off his hat and running his hand through his flowing white hair. "No, sir. I like to think we all deserved a 74 after all those years in a frigate. What does it feel like to command a ship o' the line?"

"I've only been on board about five minutes, so my feelings

are a bit mixed," Ramage said lightly. "In theory I'm looking forward to it."

"Our biggest trouble is going to be men," Southwick said. "At the moment we have less than half our complement."

"The port admiral says two convoys are due in, one from the West Indies and the other from the Cape. With luck we should get at least a hundred men from each one."

"I hope so," Southwick said gloomily. "I don't want to fill up the ship with rubbish from the prisons."

"You can't avoid having some convicts when fitting out a ship as big as this."

"I know, sir, but don't expect me to like it."

Aitken came to report: "The men are mustered aft, sir. Will you be making a speech?"

"A speech? Good heavens, the men know me well enough by now."

"I still think they'd appreciate a few words, sir. It's an even bigger change for them than it is for us, and they've been working hard since they came on board."

"Oh, very well," Ramage said, hard put not to sound surly, "but I've no idea what to say."

He was startled when, as he strode across the quarterdeck past the assembled men, they started cheering him. He spotted Jackson, Stafford and Rossi grinning among the throng, and beside them the four Frenchmen. In front of each division stood the officers. There was the willowy, debonair third lieutenant George Hill, who spoke French fluently because his French mother had been unable to learn English. And there, stiff as a ramrod, was the fourth lieutenant, William Martin, popularly known as "Blower" because of his skill with the flute. The freckle-faced Peter Kenton was standing to attention in front of his division and Ramage guessed Orsini was now on watch at the entry port. The marines were drawn up in two files athwartships, with Sergeant Ferris and Lieutenant Rennick in front. Rennick, Ramage noted, should be promoted to captain now.

The cheering had stopped and he took the commission from his pocket and unfolded it. He coughed to clear his throat and then began reading in a strong voice, hurrying over the preliminaries until he reached the important part: ". . . We do hereby appoint you captain of His Majesty's Ship the *Dido*, willing and requiring you forthwith to go on board and take upon you the charge and command of captain in her accordingly." He read out the warning to the officers and men to behave themselves, answering to the contrary "at your peril."

Finally he came to the end and rolled up the parchment and looked round at the men. Yes, Aitken was right, they expected him to say a few words.

"Well, good-bye Calypsos, hello Didos," he said. "I see that you have a larger ship than when I last saw you. The port admiral has just told me the master shipwright reports that the *Calypso* is worn out. I only hope you men aren't worn out because—" he gestured aloft at the bare masts, "—there is a lot of work to be done up there.

"But more important, we shall have about 350 new men joining the ship within the next week or two. Some will be trained seamen: some will be fresh off the farm; some will be fresh out of jail. But—as I remember telling you several years ago—none of them has a past the moment his name is written in the muster book. From then on he starts a new life as a Dido, and it will be up to him to make his own reputation. If he proves a bad man, he can expect no mercy from me. If he is a good man, then he will be treated accordingly. I mean that it is of no importance whether a man is an able seaman or fresh from the plough, he makes a fresh start.

"All this will mean extra work for you men, but also extra responsibility. I want you to help train the men that don't know their larboard hand from the hanging magazine. And I want you to make sure that trained seamen do things my way."

He looked round and concluded: "The *Calypso* was a happy ship and I hope the *Dido* will be too. But it all depends on the officers and ship's company. So, men, it all depends on you."

Ramage stopped talking, certain he had made a lame and ineffectual speech, which would have done little more than embarrass the men, so he was startled to hear them cheering again, this time even louder.

As the men were dismissed by their officers he walked under the half-deck to look at his cabins for the first time. There the cabin, coach, and bedplace seemed larger than usual because they were bare of furniture and the four 12-pounders were down on the dock, not lashed in their usual position, two in the cabin and one each in the coach and bedplace. The canvas-covered deck was painted in a chessboard pattern of black and white, and the stern-lights, six big windows with stone-ground glass, meant that the cabin had plenty of light. But, Ramage admitted, without a dining table, chairs, settee, armchairs, wine cooler and a desk, both cabin and coach were as inviting as empty warehouses.

He thought for a few minutes. The furniture that he had in the *Calypso* was very worn: the settee sagged so much that it looked more like a nest in the middle, and the armchair was even worse. His desk and the dining room table had been inherited from the French captain, who obviously had not been fussy about scratching the tops of both. No, all that furniture could stay in the *Calypso*, a present to her next captain (assuming the dockyard people did not steal it), and he would start fresh with the *Dido*, buying new furniture. It would give Sarah something to do—she could also choose material for curtains and cushions: she had excellent taste, and Jessop could take her round in the carriage to visit Portsmouth's selection of furniture shops.

And a cot. He suddenly remembered the bedplace was bare, too, and all that was fitted towards the captain's getting a good night's sleep were two eyebolts in the deckhead from which to sling the cot.

The tiny cabin of the captain's clerk was built on to the starboard forward corner of the bedplace, and he walked outside to inspect it. There was no disguising the fact that it was little more than a hutch, but luckily the man wanted little more than room for a small table and a chair and enough room to swing a hammock. Ramage was sure that Luckhurst, his clerk, was more than content: the fact that a hammock was slung showed that the man had already moved in. Well, from now on he was going to be busy—there would be plenty of reports, surveys and returns "according to the prescribed form" and applications to be made in the next few days before the *Dido* sailed.

He went back into the cabin and opened the door leading to the balcony stretching across the stern, outside the stern-lights. Extending the width of the ship, it was going to be a joy, enabling him to walk back and forth in the fresh air with privacy. And he only had to look over the side and he would see the *Dido*'s wake curling astern beneath him. Yes, a 74 was a great improvement on a frigate.

Except . . . There was one important exception. A 74 was a damned big ship. From memory, a ship as big as the *Dido* would be about 275 feet from the end of the spanker boom to the end of the jib-boom. In other words she was that long from the aftermost end to the fore end. And the actual ship, forgetting the booms? Well, about 200 feet from the figurehead at the bow to the end of his balcony.

Ramage's thoughts were interrupted by a call from the door,

and he realized that Rennick had posted a marine sentry. "First Lieutenant, sir."

"Send him in."

Aitken was carrying a small grey volume. He stopped by the door and looked around. "Bit sparse at the moment, sir," he said ruefully.

"Yes, but leave all my stuff in the *Calypso*. I'm going to buy new for this ship."

Aitken grinned and said: "A good idea, sir: that settee was getting a bit uncomfortable!"

"I'll warn her Ladyship to buy something special for you," Ramage said ironically.

"You're too kind, sir," Aitken said with a straight face. "By the way, sir, I've brought you a copy of the *Port Signals and General Orders*. They're not as bad as some I've seen, but I seem to have spent most of my time filling in forms and making reports."

"Now you hope I'm going to do it."

Aitken grinned. "I've been using your clerk, Luckhurst, so he knows his way through the *Orders*. May I ask how her Ladyship is keeping?"

"She's looking forward to seeing you all. You will be able to escort her through the ship: she is staying at The George with me, and one of her first jobs will be to furnish this cabin and the coach."

"And the marchesa, sir?"

"She's well. At the moment she is away, staying with some friends in the country. I think she'll be sad to hear we've left the *Calypso*. She had grown fond of the ship during the voyage back from Naples."

"The ship's company are always asking after her and her Ladyship. They reckon the ladies bring them luck."

"I hope so," Ramage said soberly. "Now, what reports have we got to send in today?"

Aitken gave him a grey book. "I've already done the second order, where it says the captain is to deliver a statement of defects and deficiencies of sails, rigging, and stores."

"That was quite a big job."

"It was," Aitken said ruefully. "It took Southwick and me all day. Still, having the yards down and most of the rigging stripped off made it easier."

Ramage opened the book and started reading the *Orders and Instructions*. Aitken had already dealt with the second, and the third needed no action: admirals, captains or commanders were to attend courts martial in frock uniforms with white breeches, and officers at all times when on shore were to wear their "established uniform" with swords. Subsequent instructions said no work was to be done on Sundays except loading provisions, stores or water, and applications for leave of absence from an officer of a ship refitting had to be sanctioned by the port admiral. Well, he already had permission to sleep on shore at The George.

A return had to be made daily of all men impressed the previous day but, the orders warned, men were not to be impressed from outward-bound vessels—a pity but understandable: it would be unfair to weaken a ship at the beginning of a long voyage.

And so the instructions went on, covering arriving at Spithead with sick seamen, dealing with newly raised men, and "No beat of drum is to be admitted . . . except those established, viz. the Reveille, Troop, Retreat, and Tattoo."

There were also warnings. "It being a practice with the enemy, when they make a capture, to keep an Englishman in the prize, to make answer when hailed by a British ship, particular caution is to be observed . . ."

Except in cases of "urgent necessity," boats were not to be absent from their ships at mealtimes, and all boats belonging to ships at Spithead were to leave the shore so as to be back on board by sunset. All working parties were to have their breakfast before being sent on duty, and they were to be at their work by six o'clock in summer and as soon as practicable in winter. Boats were "to attend to take them to their dinners at a quarter before twelve, and they are to return to their duty at the expiration of an hour."

There were 44 printed instructions, but several more had been added in neat copperplate handwriting, and right at the end, headed "General Order," was a long note about examinations for lieutenant. Their Lordships, it said, directed that the examination for candidates "touching their qualifications to serve as lieutenants in the Royal Navy" should take place at Portsmouth, Plymouth and Sheerness as well as at Somerset House on the first Wednesday in every month. A candidate, Ramage noted, because this would very soon concern Paolo Orsini, had to bring: a certificate from the Navy Board saying how long he had served; his Journals; certificates from captains under whom he had served of his "diligence, sobriety, and obedience to command," along with a certificate from the minister of the parish where he was born, or some other proof that he had reached the age of nineteen.

Finally, at the back of the book was glued a specimen form, twenty inches wide and with twenty-six columns, of *"A daily report of the progress made in the equipment of His Majesty's the —— the —— day of —— 18 ——."*

It was a copy of this form that, carefully copied out by Luckhurst, was filled in daily by Aitken. Many of the questions seemed redundant if they were to be answered daily, but they began with how many days since the refit began. It then went on to list the number of petty officers, able and ordinary seamen, landmen and boys, and marines, with the next column headed "Total number short of complement."

Then came the important questions: state of the rigging; stores—how far complete; water on board; number of artificers employed on board (they were divided into shipwrights, caulkers, joiners, and painters), with the almost wistful question in the next column "By what time will they have finished?" A wider column next to that asked: "Crew—how employed?"

Ramage gave the book back to Aitken. "You'd better put Luckhurst to work with his pen and ruler, then give me the details to fill in. How many men are we short of complement?"

"We brought 223 with us from the *Calypso,* and the complement of this ship is 625, so we are short 402."

"We'll be lucky to find 300 men," Ramage said. "And that will be sending out press-gangs. I hate having to press men; how true it is that one volunteer is worth three pressed men."

"It's not so bad if they are trained seamen," Aitken said. "Let's hope we are lucky with those two convoys."

C H A P T E R   T H R E E

S ARAH was excited next day at the prospect of visiting the *Dido* and meeting once again the men she had got to know on board the *Calypso.* She was wearing an olive green dress that complemented her tawny hair and she had a matching cloak. Jessop had been instructed to pick them up at The George at nine o'clock with the carriage and drive them to the dockyard.

Before leaving the ship the previous day, Ramage had filled

in the Daily Report and discussed with Aitken how the ship's company and dockyard men were to be employed. The main task for the present was to rig the ship—setting up the standing rigging and reeving the running rigging. Then the yards could be swayed up and crossed, and the ship would look less naked.

Ramage quickly saw that the most cheerful man on board was Southwick: the old master was as happy as a small boy playing mud pies at the prospect of rigging a ship of the line, a challenge he had not faced for many years, since before he first served with Ramage.

But Ramage hated the confusion and mess associated with commissioning a ship: all over the deck there were coils of rope, with men busy splicing in eyes. Caulkers were busy with hot pitch filling in deck-seams, and the harsh smell of the pitch caught the back of the throat.

His cabin and the coach reeked of fresh paint and it gave him a headache. Painters were busy lining in round the bulwarks and painting the drums of the capstans. Aloft men were busy painting the masts, while others were tarring the parts of the rigging not being used by seamen and riggers.

It seemed, Ramage thought as he settled in the carriage with Sarah, that the ship would never look seaworthy again: no yards across, no guns or carriages on board, no boats in the davits or stowed on the booms—indeed all the booms, too, were lying on the ground beside the ship. Still, there was one advantage in being alongside: the guns and carriages, yards and boats could all be painted more conveniently. There was nothing worse, for instance, than painting the yards when they were crossed: it was impossible for the men to avoid dripping paint, which spattered the deck-planking. Thought of the deck-planking depressed him—there was so much rope lying about that it was impossible to holystone the planking, and already it was looking grey, with uneven rivulets of pitch where the caulkers had been at work.

"The ship's a disgrace," he said to Sarah. "I'm sorry this will be your first sight of her."

Sarah shrugged her shoulders. "Don't worry: I'll make allowances. It is like spring-cleaning a house: one despairs of it ever looking presentable again."

"Just bear that in mind," Ramage said. "The decks look more like a chandler's, and the seams are a mess with pitch."

"'The devil to pay, and no pitch hot'—what does that mean?"

"'The devil' is the caulkers' name for a particular seam that is hard to caulk. It means some job to be done and no one to do it."

"Isn't there some other phrase about caulkers—quarrelling, or something?"

"Yes—at loggerheads. A loggerhead, or loggerheat, is an iron ball fixed on the end of the handle. The ball is heated in a fire and the hot ball is put into the pitch or a tar barrel to heat it. The point is that heating pitch or tar in a bucket over an open fire is dangerous, because it might burst into flames. But a loggerhead makes a nice weapon, and would just about stave in a man's head. So when two men quarrel, they are said to 'be at loggerheads.'"

"Well, at last I know what it means. I've heard your father use the phrase."

Jessop swung the carriage into the dockyard gates, stopped to answer the sentry's challenge, and then drove on up to the Camber, where the *Dido* was lying alongside.

Sarah was watching through the window. "Is that her? Why, she's enormous! Nicholas, however are you going to handle such a big ship?"

Ramage laughed at the question. "I wish I knew," he said ruefully. "You learn as you go along!"

"Has Southwick any experience with a 74?" she asked.

"Yes, years ago. Don't forget he's been with me for years, so he has more experience of cutters, brigs and frigates than ships of the line."

"Well, you'll all work it out somehow," Sarah said, with a cheerful confidence Ramage did not share. "Tell me, will I be in the way going round talking to the men I know?"

"No, of course not. At least, don't let them form a big crowd round you."

"First I must see what furniture you want for your cabins. And cushions, and glasses and so on."

"Ironic that instead of furnishing a home, your first experience as a married woman is furnishing a ship!"

"Well, you inherited Aldington fully furnished, so all I could do there was move some of the furniture round and change the curtains and cushions. Not very satisfying for a new wife."

Jessop swung the carriage through the piles of yards and ranks of guns and stopped at the foot of the rough gangway which had been leaned against the entry port.

Ramage glanced up and saw Aitken looking down at him. "We are expected," he said. "We'll be piped aboard. Just stop for a moment, until the piping stops."

Sarah was delighted to find all the ship's officers waiting for her when she went through the entry port, lined up according to their seniority. George Hill was the only new officer since she had met the *Calypso*'s officers. She kissed Southwick, much to the old master's delight, and to Bowen she said: "I'm glad the captain has not given you any work recently." The surgeon laughed and said: "I have never seen him look so fit, m'lady."

Finally Ramage took her off to inspect his quarters. She

walked through the coach and his cabin and said: "Compared with the *Calypso* you have so much more room, darling."

"More room, more pay, more responsibility . . . Thank goodness there are some compensations for commanding a ship of the line!"

"Now, how many chairs will you want—for dining, I mean?"

"Six," he said promptly. "That limits the number of people I can have to dinner. So I need a dining table and six chairs. A desk and chair. Four armchairs and a settee. Can you remember that so far? Let's go into my clerk's cabin—you can sit down there and write a list."

In Luckhurst's cabin Ramage continued his list. "I'll need a cot for my bedplace. A chest of drawers and a couple of chairs, too. There's not much room in there—I share the place with a 12-pounder. Now, I need curtains for the stern-lights—nothing too dark, because I like a light cabin. Cushions to match, I suppose. I'll leave the choice of patterns to you. Handbasin, water jug, soapdish . . . you know the sort of things. Wine cooler, too. Nothing too elaborate, or my guests will think they're on board an East Indiaman!"

Sarah, who had come home from India with her mother and father, travelling in an East Indiaman, laughed and said: "You'd need to be an admiral and lucky with prize-money to live as well as the captain of an East Indiaman."

She finished writing the list and led the way back to the cabin.

"You know, I am really surprised by how much room you have."

"Don't forget that in here I have to share the space with two 12-pounders, one each side, and there'll be a 12-pounder in the coach and another in the bedplace. Each has a barrel nine feet six inches long. Hang a cot in the bedplace and there's not much space. Put a desk, a couple of chairs and a gun in the coach, and I don't have much room. And with a long dining table, chairs, armchairs and a settee, wine cooler, and a couple of guns, there won't be much room to do a quadrille in here."

"Glasses," Sarah said suddenly. "You need plates, glasses, and carafes. And cutlery. Darling, we've forgotten more things than we've written on the list. Napkins, table cloths, towels. And what about some small carpets—this black and white pattern is depressing."

"No carpets," Ramage said firmly. "In a seaway they slip all over the place. Make sure you include a set of carvers with the cutlery."

Sarah was adding to her list, writing standing up. "What about lamps? There are none here."

"Yes, I need lamps. Two for this cabin, and one each for the coach and bedplace. And plates and cups and so on."

"Yes, I noted them down with the glasses and cutlery. Sheets for the cot?"

"Yes, four pairs. Silkin can't get them all washed at the right time if we have much rainy weather."

"So you still have Silkin?"

"Yes. He's not the ideal captain's steward, but he knows my ways now, which is half the battle with having a steward."

"And pillow cases?"

"What? Oh yes, four of them."

Ramage looked carefully round the cabin, trying to think of other things he needed, but they seemed to have listed everything. In any case, there would still be time to get anything they had forgotten.

"Come on," he said, "let's show you the rest of the ship, and you can meet your old friends."

The tour soon turned into something of a triumphal procession. Sarah met Martin and Kenton on the quarterdeck and stopped for a chat with them, frankly admitting to Martin that she had forgotten to bring him any music for his flute. "Can you buy any in Portsmouth?" she asked.

"Yes, there is one shop in the High Street m'lady, and I've got a good selection now."

Jackson and Stafford were squatting on the gangway, splicing rigging, and they put down their lids and stood up when Sarah came along. After the usual greetings, Sarah asked: "Any regrets at leaving the *Calypso?*"

Both men nodded their heads. "You get used to a ship," Stafford said. "I 'spect we'll get used to the *Dido* in time, but there's so much more to her." He pointed to the coil of rope he was splicing and grinned. "And so much more work to do!"

"And what about you, Jackson?"

"Well, the *Calypso* was small enough to be cosy. With a ship's company three times as big, we're going to lose some of that."

"Come now," Ramage said. "You've got to help train the new men and that way you'll get to know them. You'll soon like having some fresh faces around."

"More likely the place will be littered with clodhoppers, sir, with respect," Jackson said. "The ship will be a nursery, teaching them to knot and splice. They won't know a long splice from a long drink of water."

"There are a couple of convoys due in, so we might get some prime seamen."

Jackson sighed. "That means we'll hear dozens of stories of how they've been cheated out of their wages by the masters of their ships."

"Well, do your best with the new men," Ramage said. "I don't want the new and the old to split into two camps: that always means trouble."

The four Frenchmen whom Sarah had got to know during their escape from Brest, when the war had broken out again while she and Nicholas were on their honeymoon in France, were on the fo'c'sle, splicing some standing rigging for the fore-mast. All four men were excited at seeing Sarah again.

"Well, Gilbert," Sarah said, "how do you find life in the Royal Navy after being the Count of Rennes' valet?"

Gilbert, who spoke very good English, grinned. "It's different, m'lady, but I like it. I like the comradeship. And always something new."

She looked at Louis, who had started as a fisherman but, when his boat had been confiscated at the beginning of the Revolution, had become a gardener. "How about you?"

"I prefer it to planting cabbages and fighting weeds, m'lady, but I wish I was back fishing, my own master."

Sarah nodded understandingly. "Still, you are free of the Revolution."

Louis nodded his head vigorously. "The Royal Navy has no guillotine, and we eat regularly."

Albert, who with Auguste had sold vegetables in the market at Brest before escaping, laughed and said: "We eat regularly, yes, but always the same thing. I miss the fresh vegetables we used to sell."

Sarah looked at Auguste. "You feel the same?"

The Frenchman nodded. "I am happy enough serving with his Lordship, but it would be nice to chew at a fresh carrot, or eat an apple. These I miss."

"Don't we all," Ramage said sympathetically.

Gilbert bowed slightly towards Sarah. "There is no family yet, m'lady?"

Sarah blushed slightly and shook her head. "Give us a year or two, Gilbert. Then what shall it be, two boys and a girl?"

"At least," the Frenchman said emphatically. He thought and then added: "Three sons and two daughters would be best. Then, when the girls get married, you have five sons."

Sarah laughed musically. "I'll talk it over with his Lordship!"

It was curious, she thought, how when talking to the Frenchmen one referred to Nicholas as "his Lordship," because in the Navy Nicholas did not use his title, but the Frenchmen were always punctilious about it. Well, they had all worked for a titled Frenchman they loved and respected, and they had no sympathy with the Revolution, which had ruined their lives in France.

Sarah and Nicholas continued their stroll through the ship, with Nicholas pointing out things that were different or bigger than in a frigate. They found Rossi making up a set of foot-ropes for the maintopsail yard, and he hurriedly dropped his fid and gave Sarah a courtly bow.

"Welcome to the *Dido*, m'lady," he said. "A much more fitting ship for you to visit than that little frigate!"

"I liked the *Calypso*," Sarah said. "She had an air about her."

"Ah yes, but a ship of the line is more fitting for the captain: he deserves her! Why, next it will be a three-decker, and he will be hoisting his flag as a rear-admiral."

Sarah smiled at the Italian's enthusiasm and reflected that Nicholas was lucky to have such men serving him. "All in good time, Rossi. It seems to me you have plenty to do getting this two-decker ready for sea."

"Boh," Rossi said with a shrug of his shoulders, "a few more days and we'll be ready to sail."

As they continued their walk along the gangway, Ramage reflected how well Sarah seemed to fit in. Although looking beautiful in her olive green dress and cloak, which would have been suitable for a stroll down Bond Street, she nevertheless adapted well on board the *Dido*, lifting her skirt to step across coils of rope and ducking under pieces of rigging strung up to the shrouds.

They found Southwick under the half-deck, inspecting the

barrel of the wheel. Apart from the brief greeting at the entry port, they had not had a chance to talk. "How is the marchesa?" he asked. "Were you surprised to see her?"

"We thought Napoleon's men had murdered her in Paris, so you can imagine how surprised we were to find that she had escaped to Naples and that by chance you brought her back in the *Calypso*. She has been staying with the captain's parents, as you know, but at the moment she is with friends in the country. As you saw on the voyage from Naples, her dreadful experience in Paris has not affected her."

Southwick nodded. "She hardly recognized her nephew, he had grown up so much. He was a boy when she last saw him: now he is a young gentleman."

"Yes, I've noticed the difference, although I haven't had a chance to talk to him yet. He'll soon be taking his examination for lieutenant?"

"This month, I think," Southwick said, "although he'll have to wait until his birthday before he can call himself 'Lieutenant Orsini.' In fact, he'll probably serve as a master's mate for a few months, until there's a vacancy. We need a fifth lieutenant now, and the admiral will probably send us one before Mr Orsini can take his examination. But I gather he has all his papers ready."

"Will he pass?" Sarah asked.

Southwick shrugged his shoulders. "He'll come through with flying colours in everything but mathematics and navigation. There it'll depend on what questions the board will ask. If he does well in seamanship—which I'm sure he will—the examining board may let him off lightly."

"Well, we must hope for the best. How are you keeping? You look very well."

"Middlin' fair, m'lady. I get a touch of the screws in my back occasionally, but not bad enough to send me to bed."

"How do you like the change to the *Dido?*"

"Delighted with it, m'lady. A long overdue change for the captain. Let's hope he won't have to wait so long before getting a three-decker."

"I think he was happy enough with the *Calypso.*"

"Ah yes, you see he is a born frigate captain: plenty of dash." Southwick looked at Ramage and grinned. "I can say that now he's said good-bye to the *Calypso.* Now he's a married man with a ship o' the line. By the time you've got a couple of sons, he'll be ready for a three-decker."

"Is that how it works?" Sarah said mildly. "So all successful naval officers have to be family men. A bit hard on the bachelors, isn't it?"

Southwick's reply startled Ramage, who regarded the master as a confirmed bachelor. "Serves 'em right for not getting married."

"They might have trouble finding the right woman," Sarah said jokingly.

"Aye, luck comes into it. As the captain well knows. If we hadn't gone down to Brazil and put into Trinidade, and met you, who knows what the captain might have done?"

"Remained a bachelor who has to buy his own furniture," Ramage said.

"There you are, sir," Southwick said triumphantly. "Instead of traipsing round Portsmouth buying pots and pans, you've got her Ladyship to do it for you!"

Ramage and Sarah turned to each other and said simultaneously: "Pots and pans!"

Sarah took the pages from her bag and, using the binnacle as a table, added them to her shopping list.

Southwick, realizing what was going on, said to Ramage: "If you'd forgotten them you'd never have heard the last of it from Silkin!"

"And an iron!" Ramage exclaimed, visualizing Silkin carefully pressing his shirts and stock.

Sarah sighed. "This is hopeless—we are going to be remembering things right up to the moment you sail."

"I'll get Silkin to give me a list of what he wants. His pantry is right opposite Luckhurst's office, so Luckhurst can be in charge of the list, and I can add to it whenever I think of something."

"I hope you're including a good armchair, sir," Southwick said with a smile. "I'm getting a bit old for a straight-back chair."

"Don't worry," Sarah assured him. "Four armchairs and a settee are at the top of the list."

CHAPTER FOUR

TO RAMAGE the fitting out seemed to be proceeding with agonizing slowness: each day that Jessop brought him alongside the *Dido* the ship seemed no different from the day before. Sarah had finished all the shopping, but had arranged that it would not be delivered for several days, just before Ramage moved from The George into the ship.

One day the painters were busy down on the dock painting the ship's boats; for the following two days they were blacking the guns and painting their carriages. Then came the day when the fore and main-yard were swayed up and crossed, followed by the topsail and topgallant yards. It was at that point that Ramage began to note progress.

At last there was more to write in the "By what time will they have finished" and "Crew—how employed" columns in the Daily Report. There was more to write in the "State of the rigging" column, too. But it was slow work.

He spent a day interviewing midshipmen. As soon as it was known that there were vacancies in the *Dido*, applications came flooding in. He had been given the command too suddenly for him to have a number of relatives or friends and acquaintances asking for a berth. He had already decided he would take only ten, giving him a total of eleven with Orsini. The applicants were a mixed bunch, ranging from fourteen-year-old boys— mostly unhappy with the conditions in the ships in which they were already serving—to older men attracted by Ramage's reputation.

With his furniture not yet arrived, he had to interview them in Luckhurst's tiny cabin. As he worked his way through the list, he found he was picking more that had served in frigates than ships of the line. It was not any bias on his part in favour of frigates; it was simply that those who had served in frigates fared better in answering his questions which usually began with the phrase "What would you do if . . . ?" He was little concerned with mathematical ability and, if the applicant was young, his ability to work out a sight. What mattered most was that the applicant had initiative. By the time he had chosen his ten, he found that eight of them were under sixteen years old, one was twenty and one was thirty-two, a stocky young man already going bald.

The day after the interviews, Aitken started hoisting in the guns and carriages. The ship was filled with shouted orders, the creak of the main-yard and the squeal of the sheaves in the blocks, and then the rumble of the trucks on the deck as guns and carriages were rolled into position and secured.

It was tiring work for the men. The thirty-two-pounders, of which the *Dido* had 28, each weighed fifty-five and a half hundredweight—just short of three tons. On top of that came the weight of the carriage, which because of the shape was difficult to hoist. The twenty-four-pounders, of which she had thirty, were not much lighter, each gun weighing two and a half tons. Then there were sixteen 12-pounders, each weighing thirty-four hundredweight. Two of them were to go in Ramage's cabin, and one in the coach and one in his bedplace. Finally there were eight 12-pounder carronades, only two feet two inches long, but fitted on slides, not carriages, which would go on the poop above.

While the guns were being swayed on board, the *Dido* received her full complement of marines. Ramage had a letter saying that Lieutenant Rennick had been promoted to captain, and that was followed by the new first and second marine lieutenants, two young men of whom Rennick approved. There were now four sergeants, four corporals, two drummers and one hundred ten privates, a total of one hundred twenty-three. Ramage, looking at their details set down in the Muster Book, noted that he now had half as many marines in the *Dido* as the full complement of marines and seamen for the *Calypso*. At once Rennick offered Aitken more men to help with the fitting out, and what the marines lacked in nautical skill they made up for with strength, being only too ready to tail on to the end of a rope and give a good heave.

Once the guns had been brought on board and hauled into position so that breechings and train tackles could be secured, the purser, a newcomer named Jeremiah Clapton, was calling on Aitken, saying that he wanted to start loading provisions. Since the captain had received orders to provision and water for six months, he warned, there was a great deal to be brought on board.

Very soon carts were delivering an almost bewildering quantity of supplies alongside, and Clapton and his mates were driven almost frantic keeping a tally. Ramage, watching for a few minutes as the carts were unloaded, was always almost bewildered by the variety of stores needed. There were casks of cheese, jars of oil, bags of bread, sacks of salt, wreaths of twigs for lighting the galley fire, butts, puncheons, hogsheads, and barrels of beer, as well as a variety of measures of beef, pork, flour, raisins, suet, pease, oatmeal, rice, sugar, butter, and vinegar.

Clapton's most difficult task was keeping a tally of all the different weights and measures. His basic measurement was a tun, but the list of equivalents seemed to have been drawn up by a madman. Two butts, three puncheons, four hogsheads and six barrels all equalled a tun; but so did six jars of oil, twelve bags of bread and forty wreaths of twigs. But how many pounds in a tun was a question that only a purser with his list could answer. Just 1,800 pounds of flour or raisins was reckoned a tun, but 2,000 pounds of currants, 1,120 pounds of suet, 1,600 pounds of rice, 2,240 pounds of sugar and butter also made a tun, as did 1,800 pounds of cheese in a cask but 2,240 pounds if loose.

Nor were things any easier with liquid measures. Butts, puncheons, hogsheads and barrels, all contained different quantities, depending on whether listed in wine measure or beer measure. A butt, for example, contained 120 gallons wine measure, but only 108 gallons beer measure.

Although he had never yet met a purser whom he trusted, Ramage could not help feeling sorry for Clapton. In addition to the variety of measures which he had to deal with, there were other problems like what to issue to the men, depending on where the ship was. Within the Strait of Gibraltar, for instance, if the men could not be issued daily with a gallon of beer each, they received a pint of wine, and in the West Indies it was a gallon of beer or half a pint of spirits or a pint of wine. Nor was it only liquor—if there was any shortage of provisions, then the substitutes were listed. There were three pounds of beef for two pounds of pork, and two pounds of flour and half a pound of currants for a piece of pork and pease; and in place of a piece of beef the purser could issue four pounds of flour, or two of currants, or four of raisins.

Being a purser, Ramage had long ago decided, was an attitude of mind. Issuing one weight and charging another—which was how the purser made his living, pocketing the difference—required a certain deviousness that did not come naturally to normal men.

Ramage was still standing at the entry port watching the bustle alongside the ship when Aitken came up to him. "When do you want to bring your furniture on board, sir? With the guns stowed and the painters finished in your cabin, we're ready for you."

"Very well, let's say the day after tomorrow: that will give me time to let the shopkeepers know when to deliver."

"Have you any idea when we are expected to sail, sir?"

"No, neither when or where to. Six months' provisions can mean the Mediterranean, West Indies, America or the East Indies."

"I hope it's not back to the Mediterranean again," Aitken said. "I think I've seen enough of it to keep me going for a while."

"It's about the only place where there's any action at the moment," Ramage pointed out. "We were kept busy there with the *Calypso*."

"True, but the 74s in Naples seem to be having a dull time."

"I'm sure their officers were having a busy time socially," Ramage said ironically. "I believe Naples is one of the more favoured stations as far as that is concerned."

The new gunner and the chaplain arrived on board within an hour of each other, and it was as if a whimsical Admiralty had sent two complete opposites. The gunner, William Higgins, came from Boston, in Lincolnshire, and was a tall, thin and stooped man with a dry sense of humour. He was going bald, but what was left of his hair was fair and greying, trimmed like a monk's tonsure.

The chaplain, Benjamin Brewster, brought to mind Friar Tuck: he was a jolly, round little man whom Ramage liked on sight, thankful that the first chaplain he had ever had on board a ship he commanded looked as though he would be an asset and likely to be popular with the men. The trouble with most chaplains, he knew, was that they were too closely associated with the wardroom, more interested in their food than the spiritual welfare of the ship's company.

Ramage was determined that right from the start Brewster should understand his views, and he took the man out to the balcony of his cabin and walked him up and down while questioning and telling him.

"As far as I am concerned," Ramage said, "the chaplain is responsible for the spiritual health and happiness of every man on board—that will be a ship's company of 625 men. We have a first-class surgeon who will make sure that their bodies are healthy. I am concerned that we have a first-class chaplain who will make sure they are healthy in spirit."

"I understand you, sir," Brewster said. "But I hope you will leave me to do it in my own way."

"How do you mean?" Ramage asked suspiciously.

"Well, sir, I left my last ship because of the captain's attitude," Brewster said frankly. "He was a man with very narrow and fixed religious views. In my opinion he did not need a chaplain: he interfered so much—even to providing notes for sermons—that he did the chaplain's work for him. Except, of course, the men never went to him for help or advice, as they would have done with the chaplain."

"You mean that they did not come to you?"

"No, they didn't. They should have done, but they were intimidated by the captain giving them long sermons and conducting prayers—doing my job, in fact. That was why I left the ship and applied for a transfer to another of the king's ships."

Ramage appreciated the man's frankness and replied in kind. "Well, Brewster, I am not going to interfere with your work while you are chaplain of this ship and providing you carry out your duties satisfactorily—in fact I have only one rule for you to start with: no long sermons. Ten minutes is quite long enough, whether the men are sitting there in the freezing cold or under a tropical sun."

"I'm a ten-minute man myself, sir," chuckled Brewster. "My last captain reckoned on a minimum of half an hour. If he was delivering the sermon himself he could go on for an hour."

Ramage shuddered at the thought. "All right, Brewster, ten minutes of crisp talk, and rousing hymns where the men can sing their hearts out."

That evening he gave instructions to Jessop to call at the shops next day and arrange for deliveries on board the *Dido* on the day following.

He found Sarah sitting in their room at The George busy embroidering a cot cover for him. She had chosen a design of griffins, the Ramage family crest, sewn in the correct counts of blue and gold.

"I am having to use yellow thread instead of gold," she explained. "I can't find any gold thread in Portsmouth—gold colour, anyway: actual gold thread would be heavy, and I'd never get it done before you sail."

"Ah yes," Ramage said, "for once the Daily Report to the port admiral had some definite information today: I put down that we will be finished with the dockyard men—painters, caulkers and so on—in four days' time. We shall have taken on all the provisions and water by then, so it will be just a question of taking on powder and we are ready to sail."

"And then you pack me off back to London?"

Ramage nodded. "The admiral may want me on board before then: Jessop will be telling the shops to deliver the furniture and things the day after tomorrow, so I shan't have the excuse that the ship isn't ready for me."

"Has the smell of new paint gone? You know how that makes you ill."

"It's almost gone. All the ports are open so there's a good draught blowing through."

He suddenly realized that Sarah was quietly crying.

"The time has gone so quickly," she said, as he sat on the arm of her chair and held her to him. "I had so looked forward to us being alone at Aldington, left in peace, and we haven't even been able to go down there."

Suddenly Ramage felt a longing to be alone with Sarah at their home in Kent, walking, riding, and just lazing during the day, and making love at night, content just to be together after such a long time spent apart.

"At the end of this commission I'll go on halfpay for six months," he said. "You'll be tired of my company long before the time is up."

"Can you be sure of being employed again after six months?"

Ramage thought of all the *Gazette* letters, and his recent unexpected promotion. "Yes. I may have to wait a month or two, but Their Lordships would find me another ship."

"Are you making a promise?"

Ramage shrugged his shoulders. "How can I? I may not even survive to the end of the commission. This one may last a couple of years—I don't even know where I am going."

Sarah dabbed her eyes. "No, it's unfair of me to ask you to promise: it's enough that you think about it. But it's so lonely at Aldington when you're at sea. I love the place, but I get lonely."

"Ask your parents to stay. The marquis will enjoy the riding and your mother will enjoy chasing the gardener to plant more flowers!"

"The day after tomorrow, when the furniture is delivered, may I come to the ship again?"

"I was hoping you would, just to keep an eye on things and make sure that Silkin stows everything away properly."

"Silkin will hate having the captain's wife interfering, but I want to see how the curtains and cushions look. It's one thing seeing the material in the shop before they are made, but it will be another seeing them in the ship. I hope I've made the right choices. I'm beginning to worry now. You have to live with them."

CHAPTER FIVE

AS RAMAGE left the ship for the port admiral's office the next morning, the first ships of the West Indies convoy were sailing into Spithead and the three junior lieutenants were just setting off with press-gangs in the boats. Ramage knew that it was a gamble: there were other ships in Portsmouth and at Spithead who needed more men, and they would be sending off press-gangs at the same time. He could picture the men in the homecoming West Indiamen watching with sinking hearts as the boats approached: it must be a cruel torture to be snatched for the king's service when so near home after a long voyage abroad.

But the fact remained that the king's ships had to be manned:

there was a long and bitter war to be fought, and so far most
of it had been fought at sea, so that seamen were needed. How
many would he get from the convoy? It could be as many as
a hundred or as few as twenty-five. One thing was fairly certain—most of them would be prime seamen. He was thankful
that he now had a full complement of marines—an unexpected
bonus adding 123 men to the 225 or so brought over from the
Calypso. At the moment, then, he was short of 277 men. He
could expect to sail short of 77 men, so he needed a couple of
hundred, more if possible. A hundred men from the West Indies
convoy and another hundred from the convoy due in from the
Cape—was that too much to hope for? He decided it was. He
would end up having to send press-gangs combing the countryside, apart from printing posters appealing to men to volunteer. He wondered whether posters were really worth the
trouble. His name was well enough known to men who might
volunteer, but they would be put off by the fact that he was
no longer commanding a frigate. A frigate was more likely to
get prize-money—much more than a 74. Frigates equalled prize-
money, 74s did not: it was as simple as that.

When he arrived at the port admiral's house and was led
into Vice-Admiral Rossiter's office, he at once noticed the heap
of Daily Reports piled up on the desk. There was a smaller pile
beside it, and he recognized his own writing.

Rossiter was friendly enough: his red face, greyish-silver hair
and general manner still reminded Ramage of a landowner, and
it was still a surprise to see him in uniform.

The admiral tapped the smaller pile of reports. "You seem
to be nearly ready to sail—except for men."

"I'm hoping to get some prime seamen from the West India
convoy which is just coming in."

Rossiter sniffed. "Fifty if you're lucky. The *Dido* isn't the only
ship needing men."

"No, sir, but she's the only one that concerns me," Ramage said ruefully.

Rossiter gave a brisk laugh. "You haven't received your orders yet from the Admiralty?"

"No sir: I haven't the faintest idea where I'm going."

"Well, they ordered you to provision for six months, so you won't be hanging around the Channel, unless they want you for blockade duty off Brest."

Ramage sighed. "I hadn't thought of that."

"It's not too bad in the summer," Rossiter said. "It's the winter that sorts out the men from the boys. You know Brest?"

"I was caught on land near there when the war began again—I was on my honeymoon."

"Oh yes, I remember hearing something about it. Well, you'll be familiar with the Black Rocks. 'Close up to the Black Rocks in an easterly,'" the admiral quoted, repeating the rule for the blockade, an easterly wind being the only one with which the French could sail out of port. "You should get your orders in a day or so—I shall tell the Admiralty by telegraph today that you are nearly ready to sail. I expect your orders will come down with the night messenger."

"I still need men, sir," Ramage reminded him.

"I'll send over as many as I can. Don't be too hopeful, but I can skim a few men from some ships that have full complements. Have you all your officers yet?"

"A fifth lieutenant to come, that's all. The gunner and chaplain arrived yesterday."

"How is her Ladyship? Are you still at The George?"

"She's well, and yes, we are still there."

"I still haven't met your wife," Rossiter grumbled.

"We haven't seen much of each other since we were married," Ramage said. "I had just started some leave when I was given command of the *Dido*."

"You're hinting that you don't want me to order you to sleep on board yet."

Ramage laughed and said: "My furniture won't be delivered until tomorrow. At this moment the cabin, coach, and bedplace are bare of anything except the twelve-pounders."

"I've never met a young husband at a loss for a reason to sleep on shore," Rossiter said amiably. "Let me know as soon as you receive orders from the Admiralty."

The sails were swayed up to the yards by slings and bent on during the day: heavy and hard work. Southwick commented: "It's a miracle how much we've got done so far: fitting out a ship of the line with a frigate's complement is like being on a treadmill."

The boats with the press-gangs came back just after the mid-day meal, a delighted Aitken reporting to Ramage: "We got 97 men altogether. Clapton's busy getting their names down in the Muster Book. At least half of them should be prime seamen."

"Let's hope we're as lucky with the Cape convoy. It's due in tomorrow."

"I don't see why we shouldn't," Aitken said. "Kenton said there were not many other gangs out."

"The admiral said he would send over some men. A hundred from the Cape convoy and fifty from the admiral, and we'll be able to sail."

"We were lucky to get our full complement of marines," Aitken commented. "Rennick says they're well trained, and he's quite content with the two lieutenants."

"I'm more concerned with his four sergeants and four corporals: they are the backbone of the force," Ramage said.

"We'll soon know," Aitken said. "I've got them bending on sails, and hoisting them up from the sail room is just the work for those marines—some of them are giants."

"How many of the new men are volunteering?" Ramage asked.

"When I last saw Clapton, most of them were taking the bounty. I think about one in ten was being put down as 'pressed.'"

Every man brought on board by a press-gang was given the chance of "volunteering" and thus qualifying for the bounty paid to volunteers. It meant that "vol." was put against his name, instead of "p" for pressed. Apart from being paid the bounty, it did not affect the way that a man was treated in the ship, but it did mean that a volunteer usually served more willingly—he had none of the resentment often felt by a man who had insisted on being rated "pressed."

Ramage, feeling bored, said: "Let's make an inspection of the ship. Then I'll fill in the Daily Report and send it across to the admiral. He seemed quite content when I saw him this morning. Anyway, he did not complain."

As he followed the first lieutenant out of the cabin and crossed the half-deck, Ramage began to feel depressed again: the ship looked a mess. There were heaps of canvas, more rolled up sails waiting to be swayed up to the yards, and the decks were filthy. There was no need to comment on them to Aitken: there was no room to scrub them because ropes and sails took up every spare inch of space. Frayed ends of rope littered the gangways, thrown down as men cut them off the coil. They had various names: cows' tails—which they resembled—or "Irish pennants," a title no doubt unfair to Ireland.

At least the guns looked tidy; they stood against the ports, tackles and breechings secure, the barrels shiny with a coating of new black gun lacquer and the carriages and trucks newly painted in yellow. The thirty-two-pounders were damned big guns, he thought, his eye much more accustomed to the *Calypso's* twelve-pounders. But the *Dido* was a ship of the line: if she ever fought in the line-of-battle she would be expected to give a good account of herself, and most of the punch would come from those thirty-two-pounders.

Up on the fo'c'sle painters were giving the last few dabs to the belfry, but the ship's bell itself was in need of polishing. Ramage could see from the way that Aitken eyed it (as though it had an unpleasant smell) that he could not wait for the painters to get out of the way and the paint to dry enough for him to set men to work with brick dust restoring a polish to the tarnished metal.

The huge mooring bitts were freshly painted; the knight-heads and catheads, too, had been carefully touched up. But the *Dido* did not look like a ship yet. In fact, Ramage decided, she looked more like a warehouse where a lot of gear had been dumped on the floor without rhyme or reason.

"When do you expect the new fifth lieutenant, sir?" Aitken asked unexpectedly.

"I should have thought he'd have arrived by now. He's the last of the officers."

"I wonder if he will fit in," Aitken speculated. "We were lucky with Hill; he's settled down very well and gets on with Kenton and Martin. And Southwick; too. I think the old boy is quite fond of him."

"Yes, he has a nice dry sense of humour," Ramage said. "And plenty of initiative."

"We're lucky that all three of them have plenty of that. And young Orsini, too."

"Yes. I am going to make him a master's mate. That'll keep him ahead of these other midshipmen."

Ramage was unusual in always referring to them as "mid-shipmen:" it was usual to refer to them as the "young gentle-men," although their official rank—how they were listed in the Muster Book—was midshipmen. For years now Orsini had been the only midshipman on board the *Calypso*, and for that reason had quite unconsciously built himself up a privileged position, because it was usual for a frigate to have up to a dozen midshipmen on board. Ramage did not have a very high opinion of their usefulness, and Orsini had been lucky because, being the only one, he had been given extra responsibility, quite apart from the fact that his mathematics and navigation received Southwick's undivided attention, although mathematics were never going to be Orsini's strongest subject.

The huge foresail had been hoisted up and topmen were busy overhead securing it to the yard. The mainsail was already bent on to its yard and the maintopsail was being secured. Ramage was thankful that the shot for the thirty-two-pounders, twenty-four-pounders, and twelve-pounders had been left on board: collecting them from the stores and hoisting them in would have been a miserable job for the men. There was only the powder to come. For safety's sake every ship being refitted unloaded her powder into the powder hulks—a precaution against fire causing catastrophic explosions that could lay waste much of Portsmouth.

As Ramage and Aitken continued their inspection of the fo'c'sle, one of the new midshipmen came hurrying up. "Mr Kenton's compliments, sir, but the new fifth lieutenant has just arrived on board."

"Tell him to get his gear below and present himself in the cabin in fifteen minutes," Ramage said.

As the boy hurried off, Ramage commented to the first lieutenant: "Talk of the Devil . . ."

They went down to the mess-deck, and Ramage was glad all the ports were open, creating a draught to get rid of the smell of paint. He looked round at the guns, tables, and forms. The painters had been busy with the guns and carriages; the tables and forms were well scrubbed. Overhead rammers, sponges and wormers were held up in racks, restricting even more the limited headroom.

Aitken looked around him and said cheerfully: "It's a far cry from the *Calypso*, sir."

"Yes, nearly three times the number of men. And quite a few more guns . . ."

"I hadn't realized how big a 74 was until I found myself responsible for having it painted," Aitken said wryly. "And trying to run the ship with a frigate's complement of men isn't easy."

"Well, you've the marines and the West Indiamen to help you now," Ramage said.

"I'm afraid they've arrived when the worst part of the work has been done."

"More credit to you."

"Much of the credit is due to Southwick, he's been invaluable, especially in rigging the ship. He's forgotten more about rigging a 74 than I'll ever know."

"Well, learn as much as you can; it may be a three-decker one day!"

Aitken sighed. "I hope I've been posted by then: I don't think I could stand the strain if I was still a first lieutenant!"

Ramage took out his watch. "I had better get along to the cabin and see this new officer."

There were many cabins in a ship, but only the captain's cabin was always referred to by everyone as "the cabin." Ramage walked under the half-deck and through the coach into the cabin, thankful that tomorrow his furniture would arrive, and he would have chairs to sit in, and a desk to use.

The marine sentry suddenly knocked on the door and called: "Lieutenant Hicks to see you, sir."

"Send him in."

Ramage sat down on the breech of the starboard twelve-pounder and watched as a thin-faced young man with fair hair slouched into the cabin. He was white-faced and pimply: he was round-shouldered and walked as though he expected to keep on glancing over his shoulder to see who was following him. He was, Ramage decided at once, one of the king's bad bargains.

"Hicks, sir, fifth lieutenant." He handed over a sheet of paper that was his orders. Ramage noticed they were dated six days earlier.

"Welcome on board, Mr Hicks," he said coldly. "I notice your orders were given some time ago. Where were you when you received them?"

"In London," Hicks said airily.

"You did not hurry yourself."

"But I did, sir. I came straight to Portsmouth."

"Taking six days? Did you walk?"

"No, I've been staying at the Star and Garter."

"You've been what?" Ramage asked quietly.

"At the Star and Garter, sir. I knew the ship was still fitting out, so there was no hurry."

Ramage knew he would be hard put to keep his temper, but he said, his voice still dangerously quiet: "Fitting out needs the full cooperation of every officer. Why did you think you need not hurry?"

"I was in a card school," Hicks said in an offhand way. "The stakes were high—all of us have just received a payment of prize-money from our agent."

"So instead of reporting for duty, you stayed on shore gambling?" Ramage asked incredulously.

"Gambling and losing," Hicks said. "I'd lost so much I had to keep on playing in the hopes of recouping."

"And you failed?"

Hicks nodded. "I went down for seven hundred guineas."

"So you then decided it was time to join your ship?"

Hicks shrugged his shoulders. "I'm not finished with it yet, sir. I need permission to leave the ship before dawn tomorrow, sir, just for an hour or two."

Ramage stood up and stared at the lieutenant, hardly able to believe his ears. "What, do you want to go riding?"

"No, sir: one of the men I was playing, my biggest creditor, has called me out."

It took Ramage only a few seconds to consider his answer. "I do not permit my officers to duel."

"But sir, I have no choice. I can't pay up seven hundred guineas and I can't refuse the challenge."

"Let me be sure I understand you, Hicks. You've been accused of cheating, you owe seven hundred guineas, and you've been called out?"

"That's it, sir. If I don't fight I'll be branded a cheat and still owe seven hundred guineas."

"Who has challenged you?"

"The second lieutenant of the *Hyperion* frigate, sir. He's famous as a duellist," he added uncomfortably.

"And the weapons?"

"Pistols, sir, at ten yards."

"If you accept the challenge, you're a dead man, Hicks, and more important I'm short of a fifth lieutenant."

"I know, sir," the young man said, sounding trapped. "The trouble is that this isn't the only gambling debt I have, and he's threatened to go to my father—after the duel."

"After you're dead, you mean."

"Probably, sir. But quite a few people have been to my father, and he's refused to pay any more debts."

"I can't say I blame him. Gambling like this is a disease, Hicks. How long have you been at it?"

"Two or three years, sir. I won at first."

"By cheating?"

"Well, taking every advantage I could," Hicks said lamely.

Ramage said, his voice cold, "This means my new fifth lieutenant is a cardsharper who has been caught out cheating and called out. And you have the thundering cheek to ask me if you can leave the ship for an hour at dawn tomorrow morning!"

"But I don't have any choice, sir: my luck has run out."

"That will teach you to rely on luck. Any man who does that is a fool. That will be all. Tell the sentry to pass the word for the first lieutenant." Hicks waited, as though he had more to say, and then, white-faced, turned on his heel and left the cabin.

When Aitken arrived Ramage, who had resumed sitting on the breech of the twelve-pounder, said: "This new fifth lieutenant: a bad bargain, I'm afraid."

"How so, sir?"

"He's a cardsharper who has been caught by a lieutenant from the *Hyperion* frigate and called out. He's due to fight at dawn tomorrow."

"So we'll need a new fifth lieutenant," Aitken said unsympathetically. "Well, we've got on quite well so far without one."

"This fellow has been in Portsmouth for days. He's been staying at the Star and Garter, gambling away some prize-money. He lost seven hundred guineas, cheated and was caught. Not his only gambling debt, he tells me."

Aitken groaned. "Why do we have to get him? We've been lucky up to now."

"Well, we have two problems. How to prevent him fighting this duel, and how to get him changed."

Aitken said grimly: "Let him fight the duel and the second problem might solve itself, sir: with him dead the Admiralty have to replace him."

"No officer of this ship is going to fight a duel," Ramage said stubbornly. "Not even a grubby cardsharper. The question is how we stop him. We have to do it in such a way that it isn't a question of him refusing the challenge, though why we should be concerned with his squalid honour I don't know. He was sitting gambling at the Star and Garter with orders to join the *Dido* stuffed in his pocket."

"How many days, sir?"

"I don't know. Three or four, I think."

"That's disobeying a direct Admiralty order."

Ramage glanced at Aitken. "So I should put him under an arrest, and apply to the admiral for a court martial?"

The first lieutenant shrugged his shoulders. "It would keep him in the ship, and if we have to sail no doubt the admiral can find us another fifth lieutenant. Most admirals have a favourite close under their lee."

"Very well. Put him under arrest and confine him to his cabin. I'll pass the word to the captain of the *Hyperion*—it's his second lieutenant who is concerned. And a letter to the port admiral asking for a court martial. It's a lot of trouble, just to save that young fool's life . . ."

Vice-Admiral Rossiter was in his office, and as soon as he had greeted Ramage he held up a letter. "Your orders have arrived from the Admiralty. How is everything progressing?"

"We need another couple of days, sir; then we'll be ready to take on our powder. Oh yes, we do have one problem—our new fifth lieutenant."

Rossiter raised his eyebrows. "Why, the last time I saw you, you were waiting for him to arrive."

"He was in trouble as soon as he arrived," Ramage said shortly, handing over the letter he had written. Rossiter put the letter down and said: "Tell me about it."

Briefly Ramage described the situation, and went on to tell the admiral how Hicks had been staying at the Star and Garter gambling, instead of joining the *Dido.*

"Duelling, eh? I don't want any duels fought in my dock-yard, and I'm sure the commander-in-chief would not take kindly to any of his officers duelling. Who has called him out?"

"The second of the *Hyperion,* sir. I've little doubt he had good enough reasons—Hicks admits he has other gambling debts, and as good as admitted to me that he cheated—'taking every advantage that he could' were his words."

"If he is court-martialled, he won't be able to sail with you. In fact, come to think of it, you won't be able to sail until after the trial. He can't be tried in less than a week."

"The main thing is that I want him confined under an arrest so that he can't fight the duel tomorrow morning, sir."

Rossiter shrugged his shoulders. "You can keep him under an arrest for a few days and then decide not to press charges."

"I don't want the fellow on board, sir," Ramage said bluntly. "He's obviously a bad influence, and as he's a compulsive gam-bler, he's going to come to a sticky end."

The admiral tapped his desk with Ramage's letter. "I can send him to the guard-ship and give you another fifth lieu-tenant," he said slowly. "I am prepared to do that because I know you have your old ship's company with you, and obvi-ously it's an efficient one. This fellow could be the one bad apple in the barrel."

"That would be the best way, sir: I don't want to hang about for a court martial, but I do want to get rid of this fellow."

Rossiter gestured at the letter Ramage was holding. "Why don't you read your orders?"

Ramage broke the seal and opened the single sheet of paper. The orders were brief and simple: after provisioning for six months and completing the fitting out of his ship to the satisfaction of the port admiral, Ramage was to sail to the West Indies, placing himself under the command of Rear-Admiral Samuel Cameron, the commander-in-chief of the Windward Islands Station at Barbados. Ramage managed to avoid giving a sigh of relief: he had not been told to escort a convoy, the dreariest task he could think of.

"Well?" asked Rossiter. "To your liking?"

"Barbados, sir. I always like going back to the West Indies."

"Yes, nothing wrong with the place, as long as you avoid yellow fever, malaria and blackwater . . . You've been lucky so far, if my memory serves me. I seem to remember various *Gazette* letters from there."

"Indeed, I've been lucky," Ramage admitted. "Both in dodging disease and finding action."

"Very well," the admiral said briskly. "I take it you don't want to go ahead and bring this fellow to trial as long as I can replace him?"

"No, sir. I'm very grateful to you."

Rossiter tore up the letter he was still holding. "By the way, you can sleep on shore for another couple of days. Then you'll be ready to take on powder and sail."

Ramage arrived on board the *Dido* next morning with Sarah, and was pleased to find that there were three carts alongside the ship and seamen were already busy carefully hoisting on board his furniture, using the stay tackle. The dining table, desk, and drawers were packed in straw, which had been tied round the polished woodwork to protect it. The chairs looked as though they were growing out of a cornfield.

Sarah commented on the care that the shop had taken, and Ramage said: "Wait until the crockery and cutlery arrives. It's another shop, and they may not have dealt with a ship before."

They went to the cabin and a few minutes later sailors arrived carrying the table, having cut off the straw on deck. Ramage indicated where he wanted it put just as more men arrived with chairs. Within a quarter of an hour the rest of the furniture had been carried down and put in its place, and Ramage sat in one of the armchairs. "Comfortable enough," he told Sarah. "You made a good choice."

"The owner of the shop wasn't used to having ladies come in and choose this sort of furniture. He was most concerned when he heard you commanded the *Dido,* and promised to change anything you did not like." Sarah laughed and added: "I told him that you would like anything I chose—and he was most impressed. At least, I think he was. He may not have believed a word I said!"

The contrast between the pieces of furniture and the two 12-pounders was dramatic. The two barrels of the guns, which seemed to be crouching on their carriages, black and shiny like serpents, were in stark contrast to the yellow and white covers that Sarah had chosen for the settee and armchairs.

Ramage had not been sitting down more than a few minutes before the carpenter arrived, asking permission to fit eyebolts to the deck and the underside of each piece of furniture, so that the light chairs could be attached to stop them sliding about the cabin when the *Dido* rolled in a seaway. Soon the cabin seemed to be full of the carpenter and his mates as they up-ended each piece of furniture and started drilling for the screws to hold the eyeplates. Finally they shackled on the chains and left.

C H A P T E R   S I X

RAMAGE opened his Journal and dipped his quill in the ink. The page was headed "Journal of the Proceedings of his Majesty's ship ———, Captain ———, Commander, between the ——— and the ———."

He filled in "*Dido*" and his own name, and the dates. There were nine columns, each with its own heading, which went from the date to "Winds," "Courses," "Miles," the latitude the ship was in and the amount of longitude made, bearing and distances at noon (they were too far out to sea to give either) and the last column, which was headed "Remarkable Observations and Accidents."

He looked at the pencilled note that Southwick had given him and started filling in the columns. The wind had been north-east, the courses had been south and south-south-west, they had covered 120 miles since noon the previous day, the present latitude was 25° 7' North, they had stayed in the same longitude, and in the last column he wrote: "Weather unsettled and sighted several waterspouts. Fore-topgallant badly chafed, sent down and replaced. Exercised ship's company at great guns."

And that, he thought as he wiped the quill and put the cap on the ink, was all there was to say for a day in which the *Dido* had ploughed on just approaching the Tropics with a wind that was fitful and a sky heavy with thunderstorms.

The entry did not tell anything of the *Dido*. It did not tell of Ramage's efforts to train the two hundred or so men that had been taken from the West India and Cape convoys just before she sailed. There was the core of the Calypsos, but there were the new men to be trained in the ways of the Navy. Most of them were good seamen—that was why incoming convoys yielded a good harvest for press-gangs—but they knew little or nothing about gunnery. Few masters of merchant ships bothered to give their men any gunnery training, and few merchant ships carried anything larger than a long six-pounder.

So on most days since they left the Channel, the Didos had been exercising the guns: running in and running out the big thirty-two-pounders and the twenty-four-pounders, as well as the twelve-pounders and the carronades. Every couple of days the men were switched from one calibre of gun to another, so that they soon had experience of them all; every third day the guns were actually fired, filling the ears with the thunder of the explosions and the ship with thick smoke.

The new men were learning quickly. Most of them had got over their resentment at being snatched into the king's service just when they were expecting to go home on well earned leave, and most were thankful to find that their new ship had a firm and fair captain whose only quirk, it seemed, was an obsession with gunnery. In general the new men were sensible enough to appreciate that in these early days the enemy was not a French ship of the line ranged up alongside them but the watches held in the hands of the lieutenants, which relentlessly timed their activities.

Ramage closed his Journal, put it in a drawer of his desk, and went outside for a stroll up and down his balcony. He was enjoying the balcony: it was somewhere that he could pace alone with his thoughts with the ship's wake gurgling away below him and with just the creak of gudgeons and pintles as the rudder was turned by the men at the wheel.

What a rush those last few days in Portsmouth had turned out to be. Apart from getting the extra men—the ship had finally sailed with a complement of 602, 23 short of her establishment—it was found that a good deal of the water was bad, so much had to be emptied out and pumped over the side and fresh brought from the dockyard. And at the last moment, thanks to his strong complaints, the dockyard had produced a spare suit of sails, and these had to be struck below to the sail room a matter of hours before they sailed to get the powder on board.

Sarah had finally left—tearfully—for London with Jessop driving the carriage, and Ramage was grateful to Vice-Admiral Rossiter for leaving them alone until the last minute. Sarah had finally admitted that she could not bear standing on Portsmouth Point watching the *Dido* disappear in the distance, so she had driven off as the *Dido* left the Camber to take on powder.

Now the ship could be self-contained for six months, able to feed all her men and (he hoped) with enough powder and shot to fight off her enemies. But, he reflected, there was no getting away from the fact that a 74 was a big ship. Apart from the ship herself, 200 feet long from figurehead to taffrail, and 275 feet from the tip of her jib-boom to the end of the spanker boom, and weighing about 2,800 tons, 602 men looked to him for leadership, discipline and justice. And yes, he had to be a father to them all, as well, even though some of them—Southwick, for instance—were old enough to be his grandfather. He was the captain, with all that implied. He was responsible for feeding and fighting the ship; he had to make sure that the purser did not cheat, that the gunner looked after the guns, the surgeon the sick, the chaplain their souls, the master the sails and rigging and the first lieutenant the general running of the ship. But, he thought ruefully, if any one of his commission or warrant officers failed, the Admiralty would blame him.

He was thankful that he had managed to get rid of that card-sharping fifth lieutenant, Hicks. If he had stayed on, the ward-room would probably be in an uproar by now; Kenton, Martin, and Hill were good men, but there was obviously a limit to what they could stand. However, the new man provided by Admiral Rossiter seemed to be proving satisfactory.

He watched as a Mother Carey's chicken—known to some as a stormy petrel—flew across the *Dido*'s stern and turned to fly along her wake. Where did they sleep? There always seemed to be a few in sight. And soon they would be seeing—admittedly only occasionally—his favourite, the tropic bird. Slender and white with a very long forked tail, the tropic bird would fly steadily, never jinking, always in a straight line as though it knew exactly where it was going. But where was that? It was often 1,500 miles to the nearest land, yet the tropic bird flew on sturdily as though it was merely crossing the five miles between two neighbouring islands.

He heard shouting and knew one of the lookouts aloft was hailing the quarterdeck. What had he sighted, so far from land? It could be a particularly large waterspout to windward, so that the officer of the deck could luff up or bear away to avoid it. Although Ramage had never been in a ship hit by a waterspout he had heard many stories about their destructive force: they could rip out masts with the sails still attached, lift anything lying around the deck and suck it up, even take up boats on the booms and hurl them over the side.

Suddenly Aitken's head appeared at the taffrail and called down: "Sir, the foremast lookout reports a sail fine on the starboard bow, and perhaps another one beyond it. Steering on an opposite course to us."

"Very well, beat to quarters. I'll be with you in a moment."

That was one of the important differences between a frigate and a ship of the line: a frigate could be at general quarters in five minutes, but even with a well-trained crew it took a 74 at least fifteen minutes, and that was no time at all with two ships approaching each other at five or six knots: they would cover two and a half or three miles in that time.

He reached the quarterdeck just as the two marine drummers started clattering away, and the calls of bosun's mates were twittering below, followed by the raucous shouts of "All hands to general quarters!"

"What can you see?" Ramage asked Aitken.

"Just the hint of a sail from down here, sir."

"Send Orsini aloft with a bring-'em-near."

A sail out here? Possibly—no, in this position it would not be a convoy, or even a frigate on her way to England. In fact it was hard to guess why any ship should venture here on an opposite course, in other words beating to windward against the Trade Winds. On the same course, yes; they could be overhauling a slower ship on her way to the magic position, 25° North, 25° West, when one turned to begin one's westing. But a ship sailing north in this position?

"Hoist the private signal," he told Aitken.

The private signal was a challenge-and-reply code, changed every three months and known only to the king's ships in a particular area. When two strange ships met, one or other flew the challenge and the other—if British—flew the reply, and this was followed by both ships hoisting their pendant numbers, so they could be identified from the signal book, which gave a list of all the ships in the Navy with their pendant numbers.

He saw Orsini scrambling up the lee shrouds of the mainmast: he went up as fast as a topman, even though he was carrying a telescope.

The *Dido* was now like a suddenly disturbed anthill: men were hurriedly rigging head pumps and sluicing water across the decks; others were scattering sand. The water prevented loose grains of gunpowder being ignited by, for example, the trucks of a recoiling gun carriage; the sand stopped the men slipping with their bare feet.

More men were casting off the lashings and securing the guns and running them back ready for loading; others rolled small tubs beside the guns and filled them with water, ready for swabbing out the barrels of the guns. Rammers, mops, and wormers were put ready beside the guns.

And below, Ramage knew, the gunner had unlocked the magazine and even now was beginning to issue flintlocks, prickers, and powder horns to the gun captains, while the powder monkeys were beginning to form up ready to carry cartridges up to the guns.

In his cabin men would be shifting his furniture below to the hold to leave room to handle the guns and reduce the chance of splinters. Bulkheads were being hinged up to the deckhead or taken down, again to avoid splinters from shot smashing through the hull. It was this sort of preparation—mercifully absent when the *Calypso* used to go into action—that used up the quarter of an hour it took to prepare the *Dido* for general quarters.

The bustle of war: to the untrained eye it seemed as though many men were running about aimlessly: to an eye trained in the ways of a ship of war, every man was moving fast to do his duty.

Southwick came up and said: "An odd position to find someone steering north, sir."

"That's what I was thinking."

Southwick gave one of his expressive sniffs. "All the gunnery exercise might come in useful sooner than we expected."

"We'll soon know. I wish Orsini would hurry up and give us a hail—is this sail a privateer or a ship of the line?"

Southwick shrugged his shoulders. "In this position it could be either. Of course, it could be someone who had been heading south, spotted us first, and hauled their wind to come north to investigate us."

"If that's the case, I shall want to know why our lookouts were asleep."

"No," Southwick said, "on second thoughts it doesn't seem very likely. Damnation, Orsini's taking his time!"

A minute or two later Orsini hailed that the sail was a frigate steering on an opposite course with everything set to the royals. "There's another sail astern of her, though I can't make out if she's following or chasing."

Two ships? Two ships in this position both steering north? "Furl the courses, Mr Aitken," Ramage said. If there was any fighting to be done, let it be under topsails. With the great courses furled, only the topgallants remained to be taken in.

The bosun's mates piped the order, and men ran up the shrouds to the yards while others stood by at buntlines and clew-lines. Soon the billowing canvas was stifled, gaskets passed and the sails were rolled up on the yards, almost as neat as if they had been given a harbour stow.

Then Orsini hailed again. "The second ship is also a frigate. I think I can make out the occasional flash of guns—the bow-chasers of the second ship. She's too far away to see any smoke."

"One frigate chasing another, eh?" commented Southwick.

And that meant the first frigate was probably British, steering for the *Dido* in the hope that she was British. A frigate running away from a frigate? Why did she not stand and fight? But a moment after Ramage puzzled over the question, Orsini hailed again.

"There's a third ship, her masts are just coming over the horizon."

So the first frigate could be chased by two other frigates. That would explain why she was not standing and fighting: no one expected a single frigate to fight two others of equal or greater size.

"What do you make of it, sir?" asked Aitken.

"A British frigate being chased by a couple of French, and damned glad to see us ahead of her. They're praying we're British—they may have recognized us as British by the cut of our sails."

Orsini hailed again. "There's a fourth ship, bigger than the others. I think she's a ship of the line. She's following the frigates."

One British frigate being chased by two French frigates and a ship of the line? The British ship was lucky to spot the *Dido* . . .

The question was, would she reach the *Dido* before the frigate just astern of her ranged up alongside and began pouring in broadsides and a lucky—unlucky, rather—shot brought down a mast?

Ramage realized he had prolonged the time before the *Dido* met the frigate by furling the courses, but if the *Dido* was going to have to fight off two frigates and a 74—assuming the ship of the line was no bigger—she had to be prepared.

"Mr Southwick, go down and inspect the guns. Stop and have a word with that new fifth lieutenant—this may be the first time he's ever been in action, and he'll be a bit nervous."

There was no need to worry about Kenton, Martin and Hill: they had been in action enough times in the *Calypso*, although this would be the first time in the *Dido*. Still, the only difference was that the guns were bigger; the drill was the same.

Orsini hailed yet again: the last ship ahead was a 74, and the second frigate was fast overhauling the first one. "I think the first one is flying the private signal, but she's too far off to be sure."

"Make sure the reply is bent on the halyards," Ramage told Aitken. "I don't want any delay in hoisting it when the time comes."

Above him on the poop deck he could hear the guns' crews at work loading the carronades. Eight of them—four each side— might come in useful if there was any close fighting with the frigates, which were light and handy, much easier to manoeu- vre than the heavy 74. But for all that, one well-aimed broad- side from the *Dido* could wreck a frigate. With all his experience of the *Calypso,* Ramage found he could see just how the French frigate captains up ahead would be thinking when they saw the *Dido* was a 74. It was an interesting situation—as soon as they got closer to the *Dido* would they reduce sail and wait for their 74 to catch up with them, leaving the 74 to engage the 74?

They could not be blamed if they did: it was the convention that frigates engaged frigates and ships of the line engaged ships of the line—unless a ship of the line met a frigate, in which case the frigate could expect no mercy. That, he recalled rue- fully, remembering his own experience, was when cunning counted more than firepower if the frigate was to escape.

He picked up the speaking-trumpet and hailed Orsini. "How far off is the first frigate?" He could see her from the deck but Orsini, up aloft, would be able to judge more accurately.

"The British frigate's a couple of miles but the second frigate is almost abreast of her. The 74 is about three miles, perhaps four, from us."

Time was running out and ranges were getting shorter. Soon, he thought grimly, I shall be taking the *Dido* into action for the first time. It was a damned nuisance that it was not a clear-cut action with another 74; having a couple of frigates thrown in as well complicated the issue, though with luck they would not be such a nuisance as the *Calypso* would have been in a similar situation. That was a pardonable conceit, he decided; after all, on her last voyage under his command she had been responsible for two French 74s disabling themselves.

He lifted his telescope to his eye. Yes, he could see the first—presumably the British—frigate quite clearly now, and Orsini hailed again.

"The first frigate is flying the private signal, sir. Number 63."

"Mr Aitken, hoist the reply!"

The answer today was 91, and quickly the two flags were hoisted, and Ramage added: "And now our pendant numbers, Mr Aitken."

Three more flags, representing the *Dido*'s number in the List of the Navy, were hoisted.

Southwick, back from the gun-deck, took off his hat, ran his fingers through his mop of white hair, and said: "I'll wager he's thankful to see the right answer to the challenge. Now he's busy looking us up in the signal book. Not that he'll know you command her now."

Southwick's compliment was matter-of-fact: the man was incapable of saying anything sycophantic. Ramage was startled to think that it might encourage another captain to find that his would-be rescuer was commanded by Captain Ramage. Yes, there had been several *Gazette* letters which printed his despatches, but he had never thought of the effect they might have on his fellow captains, or that they might be building up a reputation for him that affected the attitude of other captains. Admirals yes; he had already suffered once or twice from jealous admirals.

Orsini hailed again. "She has just hoisted her pendant numbers: five seven three."

Aitken snatched up the signal book and turned to the List of the Navy at the back. "She's the *Heron* frigate, sir."

Ramage saw through his telescope that the French frigate suddenly luffed up, and from the speckles of red erupting from her side, obviously had just fired a raking broadside into the British frigate. But as, wreathed in smoke, she resumed her course it was obvious that the manoeuvre had cost her a couple of hundred yards: she was now astern of the *Heron* again.

Ramage said: "It's time to get Orsini down from aloft. Give him a hail—he can look after the poop."

Southwick picked up the speaking-trumpet and bellowed the order to Orsini, who hurried down the shrouds, still clutching a telescope.

Ramage could see now that the *Heron* was about a mile and a half away. She was steering north, hard on the wind, with the two French frigates close astern in her wake and the 74 a mile or so astern, and obviously intent on overhauling her. The *Dido* was still heading south with a quartering north-east wind. On this course she could collide with the *Heron,* so it would be easy enough to steer slightly to leeward of her—that would put him nicely to windward of the first French frigate, cutting her off from the *Heron.* What would the *Heron* do then—would she continue scampering off to the north or would she turn to help the *Dido* deal with the frigates? She would be silly to try to tackle the 74, but Ramage knew he would be glad of her help in tackling the frigates, because there would not be much time before the French 74 was in the middle of the fight and probably taking up all the *Dido*'s attention.

Which meant giving the *Heron* orders: he was startled to find that he would be the senior officer. It could be that the *Heron* was commanded by a grizzled old frigate captain whose commission was dated long before Ramage's, but he would not know it. The *Heron's* captain would instinctively obey orders signalled by a 74, and that was all that mattered until this coming action was over.

It was time to get ready for the first broadsides. "I'll have the guns run out, Mr Aitken; we'll be engaging first on the starboard side, so make sure the men are warned."

Steady, he told himself; it was quite unnecessary to tell Aitken about warning the men: he was letting himself get fussed by the thought of taking a 74 into action for the first time.

CHAPTER   SEVEN

MEN WERE wetting the decks again with the head pumps: the heat was drying the planking—an indication that they were nearly in the Tropics. More men were going round sprinkling sand. Others would be doing the same thing on the gun-deck.

As Ramage reached for the signal book he heard Orsini's voice on the deck above giving some orders.

He flicked through the pages. Yes, number 29 would do: there would not be a signal which said precisely what he intended, but 29 should cover it: *"The ships of the fleet are, independently of each other, to steer for and engage their respective opponents in the enemy's line."*

"Respective opponents" should make it clear to the *Heron* that she was expected to engage the frigates, not the 74.

"Mr Aitken, have signal number 29 bent on ready for hoisting."

There I go again, he thought crossly: there was no need to

mention "ready for hoisting;" if the flags were bent on obviously they would be hoisted in time.

His telescope showed him that the *Heron's* sails were almost new: obviously she had only recently left England. Most probably she had been bound for the West Indies, like the *Dido*, when she ran into the French force. But for sighting the *Dido*, she would have been battered into hauling down her flag. And do not forget, Ramage told himself ruefully, that even now the *Heron* and the *Dido* are outnumbered by one frigate which, in this strange contest just coming up, could be significant.

Had that Frenchman's raking broadside had much effect on the *Heron*? Ramage wondered. It certainly had not brought down any masts or yards, though the French usually aimed at the rigging and sails, firing on the upward roll, while the British always went for the hull, firing on the downward roll, making sure that a shot fired a little late would be likely to hit "twixt wind and water."

The *Heron* was fast approaching at the combined speeds of the two ships, and she was sailing as close to the wind as possible, trying to out-point the French. But these French frigates were close winded, usually able to point higher than their British opposite numbers.

He was watching the *Heron* through his telescope when suddenly she turned to larboard across the bow of the first French frigate. Ramage realized at once that she was raking the enemy and was making an attack because the nearness of the *Dido* meant that her attempt to escape from her pursuers was not so desperate.

The frigate was covered in smoke from her broadside and immediately she hauled her wind and turned north again, towards the *Dido*. Ramage could not see the effect on the enemy, but it was an impudent attack which might have been lucky in bringing down a mast.

"That might teach the Frenchman not to get too close," commented Aitken.

"The Frenchman will be slowing down very soon," Ramage said. "They won't want to get tangled up with us. They'll wait until their own 74 has caught up."

The *Heron* was now a mile away and Ramage told Aitken: "Hoist number 29."

He wanted enough time for the *Heron* to see the signal—in the excitement of having just raked her pursuer they might not be watching the *Dido*—and for her captain to understand what was expected of him.

Now was the time to plan his own move. It was—to begin with—fairly simple: he would run down between the *Heron* and the Frenchman, firing his starboard broadside into the enemy providing the Frenchman did not do the sensible thing, which would be to turn and run back to the protection of the 74. Then the *Dido* would run on and give the second frigate a broadside, and then leaving both frigates to the *Heron,* he would go on to attack the 74. She was, he knew, the main threat—both to the *Heron* and any ships on their way to the West Indies. If she got loose in a convoy, for instance—most outward-bound convoys had small escorts—the effect would be devastating.

The north-east wind was still little more than a fresh breeze; not enough to stir up whitecaps. The sky was still mottled with thunder clouds but the waterspouts seemed to have gone elsewhere. It was rather close, as though a thunderstorm was imminent. Today he had seen his first shoal of flying fish, and he had felt the usual excitement of returning to the Tropics. He freely admitted he hated the northern climate: it always seemed to be damp and cold, with usually a depressing drizzle. If he was free to live where he wanted he would buy a plantation somewhere like the island of Nevis. Not Barbados, which was too crowded and anyway too flat, nor Antigua, because he did not like the people who had settled there. Grenada, perhaps: it was a beautiful island.

But what the devil was he thinking about, considering the islands, when he had two enemy frigates ahead of him and a 74? At least he had the weather gauge. Being to windward of them all gave him a considerable tactical advantage because he could run down to attack them while they had to beat to windward to get up to him.

That went a part of the way to making up for the fact that he and the *Heron* were outnumbered by a frigate. And he was pleased to see that the captain of the *Heron* was a man with spirit, as shown by his attempt to rake his pursuer.

Now they were about to go into action for the first time. Jackson was the quartermaster—he always liked to have the American there when they were in a battle. Southwick and Aitken were with him on the quarterdeck, Aitken ready to take command if a random shot knocked his head off.

What would Sarah be doing now? Perhaps on her way down to Aldington. He was pleased that she so liked the estate he had inherited from his uncle. Given that he could not retire to the Tropics, Aldington was the next best place, sitting among the hills overlooking Romney Marsh, giving him a view extending to Dungeness.

"A point to starboard," he called to Jackson, who relayed the order to the four men at the wheel. It did not take four men to handle the wheel in this weather, but at general quarters two extra men joined the normal two, just in case any of them were killed. The two on the windward side were the ones that did the work.

That alteration of course would put the *Heron* fine on his larboard bow and kept the Frenchman to starboard. It should be clear to the *Heron* what he intended to do.

The *Dido* had barely turned when Southwick gave another of his prodigious sniffs as they saw the French frigate suddenly turn out to starboard and tack, turning south towards the 74.

"Shows he's got some sense," Southwick commented. "I was wondering how he'd stand up to our broadside!"

But Ramage now had a decision to make. The *Dido* was sailing along with her great courses furled: under reduced canvas she would never catch up with the frigate, and presumably the second one would turn away too. The question was, would the 74 stay and fight, or would she too make a bolt for it with the frigates?

There was no reason why she should bolt, since the French had the advantage; but, Ramage thought, there was also no reason why the French should stay and fight. There was a considerable difference between snapping up a single frigate and finding yourself unexpectedly in action with a British 74 as well.

He made up his mind and said to Aitken: "Let fall the courses."

The sails had hardly tumbled down and been sheeted home before the *Dido* had reached the *Heron,* and as she swept down past her the frigate turned out to starboard and tacked, so that she came round on to the same course as the *Dido.*

"He's understood what you meant by number 29," observed Southwick.

It took two or three minutes for the courses to start drawing properly, then as they added their thrust to the other sails the 2,800 tons of the *Dido* began to surge in pursuit of the French frigates.

The nearest one was now less than half a mile away, and with his glass Ramage could just make out the name *Sylphe* painted on her transom. She was fine on the starboard bow and steering directly for the French 74, like the chick running to the mother hen, but the *Dido* was overhauling her. Would she range up alongside before the frigate reached her consort?

And the second frigate: she was now swinging out and tacking before turning south, following the *Sylphe*'s manoeuvre. She was perhaps a quarter of a mile ahead of the *Sylphe,* busy trimming her sheets and braces after tacking.

Yes, the *Dido* was catching up on the *Sylphe:* he wanted to shout at the big 74 to pick up her skirts. That was the difference between a frigate and a ship of the line: a 74 was so much slower to answer—whether to the helm or random puffs of wind. Fortunately the wind was steady now so, with all her canvas drawing, the *Dido* surged ahead. She had all the advantage of a clean bottom, while the French ships were probably foul: at least he could hope so. That should knock a knot or two off their speed.

Now the *Sylphe* was close enough for him to be able to pick out details with the naked eye: she had a big patch on the larboard side of her maintopsail, and her topmasts were painted black, which was unusual. Her name was picked out in red on a white background with blue scrollwork. There was a puff of smoke as she opened fire on the *Dido* with her two stern-chase guns, but Ramage had decided not to use the *Dido*'s two bow-chasers: better to wait for the full broadside.

And that would not be long in coming: the *Sylphe* was barely a couple of ship's lengths ahead, now: Ramage could distinguish men standing on her poop and looking astern. And well they might: being chased by a lumbering 74 was, he knew from bitter experience, an intimidating spectacle, and they must be cursing that the *Dido* would overhaul them before they could reach their own 74.

"I'll have the guns run out, Mr Aitken."

Two of the midshipmen who had been standing aft on the quarterdeck were sent running down to the guns, and Aitken hailed up to Orsini on the poop. A moment later Ramage heard the heavy carronades being hauled out on their slides.

Ramage saw that the *Dido* would pass about fifty yards from the *Sylphe*'s larboard side: just the right distance for the *Dido*'s gunners to be able to see their target clearly and to be able to fire without haste. Passing too close meant that the target flashed past the gun ports without giving the gun captains time to adjust their aim.

Ramage knew the value of the first broadside: fired without haste there was no smoke to obscure the target, and the men were not too excited. It should be calmly destructive.

Now the *Dido*'s bowsprit was abreast the *Sylphe*'s taffrail and Ramage could picture the second captains cocking the locks and springing back to clear the recoil. Then the bowsprit was abreast the mizen and suddenly there was a heavy drumroll as the forward thirty-two-pounders and the twenty-four-pounders began firing. Gradually the heavy booming moved aft as more guns came to bear, and as Ramage watched the side of the *Sylphe* he saw the red flashes of her twelve-pounders firing back.

He was not absolutely sure of his feelings: the *Sylphe* was the enemy, and with her consort might well have pounded the *Heron* to matchwood if the *Dido* had not hove in sight, but she was a frigate with puny twelve-pounders while the *Dido* was a ship of the line with thirty-two-pounders: it seemed desperately unfair. Then he shook his head: it was only a few weeks ago in the Mediterranean that the *Calypso* had found herself caught between two French 74s, and he was sure that neither captain had much sympathy with him.

The *Dido*'s guns were firing quite slowly because she was not overtaking the *Sylphe* very quickly, and he was able to watch their effect. They were slowly dismantling the ship. Already the bulwarks aft had been smashed in and the starboard side of the taffrail had been battered down, as though the frigate's quarter had hit a dock. The boats stowed on the booms were smashed in and the wreckage hurled across the deck. Half a dozen gun port-lids hung down, ripped off their hinges by shot which had ploughed on to kill men serving the guns.

Now Ramage saw dust rising from amidships as more round shot hammered into the frigate's side, and Ramage could imagine the lethal showers of splinters cutting down the men at the guns. There was no doubt that the *Dido*'s men were obeying instructions and firing into the hull: there was very little damage to masts and yards—that he could see, anyway.

"Keep alongside her!" he snapped at Aitken and the first lieutenant shouted the orders that clewed up the courses, reducing their area, and under just topsails and topgallants the *Dido* slowed down, staying abreast of the *Sylphe*.

Now the guns were being reloaded and, while the smoke from the first broadside drifted across the quarterdeck, starting everyone coughing, the first of them fired again. Between the thunder of the guns Ramage thought he could hear screams from the French ship, but he was not sure: as well as the booming of the guns there was the rumble of the trucks on the deck as the guns hurled back in recoil, and some of the trucks squeaked. Squeaks and screams, it was all part of a devil's chorus.

"She won't be able to take much of this," Southwick said; and swore as a twelve-pounder shot from the *Sylphe* ricocheted across the quarterdeck and struck down one of the men at the wheel.

"She's hauling down her colours!" Aitken shouted.

Ramage swung his telescope and looked in case a stray shot

had cut the halyard, but no, there were two men—one of them looked like an officer—busy hauling on the rope.

"Cease fire!" Ramage shouted to Aitken. "Quick, send word round the guns."

He knew how difficult it was to pass orders to excited men deafened by the guns and half blinded by the smoke. Usually it was a question of sending men round to each gun, pounding the captain on the back and gesticulating. Now what? Leave the second frigate to the *Heron* and go for the 74, or attack the frigate and risk being interrupted (and put at a disadvantage) by the 74?

There was nothing more to be done with the *Sylphe:* she had surrendered, and apart from that she was almost destroyed. She could sail because her masts and yards were still standing, but her hull was little more than a shell, her vitals ripped out by the *Dido*'s punishing broadsides.

The most important target was the 74; he must not forget that. And that meant not wasting any time on the second frigate: she was the *Heron*'s affair. The 74 was beating up towards them fast, obviously hoping she would arrive in time to save the two frigates. Her captain must have been watching the smoke of the *Dido*'s broadsides and known as soon as her guns stopped spurting smoke that the *Sylphe* had been forced to surrender.

"That other frigate is *Le Requin,* I've just been able to read her name," Aitken said. "Are you going to tackle her next, sir?"

Ramage shook his head. "No, we'd better attack the 74: she'll be up with us before we can deal with the frigate."

But how to deal with the 74? Both ships were approaching each other bow to bow. Ultimately it would be reduced to a pounding match, broadside against broadside, with a big butcher's bill on both sides.

Ramage shrugged his shoulders. That was war, and now he

commanded a bigger ship, the butcher's bill was likely to be larger. He tried not to think how many dead there must be in the *Sylphe:* he could not help comparing her with the *Calypso,* and imagining what might have happened if she had been caught in a similar position.

By now the *Sylphe* was being left behind on the *Dido*'s starboard quarter and he could see that the remains of her crew were hurriedly furling sails. And was she slightly down by the bow? Ramage thought so, and guessed that several of the *Dido*'s shot had hit her 'twixt wind and water, and the leaks were flooding in water faster than her pump could clear it. Yes, with the glass he could see where the water was pouring over the side amidships as the pump started working. The poor devils— now they knew that only their own exertions could save them from sinking: they could expect no help from the other frigate or the 74.

Now to concentrate on the 74. He looked at her with the glass. Patched sails, dull paintwork. How was her rigging? Had she had a season under the tropical sun? She was pitching slightly as she butted her way to windward and occasionally, as her hull lifted, Ramage could see the green of weed growing on her bottom. She had not been docked for some time and the weed would be slowing her down and making her unhandy. Her hull was painted black, unrelieved by any colour. She seemed slightly menacing as she worked her way to windward, the occasional sheets of spray flying up from her bow as she caught an extra large wave.

Her guns were run out, naturally enough, and they stuck out down her side like stubby black fingers. She would have guns the same size as *Dido*'s: a ground tier of thirty-two-pounders, then twenty-four-pounders on the next deck, twelve-pounders on the quarterdeck and probably twelve-pounder carronades on the poop. The French had been quick to copy the carronades: at close range they were devastating and Ramage guessed that much of the damage to the *Sylphe* had been done by Orsini and his carronades up on the poop deck. He must remember to tell Orsini that would be his regular station at general quarters in future.

"Steer to pass that 74 about fifty yards to windward," Ramage told Jackson, noting that the wounded man at the wheel had been replaced by a big red-headed seaman whose peeling skin warned what trouble he was going to have from the sun as soon as they were in the Tropics.

"We'll be engaging to starboard," Ramage told Aitken. "See that the gun crews are warned."

Aitken beckoned to the two midshipmen and gave them orders.

Well, Ramage thought to himself, soon another first: just now he had taken the *Dido* into action, though admittedly only against a frigate; now he was going to match her against another 74 for the first time. It was certainly not going to be like engaging the *Sylphe:* the round shot being fired at them would be thirty-two-pounders, not twelve-pounders, and if the French followed their usual practice they would be firing high to dismantle the rigging, sails and yards, so there would be casualties on deck. The quarterdeck would be the target of French sharpshooters—just as the Frenchman's quarterdeck would be the target of Rennick's marines who were scattered round the upper-deck, muskets at the ready.

The range was closing fast: the 74 was only half a mile away now and Jackson was giving last-minute instructions to the men at the wheel while at the same time keeping an eye on the luffs of the sails.

Suddenly Ramage changed his mind. "Quick!" he told

Aitken, "send a couple of seamen after those midshipmen: we'll
be engaging to larboard."

Take the enemy by surprise: that was the important thing.
Surprise could often be the same as doubling the number of
your guns. And one thing the Frenchman would not expect
him to do would be to give up the weather gauge.

Yet there were advantages in crossing his bow and, after raking him, engaging from to leeward: the smoke of the guns blew
back on board and set you coughing, but at least it did not
obscure the target. And that was important if this fight was
going to develop into a battle of broadsides.

The French 74 was still fine on the starboard bow and
approaching fast. Ramage called Jackson over and quickly gave
him his instructions. Much rested on his skill, although Ramage
knew everything depended on his own timing.

He could make out every detail of the Frenchman now with
the naked eye: the bowsprit and jib-boom jutted out at a sharp
angle like a fishing rod from a river bank, the yards were braced
sharp up as she fought her way to windward, and he could distinguish the grey of the dried salt on the black paint of her bow.
And right aft he could make out the flapping of the red, white
and blue Tricolour.

Black and menacing: that was his main impression of the
Frenchman: the ship seemed larger than a two-decker but that
was probably because she was close-hauled and pitching into a
short head sea as she fought her way up to the east-north-east.
Ramage was not sure whether she was struggling to get up
to the other frigate and protect her, or was intent on engaging
the *Dido*. Not that it mattered either way. He glanced over
the larboard quarter and saw that the *Heron* was now bearing
down on the second frigate: her captain had understood signal
number 29.

The *Dido* swept on with the easy ridge and furrow movement of a ship that had the wind on the quarter. Sheets and braces were properly trimmed, and the sails bellied out in great curves.

He could see Rennick and his first and second lieutenants standing by their sharpshooters, and he sensed rather than saw that Orsini was ready with his carronades. Suddenly he realized the young Italian would be expecting to engage to starboard, and turned and shouted up to him. At once Orsini called to his crews and they hurried across the deck to the other side.

The Frenchman was a hundred yards away on the starboard bow and Ramage could picture all the guns' crews on her starboard side crouched down, ready to fire as the *Dido* swept past. Seventy-five yards, and then fifty. "Now!" he bellowed at Jackson and the men spun the wheel. The *Dido*'s bow gradually began to swing to starboard: slowly, agonizingly slowly. Ramage watched the Frenchman's bow and began to think he had made a mistake in the timing: instead of suddenly turning across the enemy's bow and raking him and then running down his larboard side, he imagined the two ships colliding in a dreadful tangle of jib-booms and bowsprits, each bringing down the other's foremast.

But no: the *Dido* was just going to scrape past, and even as he sighed with relief he heard the crash as the forward guns fired, flame and smoke spurting out from the *Dido* in the first of a raking broadside.

Now there was the steady thunder of the thirty-two-pounders, slamming their shot, more than six inches in diameter, into the Frenchman's bow, and the lighter boom of the twenty-four-pounders, with their shot of more than five and a half inches in diameter. Finally, as he was coughing from the smoke, the twelve-pounders joined in and as the *Dido* turned slightly to larboard to pass down the Frenchman's side there was the bronchitic cough of Orsini's carronades up on the poop, sweeping the Frenchman's decks with hundreds of musket balls. And there was the comparatively faint popping of the marines' muskets.

He began to see the Frenchman as though he was watching one of the new magic lanterns: there was her poop, with men scurrying about trying to get to the carronades after having to race across the deck when the *Dido* suddenly cut across her bow to attack on the other side. And there was the quarterdeck with a group of officers crouched down near the wheel. And a bewildering mass of ropes: shrouds, sheets and braces. And her boats stowed on the booms, two of which disintegrated into matchwood as he watched.

And he had taken the French completely by surprise: they were all prepared to fight the *Dido* on the starboard side, with the starboard side guns loaded and the locks cocked, the crews crouched and ready, when suddenly the British ship appeared on the larboard side after pouring a raking broadside into the unprotected bow.

But now the Frenchman had passed and Ramage had a quick glimpse of her stern, just having time to read her name, *Junon*. Aitken, speaking-trumpet to his lips, was shouting orders which would tack the ship and take her in pursuit of the Frenchman, who was still close-hauled and making off to the east- north-east—whether trying to escape or to cover the frigate, Ramage was not sure.

What startled him was the lack of damage and casualties in the *Dido:* instead of the decks being littered with dead and wounded—especially the marine sharpshooters—and the boats smashed and rigging hanging down torn by shot, there were perhaps half a dozen dead or badly wounded, and little sign of damage. Yes, the Frenchman had been taken completely by surprise. But the fight was not yet over; having lost the windward gauge, suddenly slipping across the bow was not a trick he could try a second time.

Quickly the sheets and braces of the *Dido* were hauled home so that the yards were braced sharp up and the *Dido* sailed to the east-north-east in pursuit of the *Junon,* which was now a good half a mile ahead.

CHAPTER EIGHT

DOWN at number seventeen 32-pounder on the starboard side, which Jackson normally commanded (along with number seventeen gun on the larboard side), Stafford, Rossi, and the four Frenchmen sat on the gun and rested, having returned there after firing and then reloading the larboard side gun.

"I don't want to fight a long action with these brutes," Stafford said, slapping the barrel of the thirty-two-pounder. "They're just so damned big. I'm used to twelve-pounders: they're more my size."

"But think of the damage they do," Rossi said. "Our broadside just stopped that frigate dead and probably not done much good to that 74 either."

Gilbert said lugubriously: "I couldn't help thinking of when we were in the *Calypso* and we met those two 74s. That could have been us, pounded to a stop and hauling down our flag."

"Well, thanks to Mr Ramage it wasn't," Stafford said briskly, "so don't get sad. They're only French."

"So are we," Gilbert said, gesturing to the other three.

"Yes, but you don't count," Stafford said, completely unaware that he had been tactless. "You're not the same sort of French."

"Thank you," Gilbert said ironically. "We are just the sort that they shoot if they ever catch us."

"Shoot?" Stafford was puzzled. "You mean execute?"

"Yes, of course. They regard us as traitors. They execute all Frenchmen they find serving the British."

"Be careful then," Stafford said, his voice serious. "We don't want anything to happen to you."

"Don't worry," Gilbert said, keeping a straight face, "we walk very carefully."

Stafford stood up and stretched himself, having to crouch because of the low headroom. "I do fink the first lieutenant was a bit 'ard on us when making out the general quarters, watch and station bill. These guns are supposed to have eight men, but 'cos we're short of complement he gives us only seven, which means six when we go to general quarters 'cos we lose Jacko who has to go as quartermaster. Six ain't enough."

"We manage," Louis said. "Stop grumbling, Staff. Always you grumble. The meat's too salty, too many weevils in the biscuit, not enough men at the gun: you're never happy."

"Oh yus I am," Stafford protested. "It's just that when you come to a new ship you 'spect things to be right. If eight men are allowed for a thirty-two-pounder, let's have eight: don't make us hump it around with only six."

"Is a compliment," Rossi said matter-of-factly. "Mr Aitken knows that we can manage."

"Most of the other guns have eight men," Stafford pointed out.

"Some have only seven, and they're all former Calypsos," Rossi said. "And we have seven except when we go to general quarters, and Jackson has to go up to the quarterdeck."

"That's the very time when we need the extra man," Stafford declared.

"Well, we haven't got him so we'll have to make do," Gilbert said cheerfully. "For me, I prefer the *Dido* to the *Calypso:* more room, a more comfortable motion in a seaway. There's no comparison between serving in a frigate and a ship of the line."

"You're right; there ain't no thirty-two-pounders in a frigate," Stafford declared. "But there's too many people in a 74. It's not friendly, like in a frigate. Too many marines, too many officers and petty officers. No, give me the *Calypso* any day."

"Well, if you were still in the *Calypso* and you had just met that French 74, you might be dead."

"No, not with Mr Ramage," he said seriously. "He'd have thought of something."

"One day," Auguste said, speaking for the first time in the conversation, "Mr Ramage might not think of something, then you are dead."

"We'll all be dead," Stafford said cheerfully. "Well, you can't expect to live forever, can you?"

"Yes," Rossi said fervently. "Well, maybe not forever, but I want to die in my bed of old age, with all my weeping grandchildren round me."

"All sobbing and sayin' prayers, eh? Some hope," Stafford said. "They'll all be damned glad to see the back of you!"

"You don't deserve to have me as second captain of this gun," Rossi said. "Dying is a very serious matter for an Italian."

"It's not exactly a lark for an Englishman either," Stafford said. "The family don't usually gather round laughing and joking."

He walked round to the gun port and leaned out. He could just see ahead, and then came back to report.

"The Frog's less than half a mile ahead. I think we're catching up slowly. We may have raked her, but it doesn't seem to have slowed her down at all. The other French frigate is further round to leeward with the British frigate engaging her. They seem to have been having quite a scrap."

"If it was the *Calypso* she'd be dismasted by now," Rossi boasted.

"If the *Calypso* was here, we'd probably be engaging the 74, knowing Mr Ramage," Stafford said soberly.

"You see, it's not so bad after all being in the *Dido*," Gilbert said quietly. "It's all death and no glory when a frigate has to fight a ship of the line. I'm not a proper sailor, but even I know that."

Stafford adjusted the strip of cloth round his forehead to stop perspiration running into his eyes. "It's hot down here. I wish I was working on the carronades, up in the fresh air."

"Not only fresh air up there," Rossi said. "Grapeshot and splinters too."

"Well, we'll get round shot and splinters down 'ere," Stafford said philosophically, "so there's not much to choose. I think I'd prefer the extra fresh air."

With that he walked to the gun port again and, holding on to the barrel of the thirty-two-pounder, leaned out to look ahead. "We're gaining on her slowly and I reckon we're pointing closer to the wind," he said.

"She must have a foul bottom," Rossi said. "Usually the French are closer winded than us."

"We may have done her some damage when we raked her," Stafford said. "That was a smart move by Mr Ramage; we threw a raking broadside into her without getting a broadside back. One up to us."

"But it's bound to end up a battle of broadsides," Gilbert said. "Gun for gun she's the same as us, so it'll be a question of who can last out the longest."

"Unless Mr Ramage thinks up some trick," Stafford said.

• • •

Up on the quarterdeck Ramage lowered his telescope and said: "We're gaining on her. Slowly, admittedly, but we're pointing higher."

"She's foul all right," Southwick growled, "otherwise we'd never get to windward of her. I don't know what's wrong with our builders, but we can't produce ships that go to windward like the French. Think of the *Calypso*. Her French builders knew a thing or two. The French can't fight, but by God they can build weatherly ships."

Ramage put the telescope to his eye again. "The *Heron* is fighting it out with the *Requin:* they're lying alongside each other, bow to stern. I hope the *Sylphe* doesn't do enough repairs to hoist her flag again and escape us."

Southwick sniffed yet again. "I think they've got all their work cut out keeping her afloat. We fairly riddled her hull. And I doubt if she has many men left alive to man the pump as well as knot and splice rigging—she took a terrible pounding. If they'd had any sense they'd have hauled down their colours *before* we got alongside her."

Ramage nodded. "Yes, she could have fired a few guns *pour l'honneur de pavillon* and then hauled down her colours. No one expects a frigate to take on a ship of the line."

He looked across at Jackson and called: "Won't she take a bit more? Can't you luff in the puffs?"

"The puffs don't last long enough, sir. But we're creeping up on her."

Southwick, meanwhile, was busy with his quadrant, measuring the angle subtended by the *Junon*'s main-topgallant masthead. He made the last adjustment, balancing himself against the *Dido*'s slight pitching, read the figures off the vernier scale, and consulted his tables. "Four degrees twenty-one minutes," he said, running his index finger down the column of figures. He read off the number opposite. "She's just 745 yards ahead of us," he said. "There's no doubt, we're gaining on her."

"Not fast enough," grumbled Ramage, lifting up his telescope once more. Although there was no doubting Southwick's quadrant, the *Junon* did not seem any closer; she was ploughing her way to windward. She obviously intended to fight: she had her courses clewed up, like the *Dido,* so she was still under fighting canvas. If she was intent on bolting, Ramage thought, she would let fall her courses. Yet that was odd: she *was* bolting—she was abandoning the *Requin,* which was still fighting and which the *Junon* could rescue by swinging away to leeward and pouring a broadside or two into the *Heron.* Why? Why had she not let fall those courses? There must be a reason. Perhaps the captain had been killed and the second-in-command was still pulling himself together. Yet the obvious thing, if you were making a bolt for it, was to set every inch of canvas without wasting a moment.

There must be a reason for it, but what was it? Ramage shrugged his shoulders: there was no point in making wild guesses—not that he could think of even a wild guess.

"Five degrees six minutes," Southwick intoned, and once again consulted his tables. "Six hundred and thirty-nine yards, sir," he reported. "We seem to be overhauling her faster now. We must have a better slant o' wind. Give us another five knots o' breeze and we'll be sheering up alongside her and boarding in the smoke!"

Ramage still watched through his telescope, puzzled by the clewed up courses. Suddenly the outline of the *Junon* seemed to blur, then he saw the foremast lean, almost lazily, and topple back on to the mainmast before slewing round and falling over the side to leeward.

"Look at that!" bellowed Southwick. "By God, our raking broadside *did* do some damage after all!"

And that explained why the courses had been clewed up: obviously the raking broadside had damaged the mast, cut the forestay or badly damaged the bowsprit, and the crew of the *Junon* had been so busy trying to make repairs that there was no question of setting the courses. Not that with the foremast in danger of going by the board, as it had just done, there was any question of setting the forecourse.

Southwick was still busy with his quadrant: the *Junon* had slowed down appreciably, with one mast over the side and the sails and yards dragging in the water like a brake. She was still under way—Ramage could see she was still leaving a wake, and the rest of the sails were still drawing. He could imagine frantic men with axes slashing at the tangle of shrouds and halyards to cut the mast free. With the main and mizen still standing they could manoeuvre the ship, though it would call for all the seamanship that the captain possessed.

"Six degrees five minutes!" Southwick said delightedly, consulting his tables. "She's only 533 yards now!"

For a moment Ramage felt sorry for the French captain: he had lost his foremast because he had let himself be taken by surprise—he expected the *Dido* to sweep down his starboard side, and instead of that she had cut across his bow, raked him and come down his larboard side, where the guns were not ready. Now he was commanding a ship which he could barely manoeuvre and with a British 74 coming up astern, less than half a mile away. Admittedly a lucky French shot could send one of the *Dido*'s masts by the board, but the French would indeed need to be lucky, cutting a stay. It would take more than one round shot to do much damage to the *Dido*'s mainmast, for instance, which was more than three feet in diameter.

One thing was certain, Ramage decided, this action was not going to degenerate into a battle of broadsides, with the *Dido* lying alongside the *Junon* and pounding away: the *Dido* could still manoeuvre, even if the *Junon* was reduced to an almost inert mass in the water. The French would have to watch their mainmast now: with stays torn away and sheets and braces ripped out, the mast might well be tottering, waiting to follow the foremast.

Ramage turned to Jackson. "Steer to pass fifty yards off along the starboard side."

Then to Aitken he said: "Pass the word to the guns that we shall be engaging to larboard at fifty yards' range. Fire as the guns bear."

Southwick was taking his last reading with his quadrant. "Seven degrees thirty-six minutes—ah, that's more like it!" He read from his tables, a note of triumph in his voice: "Four hundred and twenty-six yards, sir. We could stand off and tease her with the carronades!"

Would the *Junon* haul down her colours and save what would otherwise be a senseless slaughter? Ramage was not sure. Losing a foremast in these circumstances was a good enough reason for surrendering. Good enough, but not an overwhelming reason. Ramage thought for a moment of a French court martial, trying the captain for the loss of his ship. A case could be made out for surrendering—and an equally good case could probably be made out for fighting on, relying on that lucky shot.

He wished he did not keep thinking about the French captain's plight, but the fact was he did not look forward to what he had to do: it had been bad enough pounding the *Sylphe* in an action which would bring him no credit—a 74-gun ship was expected to pound a frigate into submission. Admittedly it would be different with the *Junon*, because two equally powerful ships had started off on level terms, and the *Dido* had gained the advantage by using surprise. But he hated the idea that the French captain would fight on because of pride, and probably cause the death of fifty of his men and the wounding of double that number.

Would a French captain be having these thoughts? He shook his head impatiently: no, he almost certainly would not. So it was his job to get fifty yards to windward of the *Junon* and pour in a full broadside to start the proceedings.

This was the first time he had been able to compare the windward ability of the *Dido* against another ship, and he was quite impressed by her performance: she had pointed higher than the *Junon*, which at the time had been all that mattered. One learned about one's ship at the oddest times.

They were approaching the *Junon* fast now. The thunderclouds were clearing; blue patches of sky were hinting at a clearance. The wind was less gusty and perhaps a little stronger: there were hints of whitecaps on the water.

And now the *Dido* was within a few minutes of firing her larboard broadside into the *Junon,* and it was important to remember that although the French ship had lost her foremast and some of the larboard guns were obscured by sails hanging over the side, her starboard broadside was unaffected: every one of those guns would be loaded; at this very moment the French gunners would be waiting for the *Dido* to come into their sights.

Ramage had one big advantage—he could manoeuvre the *Dido*. Use that advantage, he told himself; do not lie alongside the *Junon* and indulge in a slugging match. The way to fight this action was to keep on making darting attacks—raking the Frenchman across the bow and across the stern, keeping out of the way of her broadsides as much as possible while pouring a heavy fire into her unprotected ends. So after his first broadside the *Dido* would be raking her.

He watched from the quarterdeck as the distance rapidly lessened: four hundred yards, three hundred, two hundred, and then the tight feeling of anticipation as the *Junon* seemed to come into fine focus: all the colours seemed intensified, from the sea to her copper sheathing (revealed as she rolled gently), from the scroll bearing her name (at this distance the red seemed gaudy) to the flax colour of her sails and the black of the muzzles of her guns poking out of her side.

Ramage could see the marines raising their muskets as Rennick and his lieutenants gave them orders. He imagined the second captains of guns cocking the locks and leaping back out of the way of the recoil, while the captains would be taking up the strain on the trigger-lines, ready to give that tug that would fire the guns. And, of course, the French gunners would be going through the same drill.

A hundred yards, fifty, a ship's length . . . and then the deep cough and spurts of smoke and flame as the first of the *Dido*'s guns opened fire, punctuated by the sharper crash of the *Junon*'s opening broadside. Almost at once the smoke drifted aft and set them coughing, and as the broadsides continued Ramage heard the tearing calico sound of round shot passing close. There was a crash and he saw one of the cutters disintegrate: a reminder that he had not paused earlier to hoist out the boats and lower them, to tow them astern out of harm's way, and where they would not be smashed into showers of lethal splinters.

He could feel the thuds as some of the French shot slammed into the *Dido*'s side, but so far no yards had been damaged. Were the French gunners not firing into the masts and spars as they usually did? Perhaps the *Dido*'s steady fire after raking her had shown the French how devastating was a broadside fired into the hull.

The popping of the marines' muskets seemed laughable, too light to be lethal, but he reminded himself that every pop meant a musket ball, each one of which could kill a man. Now the twelve-pounders on the quarterdeck were firing, and almost immediately Orsini's carronades joined in. And by now the *Junon*'s quarterdeck was abreast that of the *Dido* and he could see a small group of French officers standing at the forward end, looking across at the *Dido* just as he was watching the *Junon*.

He could see pockmarks, holes surrounded by rust, where the *Dido*'s round shot had hit home, and smoke was streaming out of her gun ports and there was the red winking as guns fired. The din was greater than he had ever experienced; twice as loud as anything he had heard in the *Calypso*. On top of the dreadful crash of the guns there was the rumbling of the trucks as they recoiled, the shouting of men giving orders, the screams of those cut down by shot or splinters, and the ominous thud of shot striking home.

Then, as the *Dido* shot past the *Junon*'s bow, the noise stopped as neither ship's guns would bear. Ramage felt as if he had been standing there with his eyes shut but realized everything had happened too quickly to be fully appreciated and absorbed. Now the gunners would be scurrying round reloading their guns, and he said to Aitken: "Bear away across his bow; we'll rake him again."

Hurriedly sheets and braces were trimmed as the *Dido* turned to larboard to cross ahead of the *Junon*, out of reach of her guns but able to batter her with the larboard broadside. The *Dido* was crossing the *Junon*'s bow diagonally and as soon as the broadside was fired Ramage said: "Luff up, Mr Aitken; we'll tack and give him our starboard broadside as we pass across his bow again."

The sails billowed and filled again with a bang as the *Dido* tacked. The two midshipmen were sent hurriedly below again to warn the lieutenants of divisions to be ready to fire the starboard broadside.

Once again the *Dido* raked the *Junon,* each gun fired deliberately and the round shot crashing home into the French ship's unprotected bow.

"Just look at that foremast," commented Southwick. "If they try to fire those forward guns on the larboard side they'll set the sails on fire!"

The canvas was hanging down over the muzzles of the forwardmost guns like huge curtains, held out at strange angles by smashed yards. There was no sign of men cutting it clear: Ramage guessed that the Frenchmen were too busy at the guns to spare anyone to clear away wreckage.

Well, he thought grimly, they will have plenty of opportunity now because, unless I make a bad mistake, those guns will not be firing for many minutes.

He was beginning to feel more confident handling the *Dido* now: probably the first encounter with the *Sylphe* and now attacking a crippled enemy was showing him that a 74 was simply an overgrown frigate; the tactics remained the same. The noise was worse, the casualties would be higher, and the penalties for mistakes would be higher also: otherwise handling the *Dido* was like fighting the *Calypso*. With the increase in size of ship, of course, went an increase in the size of the enemy. A frigate was only expected to tackle a frigate or smaller.

As the *Dido* bore away to start her third diagonal run across the *Junon*'s bow the French ship was broad on the larboard bow, still making headway. Although her foremast had gone by the board, almost miraculously the bowsprit and jib-boom were still standing, thrusting out like fishing rods. The *Dido*, now speeding down with the wind on the quarter, was hardly rolling: the gunners could not hope for a steadier gun platform.

Ramage decided he would give the helm orders: he wanted
to pass only a matter of a few yards ahead of the *Junon,* and
since she was still making headway it needed fine judgement
to avoid a collision. But a raking broadside at that range should
do enormous damage to the Frenchman, the round shot smashing through the beak-head bulkheads at the bow to travel the
length of the ship, overturning guns, cutting down men and
sending up a lethal shower of splinters.

Aitken, speaking-trumpet to his lips, bellowed orders which
sent seamen rushing to the sheets, hauling on them to trim the
sails more precisely. Ramage could hear the creaking of the
yards above the whine of the wind and the hissing of the sea.

Judging the forward motion of the *Junon,* he gave a brief
order to Jackson, and the *Dido* turned slightly to starboard. The
range was closing fast now and Ramage found he was still
underestimating the *Junon*'s forward speed. He gave Jackson a
second order, and the *Dido* turned a fraction more to starboard.

The flintlocks on the guns along the larboard side would be
cocked; the gun captains would be holding the lanyards taut,
watching through the gun ports for the *Junon* to come in sight.
Ramage looked again at the *Junon:* yes, he had judged her speed
just right: the *Dido* would, in a few moments, pass across her
bow.

He heard Orsini shouting orders up on the poop and noticed
that both Southwick and Aitken were now watching the
approaching *Junon* with all the fascination of a rabbit trapped
by a stoat.

Then, in a bewildering swift blur, in which colour seemed
to vanish and give way to a grey smear, the *Junon* was passing.
Guns thundered out, the noise advancing down the *Dido*'s side
like a procession. The smoke billowed out of the ports and then
drifted aft as the ship sailed through it. They were so close to

the *Junon* that Ramage could see clouds of dust erupting where the round shot smashed through the bulkhead. But, apart from the dust, the *Junon* seemed to be little damaged. However, Ramage knew what that dust indicated: it was a strange thing how round shot smashing their way through woodwork sent up the dust: a lethal fog behind which was often hidden dreadful damage.

And then the *Dido* was clear, the last crash of guns being from Orsini's carronades on the poop, no doubt blasting the Frenchman's quarterdeck where the targets ranged from the binnacle to the wheel.

As the *Dido* sailed away at an angle from the *Junon* the French ship's larboard side erupted smoke and red flashes as they poured a broadside into the *Dido*'s larboard quarter. Ramage could picture the *Dido*'s gunners hurriedly swabbing out the barrels of their guns and ramming home wads, cartridges and round shot before running out the guns, ready for the next broadside.

The *Junon*'s broadside did no damage that Ramage could see: but there was no telling, from the quarterdeck, what had happened in the vitals of the ship. The carpenter at that moment came up on to the quarterdeck to report to Ramage that he had just sounded the well and there was nothing to report. In answer to Ramage's question he said there were no shot-holes yet 'twixt wind and water that needed any shot plugs.

Were the Frenchmen firing high, to dismantle the rigging? He had not heard many shots passing overhead and decided they must be still firing into the hull. Well, it might mean more casualties but he did not want masts to come tumbling down. There was one thing about it—the *Junon* could not fire a full broadside on the larboard side because of the sails still draped over the forward guns.

He told the first lieutenant: "We'll haul our wind as soon as we're in position to cross his stern and rake him again. Warn the lieutenants that we'll be firing to larboard again."

Ramage realized that the *Dido* was sailing in a huge figure of eight round the *Junon* and because of the direction she was going the larboard guns were doing most of the work. Not that it mattered to the gunners: there were only enough men on board to work the guns on one side at a time; no ship in the king's service ever had a large enough complement to fight both sides at the same time, so the gunners had to dash from one side to the other as required.

As the *Dido,* now out on the *Junon*'s larboard quarter, bore up and turned to larboard to begin her run across the French ship's stern, Southwick said diffidently: "The smoke coming from those forward ports—it seems to be coming from under the sails. Surely they didn't fire those guns?"

Ramage shook his head. "No, I'm sure they didn't." He put the telescope to his eye. "Doesn't look like gunsmoke, either: it's the wrong colour."

"What on earth's going on, sir?"

It was a puzzle: the gunsmoke had blown clear of the *Junon*'s afterports, but there were still trickles of smoke which seeped, rather than spurted, from underneath the sails.

"Perhaps some fool fired a gun and the flash set the sails on fire. That could easily happen."

"Yes, sir, but," Southwick persisted, "I can't see any sign of a sail actually burning: the flames'd move pretty quickly."

Ramage hurriedly examined the sails with the glass. Southwick was right: the sails were not on fire, but nevertheless smoke was coming from beneath them. And yes! From some of the ports just aft of the sails, the wisps were just starting, barely distinguishable. In fact without a glass they would not be seen and anyway Southwick was sharp eyed to have noticed the smoke under the sail.

But even as Ramage watched the smoke from the forward ports, just abaft the draped sails, got thicker. He could see it with the naked eye now, and yes, it was moving aft, coming from other ports.

"She's on fire!" he suddenly exclaimed. "She has a big fire forward, and it's spreading aft rapidly. It might reach the magazine! Mr Aitken, bear away—we don't want to be near an explosion."

He could picture blazing wreckage raining down out of the sky and lodging in the *Dido*'s sails, apart from falling on her decks which, fortunately, were still wetted and sanded.

CHAPTER NINE

THE SUDDEN order shouted by the bosun's mates, "Firemen to the upper-deck!" startled Stafford and his gun's crew as they waited for the *Dido* to cross the *Junon*'s stern. None of them were down in the general quarters, watch and station bill as firemen, but fire in a ship was a seaman's greatest fear. To begin with they thought the *Dido* was on fire, and Stafford was already looking round at the powder monkeys, ready to order them to throw their cartridges of powder over the side. But quickly the word spread through the ship: it was the *Junon* that was on fire, and the reason the *Dido*'s firemen were being ordered to the upper-deck was to deal with any blazing debris should she blow up.

Stafford immediately ran to the gun port and looked at the

Junon, now broad on the *Dido*'s beam. His sharp eyes soon spotted the smoke coming from under the foresails draped over her side, and then saw the wisps of smoke curling out of the after gun ports.

"It's her all right!" he shouted to the others. "She has a fire forward—I reckon it's right over her magazine. No wonder they passed the word for firemen; if she blows up she could shower us."

"Fire," Gilbert muttered. "The poor devils. She's an unlucky ship. To be raked four times . . ."

"She was unlucky to meet Mr Ramage," Rossi said. "Don't waste too much sympathy on them!"

"Yes, but we weren't."

"No, thanks to Mr Ramage having some tricks to play. But we could have been blown out of the water. Look what we did to that frigate, and we're only one 74. Imagine what it would have been like to have one each side."

"No," Gilbert said emphatically, "I don't want to imagine it."

"Well, just because you're French don't get weepy over the *Junon*."

"I'm not weepy. I'm thinking of six hundred men who risk being blown to pieces."

"But they're French," Rossi protested. "If we were on fire no one in the *Junon* would give a damn; in fact they'd be cheering."

Stafford called from the gun port: "We're bearing away, putting a distance between us."

"Thank goodness for that," Louis said. "It will soon be raining burning beams."

Stafford inspected the *Junon* again and announced: "The fire's getting worse: the smoke is beginning to pour out of her hatchways, too. It's even coming out of her stern ports: she's making just enough headway to make a draught through the ship."

A minute or two later he added: "She's trying to heave-to. They're backing the maintopsail. Ah, they've got a fire engine to work. They're squirting water down the forehatch."

Rossi went to the gun port to have a look for himself and announced: "No fire engine is going to put out *that* fire!"

"I 'ope they've flooded the 'anging magazine," Stafford said. "Otherwise she'll blow in the next five minutes. Oh, we're heaving-to as well," he added, as he watched the waves and heard the slamming of sails overhead. "That's nice o' 'em; we'll have a good view."

The words were hardly out of his mouth when there was an enormous red and yellow flash, as though someone had suddenly opened a huge furnace door, and then a thunderclap as if they had just slammed it shut. The *Junon's* outline was replaced by a cloud of smoke from which yards, masts, beams and dozens of pieces of burning wood lanced up into the air in geometrically precise parabolas and splashed down into the sea.

Slowly the wind dispersed the cloud of yellow, black and grey smoke, and there was no sign of the ship: simply a turbulent ring of water pitted with splashes.

Up on the quarterdeck Ramage shut his telescope with a click and said to Aitken: "Hoist out the boats and let's get under way: make for the spot where she exploded, then the boats won't have to row so far."

Southwick sighed and took off his hat, running his hand through his hair in a familiar gesture. "I think that's the biggest explosion I've ever seen. I don't suppose we'll find many survivors."

"No, but we'll look. Anyone who survived that deserves to be rescued." He pulled out the tubes of his telescope again and adjusted it, then he looked over the larboard bow at the two frigates, which were about a mile away. "The *Heron* and the *Requin* are still at it. As soon as we've got the boats in the water, we'll leave them to search for men and go up and put a stop to those frigates squabbling. They must be causing a lot of casualties."

The maintopsail yard was braced sharp up as the last of the boats were lowered into the water and the crews scrambled down rope ladders into them. Ramage directed Jackson to steer for the oily-smooth patch of water in which an almost incredible amount of debris was floating.

"Enough wreckage there to build two ships—or so it seems," commented Aitken. "Plenty for survivors to cling to."

The *Dido* hardened in sheets and braces and headed up towards the two frigates which, almost hidden in a cloud of gunsmoke, were now lying with their bows to the north, and side-by-side, pounding each other with their broadsides.

"Damned hard to make out which is which with all the smoke," commented Southwick.

"The nearest one is the Frenchman," Ramage said. "She has something about her sheer that reminds me of the *Calypso*."

"Funny how we keep thinking about her. I'm beginning to see the advantages of a ship o' the line at long last: you've more between you and the enemy's shot!"

"I don't know that's such an advantage: there are many more shot flying around."

"Aye, there's that to it, and I suppose most of them are bigger. Still, up to now we've been lucky."

"Yes, a frigate and a ship of the line isn't a bad score to start with. We were lucky with the *Junon*, though: raking her bow so many times must have smashed her up forward. And a lucky shot started that fire. I wonder what it was."

Southwick shrugged his shoulders. "Could have been anything. Most probably a round shot hit a cartridge. Or maybe it wasn't us at all: it could have been started accidentally by the French. Must have been chaos forward, after our broadsides."

It took fifteen minutes for the *Dido* to work her way up to the frigates: the wind turned fitful and once the big ship was left almost becalmed, Ramage tantalized by the thunder of the frigates' guns.

Finally the *Dido* was in position, two hundred yards on the *Requin*'s larboard quarter, and ready to make the final run in to pour a broadside into her. The gunners on the starboard side were warned to be ready, and Ramage found himself feeling slightly queasy: he could remember only too vividly what the *Dido*'s broadside had done to the *Sylphe*.

The *Requin,* like the *Heron,* was almost hidden in smoke and the flash of her guns firing played in it like summer lightning among evening clouds. The *Dido* approached slowly on her larboard quarter, Ramage watching her closely with the telescope. Not watching the ship, but watching the Tricolour, now hanging limp in a cloud. Suddenly he saw what he had been waiting for—the flag came down at the run: the French, seeing the *Dido* coming, had very sensibly decided the only way of escaping complete destruction was to haul down their colours before the ship of the line had a chance of firing a broadside into them.

"Put us alongside, Mr Aitken," Ramage said. "I doubt if the *Heron* is in much of a shape to take possession of her."

Ramage waited for Aitken to pass the necessary orders and then sent one of the midshipmen to fetch Rennick. The marine captain arrived in a hurry and stood to attention in front of Ramage.

"As soon as we get alongside I want your marines to take possession of the frigate," Ramage said. "Be very careful they don't get mixed up with a boarding party from the *Heron*. The smoke should be clearing very quickly, so there'll be less chance."

Rennick strode off, glad to have something specific for his marines to do, and quickly the men were drawn up in files under the two lieutenants, one to board from forward, the other aft.

The *Dido* was carrying more way than Aitken expected and he gave the order to clew up the topsails a minute too late, so that she crashed into *Requin* with a thump that threw some of the marines off their feet. But almost at once Rennick was bellowing orders and the marines swarmed across the gap between the two ships, while Ramage was thankful that in addition to telling the *Dido*'s gunners not to fire he had ordered them to run their guns in, so their muzzles would not be torn aside by the *Requin*'s topsides.

Ramage suddenly remembered that the French captain would probably formally surrender to the larger ship—the *Dido*—rather than the *Heron,* and sent a midshipman hurrying down to his cabin to fetch his sword. As soon as the boy arrived back with it he put it on, saying to both Southwick and Aitken: "You ought to be wearing swords: these French have fought well and we owe them the courtesies."

Five minutes later, Rennick came back on board with the French captain escorted by two marines. The Frenchman was about thirty years old, with a lean face, aquiline nose and sallow complexion. He spoke some English and, proffering his sword, haltingly began explaining why he had surrendered.

He had only just started when, helped by two of his lieutenants, the captain of the *Heron* hobbled on board, his shin tied up with a bloodstained bandage.

He was an older man, heavily built and with a chubby face and grey eyes. "Edward Eames," he said as he introduced himself to Ramage. "I'm sorry I took so long to get over here, but the beggars winged me just before they hauled down their colours, and I had to get a lashing put on it—it was spilling a lot of blood and filling m' boot."

Ramage introduced himself and spoke quickly so that the Frenchman would not understand what he was saying to Eames. "I've only just arrived alongside so I'll go by what you say. This fellow seems to have put up a good fight: do we let him keep his sword?"

Eames nodded vigorously. "It was touch and go before you arrived: he fought well enough."

Ramage turned to the Frenchman and said in French: "Please keep your sword and regard yourself as a prisoner at large: you could not be expected to fight on."

"The *Junon*—what happened?"

"She caught fire and blew up: my boats are looking for survivors—though I don't expect there to be many."

"We saw the explosion," the Frenchman said, "and we realized our last chance had gone: we just had to fight on against the frigate, but when you approached . . ." The man shrugged his shoulders.

"You did the wise and honourable thing," Ramage said. "Now you'll be taken back to your ship."

He repeated it to Rennick. "He's a prisoner at large. I'm just going to discuss with Captain Eames here who takes possession of the ship."

He turned to Eames. "Is your leg all right? Would you like my surgeon to have a look at it?"

"No, thank you. I'm all right. That Frenchman seems a decent sort of chap. Put up a deuced determined fight."

"Yes. It must have been very depressing for him when he saw the 74 blow up: she was his last hope."

"Yes, you'd already put paid to the other frigate. By Jove, your broadsides smashed him up."

Ramage nodded. "I was commanding a frigate until recently," he said dryly, "and I ran into a couple of 74s in the Mediterranean. I speak with experience of both sides when I say there's no disgrace in a frigate hauling down her colours when she meets a 74."

"I hope a court of inquiry would agree with you," Eames said. "I think some of them expect you to run up a butcher's bill before striking."

"Then they've neither experience nor imagination," Ramage said. "Now, let's go down to my cabin and decide what we do next."

As soon as Eames was seated comfortably in the armchair, his wounded leg supported by a stool, he explained that the *Heron* was on her way back to England after escorting some John Company ships south of 25° North. "A couple of them were carrying specie for the Honourable East India Company," Eames said, "so it was decided to escort them further south than usual. I was on my way back when the French 74 and the two frigates appeared. I was making a bolt for it—though with not much hope of escaping—when I sighted you and you answered the private signal. That was a relief, I can tell you!"

"I'm bound for the West Indies, as you've probably guessed. What are we going to do about all these French prisoners?"

"I don't have enough men both to guard and sail two frigates," Eames said. "If you can spare me some men to guard one frigate, I'll probably be able to get them both to England."

Ramage nodded his head but said: "I don't know if the first one, the *Sylphe,* will make it. We'll inspect her, but we may have to set fire to her and just leave you with the *Requin.* It means you'll lose some prize-money, but we may not have the choice."

118 : RAMAGE e) The Dido

Under the prize rules, if there was another ship in sight at the time that an enemy was captured—in this case the *Heron*—she shared in the money because the sight of another ship might have affected the enemy's decision to surrender.

Ramage thought Eames was not a man who could afford to lose prize-money, but the other captain said: "I did notice she was down by the bow when you left her."

Ramage realized he had not looked at the *Sylphe* for a long time and he called to the marine sentry to pass the word for the first lieutenant. When Aitken arrived he asked him if he had looked at the *Sylphe* recently. When he said he had not, Ramage sent him back on deck to look with the telescope.

The Scotsman returned almost immediately with a long face. "I think she is sinking, sir: she's down by the bow and she's rolling heavily, as though she has a lot of water in her."

Ramage grimaced: "Looks as though we are going to spend most of the day fishing Frenchmen out of the sea."

"Our boats are heading back from the *Junon*," Aitken said. "So they'll have done the best they can there."

Ramage looked at Eames. "I think you'd better take the *Heron* over to the *Sylphe* and see what's going on. There's no point in my going over because I don't have any boats yet."

Eames lifted his wounded leg off the stool. "Very well. What shall I do if she isn't actually sinking?"

"If you think a prize-crew can get her back to England, make sure the French keep at the pumps, and put some men on board. If it looks as though she's going to sink—that the pumps can't keep up with the leaks—take off the French and set fire to her."

The *Dido*'s boats came back with a total of nineteen men from the *Junon*. "We searched every bit of wreckage there was," Hill reported, "but the only survivors were men who were on deck when she blew up. They tell me there were more, but they drowned because they couldn't swim."

"Any of them injured?"

"Yes, sir: one broken leg, two broken arms and two badly burned. The rest don't have a scratch between them."

"Have Bowen deal with them."

"They're already down in the cockpit, sir. Rennick has put a guard on the rest."

Nineteen survivors out of more than six hundred men. Ramage felt a black depression spreading over him. Being given command of a ship of the line meant, in effect, that all figures had been multiplied by three. The *Dido* had almost three times the number of men that the *Calypso* had. In turn that meant that if she sank a ship of the line—the *Junon* for instance—she was likely to cause three times the number of casualties. Altogether more than twelve hundred men were involved. The figures were quite horrifying. He had just killed more than six hundred men in the *Junon,* quite apart from any he had killed in the *Sylphe,* which even now was probably sinking.

The sentry reported that the master was at the door and Ramage called him in. Southwick seemed to sense Ramage's mood without anything being said, and as he settled in the armchair he said: "Bad business about the *Junon.*"

"I was just thinking about it," Ramage said. "More than six hundred dead."

Southwick nodded and said quietly: "Of course, it could have been us. A lucky shot could have set us on fire, and the fire could have spread to the magazine. Hill tells me they picked up nineteen Frenchmen. It could have been nineteen Didos. That really doesn't bear thinking about."

"No, it doesn't," Ramage agreed.

"Once you realize it's a 'them or us' situation, though," Southwick said conversationally, "it's surprising how you see it all in a different light."

And, Ramage admitted to himself, Southwick was quite right. He had summed up what war really was. Whether you served in a sloop, a brig, a frigate or a ship of the line, in the end it all boiled down to that one phrase: it's either them or us.

Yes, Southwick was quite right, but Ramage knew that as far as he was concerned he still had a guilty feeling about being the cause of the death of more than six hundred Frenchmen. Yet another part of him knew that if he had not been able to take the *Junon* like that, it might have been the *Dido* blowing up. He found he was getting confused.

"What about the *Sylphe?*" he asked Southwick, determined to break the train of thought.

"The *Heron's* hove-to close to her. She seems to be well down by the bow. If you want my opinion, she's sinking, and there's not a chance of holding on with the pump."

"Well, I told Eames that if he didn't think she could be saved he should take off the men and set fire to her."

Southwick sniffed and said: "We don't have much choice. And good riddance to her: the *Heron* will have her work cut out getting the *Requin* back to England."

"Her share of the prize-money should make up for it," Ramage said.

"Yes, Eames is a lucky fellow. Or he will be, if he gets the *Requin* home safely."

"We'll have to let him have some marines," Ramage said. "He'll have nearly five hundred prisoners to guard from the two Frenchmen."

"As long as we don't have to take any to the West Indies with us," Southwick said. "Eames realizes the problem?"

"Yes, but I think he'll be glad of some extra marines."

Eames returned in the *Heron* an hour later to report that he had taken all the French off the *Sylphe* because in his opinion she would sink of her own accord within a couple of hours, and for that reason he had not set fire to her. Ramage could not see why the fact that she was going to sink should prevent him from setting fire to her, but he decided to say nothing.

The more immediate problem was that the *Heron* had 211 Frenchmen from the *Sylphe,* and there were still 186 on board the *Requin.* How many men were needed to guard 397 Frenchmen? Plus nineteen from the *Junon.*

When Eames came across to the *Dido* again, Ramage proposed dividing the prisoners into two sections, half in each frigate. The *Heron's* marines could guard the ones she had on board, and Ramage would provide 25 marines from the *Dido* to guard those left on board the *Requin.*

"I'll let you have my fifth lieutenant and two midshipmen to handle the prize," Ramage said. "Fifteen of your seamen should be enough to sail her. Can you spare them?"

"Yes. I'll get 'em back as soon as we get to Plymouth. 'Fraid you'll be losing your people permanently."

Ramage shrugged his shoulders. "That's the problem with prizes taken when you are outward bound. If I meet many more people like you, I'll arrive in the West Indies with a skeleton crew!"

Two hours later, as Ramage watched, the *Sylphe* finally sank, as Eames had predicted.

Southwick said: "That makes two out of two. We've attacked two ships and both have sunk. Or rather one blew up and the other sank. Either way they're destroyed."

"Regard it as a precedent," Ramage said. "We must make a habit of it."

To Ramage's surprise Southwick shook his head and took his hat off, running his fingers through his hair in a familiar gesture. "I can never get used to watching a ship sinking or blowing up. One minute she's a beautiful object, floating and pleasing to the eye. The next minute, nothing. No, I'll never get used to it. Not," he added hastily, "that that isn't the way we should deal with the French. It's just that I love the sight of ships, whatever nationality they are, and I hate to see them destroyed."

Ramage nodded his head in agreement. "I feel the same way, but while there's a war on we must get used to it."

Ramage had to admit that the Reverend Benjamin Brewster was handling the funerals well, and he was thankful that the *Dido* carried a chaplain: he hated reading the funeral service, though he had done so all too often in the *Calypso*.

Looking at the bodies lying on the deck, sewn up in their hammocks, Ramage could hardly believe how lucky the *Dido* had been. Bowen had eight wounded that he was treating down below, but only five men had been killed. Five, and he thought of the more than six hundred who had perished in the *Junon*.

A plank had been fitted to the bulwarks by the main chains, hinged so that the inboard end could be lifted up, and at the moment a body rested on it, covered by a Union flag. Brewster read the service in a low, even voice and most of the Didos were gathered round him, bareheaded and listening attentively.

The body belonged to one of the new Didos: Ramage did not recognize the name, except as an entry in the Muster Book, and he was relieved that it was not a Calypso. In fact, not one of the men killed had been a Calypso, a piece of chance which gave him grim satisfaction. Yet he felt it was wrong: he should not favour the former Calypsos; he now commanded the *Dido*, and every man on board should have an equal status.

Now Brewster was saying that the men had lost a shipmate, and that somewhere a family had lost a son or a father, and a woman had probably been left a widow. The good thing was, Ramage realized, that Brewster sounded as though he cared. Ramage was reminded of a line by John Donne—something to the effect that "Each man's death diminishes me." Brewster gave the impression of being diminished, and Ramage guessed that the men sensed it.

Then Brewster reached the end of the brief service and a couple of burly seamen up-ended the plank while a third held on to the Union flag. The body in its hammock slid into the sea and vanished, the body weighted down by a couple of round shot placed at the man's feet before the hammock was finally sewn up.

Brewster stood still, Prayer Book in hand, his vestments tugged by the wind, while the next body was placed under the flag on the plank. Once again he read the funeral service, and he had a happy knack of making it sound fresh; there was no sense that he was repeating parrot-fashion a service that he would have to repeat five times.

Finally the plank tilted for the fifth and last time and Brewster led the men in a hymn. He had chosen one which was a favourite. The men sang it with gusto, and Ramage realized that as soon as they dispersed they would be chattering among themselves, happily, the last few grim minutes forgotten. It was not that these men were cold-blooded or hard-hearted: death was something they had to take in their stride. Dwelling on it would probably drive a man mad, so he mourned at the funeral, sang a hymn and meant it, and then went about his business, ready to go into action again.

C H A P T E R   T E N

R AMAGE took his Journal from the drawer. He noted the latitude—the *Dido* was now sweeping south and already down level with Guadeloupe—and the longitude, which put them about seven hundred miles short of Barbados.

He still had to write his report on the *Junon* and *Sylphe* affair, ready for the admiral at Barbados, and he knew he must get it done quickly because the details were already fading in his memory.

How was Eames getting on? He decided he did not envy him: getting the *Heron* back to Plymouth with all those prisoners on board, while shepherding the *Requin,* would be a constant worry. Apart from fearing that his own prisoners would rise on him, he must watch the *Requin* all the time, looking for signs of trouble on board. Ramage shrugged: Eames was quite content because—as he had freely admitted—he had never been lucky with prize-money, and now he had head-money, too, for all the prisoners he had taken from the *Sylphe:* head-money— calculated on the number of prisoners taken—which had come without having to fire a single shot. Ramage could have made a claim for a share, but had decided against it because Eames had put up a spirited fight against the *Requin.*

Distances, noon positions, wind directions and strength, courses steered: the facts required for his Journal were mundane: nowhere could he write how exciting it was to be commanding a ship of the line sweeping down to the West Indies in the Trade Winds, feeling alive as the ship pitched and rolled her way westward and the sun was warmer every day.

Nor, for instance, could one mention the flying fish spurting like small silver arrows out of the sea and following the crests and troughs until they vanished into the water again. Occasionally they flew high enough to land on deck—twenty or thirty feet—to flap about helplessly until snatched up by seamen who would then try to bribe the cook to boil them. They looked like fat herrings with wings and had much the same colouring and, one of the men had once told Ramage, much the same taste.

The men liked watching the schools of dolphins which played round the ship from time to time. Play was the right word: they raced and cavorted round the ship like children playing chase in a street; they delighted in swimming fast across the *Dido*'s bow, as if in competition to see which could pass closest to the stem without actually touching. Their speed was amazing: they made the *Dido*, doing eight knots, look as though she was stopped in the water.

And then, hundreds of miles from the nearest land, there were the birds—Mother Carey's chickens, swooping low over the water but never seeming to eat or, for that matter, rest. And then came the—to Ramage—exciting day when they sighted their first tropic bird. All white, it always flew with strong wing beats, and was usually going east or west. The first he had seen this voyage passed eastward at eight o'clock in the morning and returned westward at six in the evening. Where had it come from? Where was it going?

Ramage had often seen colonies of them on the islands: they nested among the cliffs away from people—he remembered seeing them on the west coast of St Eustatius, the north-western side of St Martin and the south and west sides of Antigua, but one rarely sailed from one island to another without at least one of them flying overhead. The odd thing was one could never determine their destination: they never seemed to be bound for any particular island, yet they always flew in a dead straight line.

Then there were the whales. One would suddenly become conscious of them surfacing almost alongside, silent and enormous, but occasionally one heard and saw them spouting water into the air. They, like the dolphins, were not alarmed by the sight of a ship of the line ploughing through the water: in fact the bulk seemed to attract them closer, instead of frightening them off.

But one of the joys of a 74, as far as Ramage was concerned, was "the captain's walk," the balcony built outside the cabin across the stern and stretching from one side to the other. He could pare along it, looking down at the *Dido*'s curling wake, and he found himself fascinated by the loops and whorls the ship left in the water. At night there was often heavy phosphorescence, when the *Dido* would seem to be leaving a wide trail of light in the water. At times it was light enough to read a newspaper, and once when talking to Aitken out there he had been able to see every detail of the Scotsman's features.

More surprising in the darkness were the antics of the fish caught in the *Dido*'s wake: he could see them swimming under water, leaving trails of phosphorescent light. It was ironic that one only saw them in the dark of night: in daylight the reflection from the top of the water prevented any sight of them. Then occasionally in daylight—as if to remind one that the sea was unfriendly—Ramage saw the fin of a shark cutting through the water. And from time to time there would be a sudden flurry as dozens of flying fish suddenly took to the air, or other fish leapt out of the water in a desperate attempt to escape, as some predator attacked them. The effect was the same as throwing a heavy stone into the middle of a pond—the splashes of escaping fish radiated outwards like the spokes of a wheel.

• • •

Stafford put down his mug and pointed at Gilbert. "Yus, you're going to enjoy the islands. Why, you'll be sucking the monkey with the best of them!"

"Shall I? Why should I like the islands?"

"They're so beautiful—every one different. And the sea so clear that in places you can see the bottom in ten fathoms."

"But what is this monkey?" Gilbert inquired.

"Ha, that's a treat in store. You know what a coconut is like?"

Gilbert shook his head, so Stafford described it.

"This shell," he added, "is full o' what they call milk, or coconut water, and it's very refreshing to drink. You just cut off the top o' the shell or punch an 'ole in it."

"What's all that got to do with monkeys?"

"Well, last time I saw it done a young midshipman was taking a party of us on shore, and it was very hot. Very green, this young lad; he'd never heard of sucking the monkey. So we asked him if we could buy some of this old lady's coconuts, so we could drink the coconut water. He agreed, so we paid up and soon all of us were sucking the monkey."

"Oh, I see: drinking the coconut water is called sucking the monkey," Gilbert said. "I don't think that's very funny."

"It's not. We weren't drinking coconut water! We were drinking rum: what the old ladies sell is not a coconut full of coconut water but a coconut filled with rum—that's sucking the monkey! The poor midshipman never did find out why we suddenly got so cheerful."

"Drinking rum in the hot sun just gives you a headache," Gilbert protested.

"It does," Stafford agreed. "I was a lot younger then. But you've come across it, haven't you Jacko?"

The American nodded. "I remember once every man in a working party had two coconuts each and got so drunk he couldn't walk straight. Neither the midshipman nor the first lieutenant had ever heard of sucking the monkey, so they never did discover how the men got at the rum."

"Rum must be very cheap."

"Yus, and easier to find than water. You'll see the sugar growing—like 'normous grass when it's ripe—and you'll get fed up with the stink of molasses, which is what they make from the sugar. Strange to think that rum comes from stuff that looks like overgrown grass."

"Very overgrown," Jackson said. "It stands higher than a man when it's ready to be cut."

"That's what the slaves are kept for," Stafford explained. "They plant and weed and then cut the cane. Hard and hot work in the boiling sun."

"What else is there beside sucking the monkey?" Gilbert inquired.

"If you mean tricks to play on midshipmen, that's about the only one. But to eat—there's more fruit than you could dream of. Oranges you buy by the kitbag, then there's bananas and pawpaw—just you wait until you go to market: the old ladies have it all spread out on the ground and you just choose what you want."

"But I hear there are things like yellow fever and blackwater which take you off in a couple of days . . ."

"Oh yus, there's plenty of that. I know of one frigate that lost thirty men from yellow fever in a week. Ho yus, yer got to stay alive if yer going to enjoy the West Indies."

"How do you do that?"

Stafford shrugged his shoulders. "Yellow fever can strike whether you've just come out or you've been in the islands for years—so I'm told, though I reckon the longer you've been out, the less chance o' getting it. But there are a lot more fevers, and bad cuts can go gangrenous very quickly, so watch out. Mr

Bowen's been out here a lot and he's very good—about as good a surgeon as you could wish for. He won't make much work for that parson—leastways, I don't 'spect so. That parson's got a burying sort o' voice, I must say. He let himself go when we buried those five chaps. Still," he added philosophically, "if you're going ter go, he gives you yer money's worth."

"I must say you make it all sound very inviting," Gilbert said mildly. "If the rum doesn't get you, the yellow fever will, and if you cut yourself there's always gangrene!"

Stafford laughed and said: "Don't get too depressed. The West Indies is the favourite station for Jacko and Rosey and me, better than the Mediterranean. You'll like it—if you live long enough!"

Barbados came up out of the haze, long and low on the western horizon, just as Southwick had calculated. As usual the outline of the island was faint, blurred by the spray blowing inland as the rollers crashed into the rocky shore, rollers which were uninterrupted as they swept across the Atlantic from the coast of Africa.

Ramage's clerk, Luckhurst, had made a fair copy of the captain's report on the actions against the *Sylphe, Junon,* and *Requin,* and Ramage had signed it. The weekly accounts were up to date and Ramage had inspected the midshipmen's journals, which were supposed to be filled in daily and shown to the captain each week. As far as Ramage could see they were an indictment of the midshipmen's literacy: only two of them had produced anything which could pass for a journal. On the other hand, one of them was almost outstanding: he had drawn in charts showing how the *Dido* had manoeuvred in the actions against the frigate and the ship of the line, and he had done a watercolour painting showing the *Junon* blowing up. It was what a journal should be. Ramage had rejected six others, telling

Aitken to warn the owners that they must do better.

Gradually Barbados changed from a bluish blur to a brown curve on the horizon and then, as the *Dido* approached, slashes of green could be seen. Through the glass these showed up as stands of palm trees and fields of sugarcane. The palms were mostly along the coast with the cane spreading inland, acre upon acre. There was no doubt where Barbados's wealth came from.

Southwick tucked his telescope under his arm and remarked to no one in particular: "Well, welcome back to the land of the sugar barons."

"Are you glad to be back?" Ramage asked.

"I am at the moment; but whether I stay that way depends on what the admiral has for us."

"It can't be anything too bad."

"Don't trust admirals," Southwick said darkly.

"Well, I haven't heard much about Rear-Admiral Samuel Cameron, so he can't be too bad."

Southwick shook his head and sniffed. "Don't forget we've been in the Mediterranean. Time flies. Trafalgar was months ago, hard as it is to believe. I didn't get a chance to talk to anyone from the West Indies convoy that came into Spithead just before we sailed."

"Well, we'll soon know," Ramage said. "One thing about being in a ship of the line, it's unlikely to be escorting a convoy!"

Slowly the *Dido* followed the coast round to the south-west, closing with the shore until they could make out the line of pale blue water, where it shallowed. Then, with a surprising suddenness, they were at Carlisle Bay, and Ramage quickly picked out Admiral Cameron's flagship, the *Reliant*, and began the salute.

As the *Dido* anchored and the ship swung head to wind, Ramage felt the heat: until now the *Dido* had been out in the open sea, with the Trade Wind blowing steadily across the deck and keeping the ship reasonably cool. Now, at anchor, the heat was coming off the land, humid and uncomfortable.

"Get the awnings rigged as soon as you've finished squaring the yards," Ramage told Southwick. "I'm going across to report to the admiral."

As he changed into his best uniform, tied his stock and put on his sword, he heard Aitken shouting orders as the boat was hoisted out ready for him.

So far so good, he thought: there were no strings of signal flags from the flagship telling him where to anchor, so Cameron was not one of the fussy sort of admirals who did not trust a captain to anchor properly. Perhaps he guessed that Ramage had anchored in Carlisle Bay a dozen or more times. Perhaps he did not care, Ramage thought.

He put his papers into the leather case, picked up his hat and, acknowledging the sentry's salute as he went out of the door, made his way to the entry port. There the red cutter was alongside and sideboys were holding out the side-ropes for him to hold as he climbed down.

As he went down he could smell the weed which had grown on the *Dido*'s hull as she crossed the Atlantic, and as he sat in the sternsheets he glanced along the waterline and could see dozens of goose barnacles growing like toadstools. It always amazed him how they could attach themselves to the ship and grow when she was ploughing through the water at a rate of knots, but they not only could but did in their hundreds, not deterred by the copper sheathing: in fact it almost seemed they had an appetite for copper.

Ten minutes later he was climbing on board the *Reliant* to

the shrilling of bosun's pipes, and on deck a man in a post captain's uniform with epaulets on both sides, denoting more than
three years' seniority and showing he was probably the captain
of the *Reliant,* came up with outstretched hand. "I'm Simpson,
welcome on board."

"Ramage. Thank you: I'm reporting to Admiral Cameron."

"Yes, indeed, come this way." Then Simpson said: "Been in
command long? We don't have an up-to-date Navy List, and
mine shows the *Dido* out of commission."

"I've only had her a few weeks. Commissioned her in
Portsmouth and sailed at once for here."

"The admiral will be glad to see you: we're very short of 74s
and he's grumbled to Their Lordships. I expect you're their
response."

Ramage found Rear-Admiral Samuel Cameron a burly, red-
faced Scot with mutton-chop whiskers, who greeted Ramage
cheerfully and seemed very glad to see him.

"Did ye have a good trip m'lad?"

"Yes, sir. We ran into a French 74 and a couple of frigates,
but that was the only excitement."

"I hope you saw them off?"

"We blew up the 74 and one frigate sank. The other was
captured by a British frigate that happened to be on the scene."

"Splendid, m'lad, splendid," Cameron said enthusiastically.
"You've written me a full report? Now, can I offer you a rum
punch, or would you prefer a glass of wine?"

Ramage declined politely, and Cameron said: "Let me see
your report on the action. I hope you haven't brought me a lot
of French prisoners."

Ramage explained they were on their way to England in the
frigates. He handed over his despatch and sat back comfortably
in an armchair while the admiral started reading. The cabin was

RAMAGE & The Dido : 133

well furnished: obviously Cameron was a wealthy man—probably the Windward Island station brought him a good share of prize-money. The admiral would have frigates cruising along the Main, and they would make a good number of captures.

Finally Cameron finished reading, and he grunted as he refolded the despatch. "Very creditable," he said, "and I shall say so in my letter to Their Lordships. The *Heron* was fortunate to meet you. It would have been all up with her otherwise."

Ramage nodded. "A frigate doesn't stand much chance against a 74."

"As you showed," Cameron said. "Well, I don't know that we can offer you that sort of excitement out here. But the fact is I am very short of 74s. At the moment I have only two— one refitting at English Harbour, and the other down off Surinam. It was in anticipation of the one having to go into Antigua for a refit—long overdue—that I wrote to the Admiralty asking for a replacement and that's why you were sent out."

Ramage nearly sighed: so it was going to be a boring old routine: no excitement, nothing out of the way. Simply, in all probability, just patrolling among the islands. Well, at least he knew his way around, which was something. And it was better than patrolling up and down the English Channel, with its abominable weather and the constant battle against south-westerly gales which blew their way through with monotonous regularity. All he had to do was to keep his ship's company fit: make sure that they were not hit with yellow fever.

"You know your way round out here, I believe," the admiral said. "You were out here with a frigate, I hear."

"Yes, sir, the *Calypso*."

"Ah yes, I remember: the Diamond Rock affair, when you captured the island. It was sheer carelessness on our part that we lost it again after you had returned to Europe. Well,

I'm proposing sending you up to Martinique again."

He tugged at his mutton-chop whiskers, as if trying to decide how he was going to explain to Ramage. "The fact of the matter is, our blockade o' Martinique has more holes in it than a boarding net, and the French now have a 74 in Fort Royal which they are using to escort their convoys for the run into the island—the time when our frigates used to be able to capture a few ships and disrupt a convoy.

"I can't spare the 74 that is patrolling off Surinam, and as I mentioned, my other 74 is refitting in Antigua, and if I know anything about English Harbour the work is going to take an age and be badly done. Which leaves you and the *Dido* to do the business for me."

"The business of stopping the convoys?" Ramage asked.

"Aye. How ye'll set about it I don't know. You might intercept one of the convoys and deal with the 74—which means finding them several days out, I have no doubt. Or, ye can settle with the 74 before she gets far away from Fort Royal. It'll be up to you, depending on how you find things at Fort Royal."

Ramage nodded. "I understand, sir. It rather depends on how the French react to a 74 cruising up and down outside. They might sail their own 74 to drive it off—or they might keep her in harbour . . ."

"I wouldn't try and guess which it'd be," Cameron said. "You're lucky that the convoys have to come round the south end of the island—that's about the only advantage you've got."

For an admiral giving orders to a newly joined captain, Ramage thought Cameron was surprisingly frank: in his experience, admirals never pointed out, or made any allowances for, any slight advantage there might be. But Cameron was remarkably friendly. Or was it that as one became older and more experienced, and commanded bigger ships, then admirals became more confiding? He was far from sure, but whatever the reason it made a pleasant change.

Cameron's comment that the convoys had to come round the south end of the island was a sensible one for him to make, because a captain who did not know the island probably would not know that peculiarity, caused by currents and calms.

Martinique's size and her mountains meant that the island blocked off the usual north-east and easterly winds, creating a calm area stretching several miles to the westward. In addition, the north-going current was strong along the west side of the island, through the calm area. All this meant that any ship— especially a heavily laden merchantman, which would in any case be a dull sailer—approaching round the north end of the island and bound for Fort Royal, which was also on the western side, would run into the area of calms, and lying becalmed she would find herself swept to the northwards by the current, away from Fort Royal. If she managed to find a whiffle of wind, it was unlikely to be strong enough to let her make any headway against the current. So ships made sure they approached round the south end of the island where, because of the lie of the mountains, the calms started further north and anyway the current swept a ship along the way she wanted to go, up to Fort Royal.

Fort Royal itself was on the north-west corner of a large bight which was in turn the wide entrance to a river. At first glance it seemed to be an open anchorage, but the chart showed that Fort Royal was set well back into the river entrance so that it could be protected by a fort and batteries, which could also cover any ships anchoring in the roads.

Cameron said: "I've just had to send a couple of frigates off to England with a convoy, and two more are cruising off the Main for another three or four weeks. The only ship I have off

Martinique at the moment is a brig, which is keeping a watch on Fort Royal with orders to report back here at the first sign that a convoy is due. Not," he admitted ruefully, "that I could do much about it until you arrived. I'd take the *Reliant* out, of course, but she's a damnably dull sailer: about all she's fit for is being anchored here in Carlisle Bay as the flagship."

He tugged his whiskers again, and said: "I suppose every commander-in-chief complains he doesn't have enough frigates, whether he's commanding a fleet or a station, but I'm supposed to keep a watch on the Windward Islands—including blockading Martinique—and assemble and sail convoys to England, providing the escorts, as well as covering the whole of the Main. All this with four or five frigates, a couple of 74s, and a brig or two. Their Lordships ignore my requests for frigates—in fact I often have to sail convoys with the same escorts that brought them out, which isn't really fair on the frigates, which are doomed to sail back and forth across the Atlantic escorting convoys and never getting a penn'orth of prize-money."

He paused for a minute or two and then said briskly: "Well, my problems don't concern you. I'll have your orders ready for you by tomorrow morning. You've got to water and provision, so I hope you'll be on your way to Martinique in a couple of days."

CHAPTER ELEVEN

THE Windward and Leeward Islands lay in line north and south like the blade of a sickle, with Grenada at the southernmost point. Next to the north came St Vincent, on almost the same latitude as Barbados, which was nearly a hundred miles to the east, a lonely outpost in the Atlantic.

Just north of St Vincent was the mountainous island of St Lucia, and then came Martinique, followed by Dominica, Guadeloupe, Antigua and then the group of French and British islands forming the north end of the Leewards.

From Barbados, Martinique was about 125 miles to the north-west, and a few hours after sailing, the *Dido* was rolling and pitching her way along with a brisk quartering wind from the east, with the white cotton balls of Trade Wind clouds scudding along overhead in their relentless march to the westward.

The *Dido* had left Carlisle Bay in the darkness, and as soon as dawn broke and the ship's company stood down from general quarters—where they always went to meet dawn and dusk—the deckwash pumps were rigged over the side while seamen collected buckets of sand and holystones, ready to scour the decks. The holystones were blocks of sandstone about the size of house bricks and once the deck had been swilled down with water and sprinkled with sand, the men on their hands and knees used the holystones to scour the planking. It was backbreaking work, but since it was done daily the men were used to it, thankful that they were doing it in a warm climate, instead of the Channel, where often there was a bitterly cold wind as well as icy water spurting from the deckwash pumps.

"Holystoning is almost a pleasure in the Tropics," Rossi commented to Stafford as they worked the blocks back and forth.

"Where's the pleasure?" demanded the Cockney.

The Italian seaman sighed. "Nothing ever pleases you, Staff. The water's warm, the wind is warm, and soon the sun will be up, bringing another nice day. Be cheerful!"

"That'll be the day," growled Stafford. "You'll never find me 'appy 'olystoning: you oughta know that by now, Rosey. It's m'knees. I must be getting old: the joints creak."

Rossi called across to Jackson, who was holding the hose of

a pump. "Here, Jacko: we need more water." Then he waved at Gilbert, who was holding a bucket. "Come on, we want some sand over here, or we'll never get these decks clean."

"I swear we'll wear out the wood afore we've finished," Stafford said, giving the holystone he was holding an extra flourish.

Finally the deck was scoured and Jackson directed the stream of water from the pump to wash the excess sand over the side. While some men had been holystoning the deck, others had been polishing the brasswork, using strips of cloth and brick-dust.

The men were just beginning to go below for their breakfast when from the masthead came a familiar hail. "Deck there!" Martin, who was officer of the deck, snatched up a speaking-trumpet and answered.

"Sail dead ahead, just lifting over the horizon."

Ramage, who was listening, said: "What does he think it is?"

Martin shouted up the question and the lookout answered: "Probably no bigger than a frigate but on the same course as us."

Ramage looked round aloft. The *Dido* was sailing along under courses, topsails, and topgallants. "Rig out the stunsails, Mr Martin; he ordered. "There's no British warship around here."

It took time to rig out the studding-sails, which were extensions to the ordinary sails, the head extended by a short yard with a boom which slid out along the yards to hold out the foot.

As soon as they were trimmed, Ramage could feel the effect: the *Dido* had increased her speed by a couple of knots. Southwick had come to the quarterdeck and he said: "Whoever she is, she seems to be steering for Martinique. But she's come from the south. From French Guiana, perhaps."

"Maybe she's a privateer," Ramage said. "Anyway, we shan't know until we get a closer look."

Orsini, sent aloft with a telescope, was soon hailing that the sail was a frigate, on the same course, and that she had just set her royals.

"That settles it, she's French," Ramage said. "If she was British she wouldn't set royals just because a two-decker came up astern: she'd be certain the two-decker had come from Barbados: it's obvious from the course."

But, Ramage wondered, what was a French frigate doing out here? As Southwick had speculated, she *might* be coming up from French Guiana, but it was unlikely. Cayenne, the only town in French Guiana, had only one use and that was because Devil's Island, just up the coast, was used as a penal colony. The ships visiting Cayenne were usually frigates or transports carrying royalist prisoners from France. Usually they were frigates armed *en flûte*, in other words carrying only a few guns, the rest of the space being used as accommodation for the prisoners.

Ten minutes later Paolo Orsini was hailing again. The frigate was definitely French, judging from the cut of her sails and her sheer, and they were gaining on her rapidly: she seemed to be a very slow sailer. He stopped talking for a few moments and then added: "She's just rigging out stunsails."

Ramage could see the ship clearly with his glass and he could distinguish that the frigate was beginning to look wider as the stunsails were set. Aitken had come up to the quarter-deck and Ramage nodded to him. "You've arrived at the right time: I was about to tell Martin to beat to quarters. Bend on the challenge."

A minute later the *Dido*'s two marine drummers were striding up and down the upper-deck, thudding away at their drums,

and at once the ship's company ran to their stations, remind-
ing Ramage yet again of a disturbed anthill.

Again it was the same procedure: the deckwash pumps, only
just put away after holystoning the deck, were brought out
again and rigged, the gunner collected the big bronze key of
the magazine and went below, and the crews began hauling on
the lanyards that raised the gun port lids. As water was sprayed
over the deck, men scattered sand, and soon Ramage heard the
report from Aitken that all the guns were loaded and ready to
be run out. "Can I bring Orsini down now, sir, so that he can
look after his carronades?"

"Yes, we can see what we're about from down here."

He could imagine just how the French captain felt now, with
a 74 rapidly overhauling him. There was no chance of him
reaching Martinique in time to seek shelter: even now the island
was just coming into sight, a bluish bruise on the horizon to
the north-west.

Now, with every stitch of canvas set in the *Dido*, it was only
a matter of time before they ranged up alongside the frigate
and started firing broadsides into her.

He saw Orsini coming down from aloft and watched him
hurry up to the poop, to take command of the carronades. He
knew that the three lieutenants, Kenton, Martin and Hill, were
standing by at their divisions of guns, as were some of the
senior midshipmen. He knew that every available telescope on
board the French frigate was trained on the *Dido*. "Run out the
guns," he told Aitken. It would depress the French even more,
once they saw those stubby black fingers sprouting out along
the *Dido*'s sides.

"Hoist the challenge, if you please, Mr Aitken."

Ramage watched as the flags rose on the halyard. He put
the glass to his eye, watching the frigate as a matter of routine.

But no answer was hoisted, not that Ramage had expected one. Still Ramage puzzled over why a French frigate should be out here. If she had come from French Guiana—which he finally decided was a remote chance—there was no reason why she did not go up the inside of the island chain, keeping to the westward. That way she would not risk interception by any British warships on passage between Barbados and other islands such as Grenada and Antigua. Could she have come from France and made a landfall too far south? That too seemed unlikely. A mistake in longitude, yes, putting her too far east or west, but not in latitude, taking her too much to the north or south: a latitude sight did not have to depend on the accuracy of the clock: the highest altitude around noon was sufficient.

No, it was a puzzle, but now the *Dido* had closed the distance to a mile, and Ramage could see that the ship was black with two white strakes, and the sails were very patched. The main course seemed to have more patches than original cloths and he thought he could see small holes in the stunsails—probably where rats had been chewing, and showing that the stunsails were not used very often. Or that the frigate had a lot of rats on board.

Southwick was busy with his quadrant and, after consulting his tables, reporting distances. Three quarters of a mile, and the *Dido* was making at least nine knots. The stunsails were going to be a nuisance and Ramage gave Aitken the order to take them in.

The master had just reported the distance was down to half a mile when Ramage told Aitken to clew up the courses. What about topgallants? Would the frigate try to escape at the last moment by some cunning manoeuvring? He decided to leave them: the *Dido* handled well under topsails and topgallants.

The Tricolour was very obvious now, and Ramage could see

that it was very faded, either from age or too much tropical sun. And the black paint of her hull had no sheen; it was a long time since her topsides had last been painted. In fact, he thought, what with the patched sails and faded paint, the frigate looked as though she was at the end of a long voyage.

There was no need for Southwick to call out any more ranges: in fact Ramage just managed to read her name, even though the paint on her transom was faded. She was the *Volage*, and Ramage was surprised she had not opened fire with her stern-chasers, in the desperate hope that a lucky shot might bring down the *Dido*'s foremast, or damage her bowsprit.

Then he noticed, for the first time, that the *Volage* had run out her guns, some of them, anyway. He watched through the glass, waiting for the rest to be run out, but nothing happened, and he realized there would be no more: only eight guns were run out on each side.

"That poor devil's armed *en flûte!*" he exclaimed to Southwick and Aitken. "They've only run out sixteen guns, eight a side."

"What unlucky fellows," growled Southwick. "A lot of them won't live to see the sun set."

But what was a frigate armed only *en flûte* doing here? Had she been carrying prisoners to French Guiana? Was she bringing stores from France to Martinique, urgently needed stores which could not wait for a convoy?

There were many questions, Ramage decided, but no one was going to find the answers—yet. "Pass him fifty yards to larboard," Ramage called to Jackson, who once again was acting as quartermaster.

"Warn the gunners that we will be engaging to larboard," he told Aitken, who immediately sent off two midshipmen who had been waiting on the quarterdeck.

The *Dido* seems to be making a habit of sinking or capturing frigates, Ramage thought to himself. In fact the thought would be depressing but for the *Junon:* she had also accounted for a 74, so no one could say she was a bully!

Now the range was closing fast: two ship's lengths would do it. Just as Ramage was preparing himself for the thunder of the *Dido*'s broadsides he was startled to see spurts of smoke from the *Volage*'s starboard side, and almost immediately the Tricolour was hauled down.

She had fired a broadside *pour l'honneur de pavillon*, and then hauled down her colours. No one could accuse her captain of surrendering without firing a shot . . .

The whole question of firing a broadside for the honour of the flag was one for which Ramage had little sympathy: any court of inquiry afterwards should be able to decide whether or not the odds were so overwhelming that it was pointless to fight. But maybe the French courts were tougher; maybe they had to make sure their captains were full of revolutionary zeal. And being revolutionary, perhaps they were more sensitive about insults to their new flag . . .

He saw that the frigate was heaving-to, and he ordered Aitken to back the maintopsail. "We'll heave-to to windward, and prepare a boat to take over a boarding party. Pass the word for Hill."

While a boat was being lowered into the water, Ramage gave the lieutenant his orders, thankful that he had someone on board who spoke fluent French.

"Take ten marines with you and bring back the captain. Since she's armed *en flûte* I presume she's carrying a special cargo. Ask the captain about it but, if necessary, inspect it yourself. Leave the marines on board with orders to secure the wheel, and put the officers under guard."

Just under an hour later Hill returned on board with the

French captain, who very punctiliously surrendered his sword to Ramage, Hill explaining that he had refused to receive it earlier. The man introduced himself as Furneaux.

"Where have they come from?" Ramage asked.

"Mauritius, sir, and she's bound for Fort Royal, Martinique."

"And what is she carrying?"

"It's all very strange, sir: she's loaded with boxes and boxes of plants. Captain Furneaux says they were carrying them from Mauritius for the French to try and grow them. They came from India originally, and were first taken to Mauritius. Now the French were going to try to grow them in Martinique—it's an experiment."

"But what plants are they?"

"Furneaux calls them *les mangues*. He says they grow an oval-shaped fruit which is orange inside. He says the Indian name for them is 'mango.' You can either eat them as a fresh fruit or boil them up and make them into a preserve: something the Indians call 'chutney,' apparently."

"So the French are experimenting with plants, eh? Well, Captain Bligh brought the breadfruit here from the Pacific not so many years ago, and that has been a success. And Louis de Bougainville brought a plant from Brazil in 1768—if my memory serves me—which has a very pretty purple flower, and which was named after him."

He thought a moment and then asked Hill: "Have any of the plants got fruit on them?"

Hill shook his head. "No, sir: I looked carefully at all of them. The plants are in good condition, though: the French have been watering them regularly, and they look to me as though they'll grow all right."

"Mangoes . . . well, we'd better send them to Barbados. She looks a fairly new ship, although she needs some paint."

"Four years old, according to Furneaux, sir. Built at La Rochelle."

"Well, Admiral Cameron will almost certainly buy her in. He's very short of frigates. I don't know what he'll do with the plants—probably grow them and call them 'camerons'!"

Ramage started thinking about sending the *Volage* to Barbados. It was a voyage which, even though it was to windward, should not take more than a few hours, but he was reluctant to lose any more lieutenants. He decided to send the two senior midshipmen, mature men, along with a few seamen and some marines.

"How many men on board her?"

"Ninety-eight, sir. Apparently they had a lot of fever in Mauritius and lost many men. Furneaux was complaining that he had only a few men and they spent most of their time gardening. He's not very pleased with the idea of introducing *les mangues* to the West Indies, and he's blaming himself for being too far to the eastward, so that he passed Barbados closer than he intended."

Ramage smiled and said: "Well, if *les mangues* grow successfully and people like them, perhaps his name will go down in history as the man who nearly brought them to the West Indies!"

"I think he can claim to have brought them to the West Indies, sir, but he failed to get them ashore anywhere!" Hill said.

Ramage laughed. "Well, Captain Bligh is known as 'Breadfruit Bligh' despite the *Bounty* affair, so perhaps we can invent something for Furneaux or the *Volage*."

Furneaux was a very nondescript man; the sort, Ramage thought, who would be given the job of taking *les mangues* to Martinique with too few crew, and who would make the mistake of passing too close to a British island after a voyage of thousands of miles. Every time his name, or that of his ship, was mentioned he jerked his head round to look at the speaker, a nervous gesture which showed the strain that he was under.

Ramage sent orders for the two midshipmen to make ready to embark in the frigate. "Give them a course for Barbados, Mr Southwick. They should sight it in a few hours."

He then turned to Furneaux. "Tell me, Captain: about these plants you are carrying, have you any special instructions for planting them?"

Furneaux shrugged his shoulders in a typical Gaelic gesture. "I was told to give them plenty of water, that was all. We carried extra water for them. But special instructions—no. I received none."

"Take him back on board the *Volage*," Ramage told Hill. "I'm sorry I can't make you prizemaster, but the *Dido* can't afford to lose any more lieutenants."

C H A P T E R   T W E L V E

R AMAGE had written a brief but tactful letter to Admiral Cameron outlining the capture of the *Volage* and describing the new plants, mangoes, that she had on board. Without mentioning Captain Bligh or breadfruit, he had tried to draw the admiral's attention to the fact that the mango might become an important fruit in the West Indies—a welcome change from the usual round of oranges and bananas and paw-paw. How did one tell an admiral that the mangoes in the *Volage* might be as important to the West Indies as the breadfruit, and obtained without having to send a special ship all the way to India to collect them?

Had the French split the journey up, first taking them from India to Mauritius and planting them out there, then a year or so later taking plants from Mauritius and bringing them here, thus cutting the length of the voyage almost in half?

How could one persuade an admiral in a letter to have the plants brought ashore and planted out, instead of throwing them overboard and fitting the frigate out with more guns, because he was so short of frigates? Better still, send the *Volage* on to Jamaica, the biggest British island and the most suitable, he thought, for experiments. They had big botanical gardens there: the staff would be just the right people to plant the mango and see how it prospered in the West Indies.

Anyway, the *Volage* was now carrying the letter to Admiral Cameron. If the admiral was really interested, there must be someone on the station who spoke French and could question Furneaux further.

Southwick, who Ramage suspected was a frustrated gardener, gave a sniff and said: "If anything comes of this plant business, they'll probably call you 'Mango Ramage'—you'll be as famous as 'Breadfruit Bligh.'"

"Bligh is famous for the *Bounty,* not the breadfruit," Ramage said sourly, "so I'll thank you for not making any comparison."

"Well, mangoes sound tastier than breadfruit, so perhaps it won't be too bad."

"Martinique," Ramage said, to change the subject. "Is the current playing tricks with us?"

"There's a bit o' west-going current here, but not enough to worry about. We should have Diamond Rock abeam in about three hours. That'll bring back some memories, eh?"

Ramage nodded. "It seems a long time ago. I still don't know how we captured it!"

"I don't know about capturing it: the miracle was how we

swayed up those guns to the top. And how we captured the *Calypso*."

"Well, we may have captured it, but it was retaken by the French because of the drunken antics of an officer long after we had gone back to England."

"Yes, the loss of the Rock was a shameful business," Southwick said. "If we'd have held on to it we would have continued to control everything that tried to get into Fort Royal."

"And we wouldn't have the present trouble either. At least, Admiral Cameron wouldn't. And we wouldn't be here. Curious how the wheel seems to have turned full circle. It's about time for us to recapture Diamond Rock."

"I should imagine the French have a proper garrison there now," Southwick said speculatively.

"Well, I'm certainly not going to try it," Ramage said. "Times have changed. What a young officer commanding a brig can do, and get away with, is different from the circumstances of a post captain commanding a 74 and with definite orders in his pocket."

Southwick put his telescope to his eye. "I can just make out Cabrit Island," he said. "You'll remember that is the southernmost tip of Martinique. We'll soon be up to Fort Royal, and loosing off a broadside into Fort Louis. Ah," he said sentimentally, "it's quite like old times!"

Half an hour later, when the *Dido* had hauled around to the north-west, a lookout hailed the deck to report a sail in sight in line with Diamond Rock, which it had just rounded.

Ramage immediately sent Orsini aloft with a telescope, and the young Italian was soon shouting down that the sail was a brig, which had just altered course towards the *Dido*.

Aitken, who'd answered the hail, put down the speaking-trumpet and said to Ramage: "Didn't you say, sir, that there was one of our brigs patrolling off Fort Royal?"

"Yes, the admiral was grumbling that he had not got a frigate. Hoist the challenge."

At dawn each day Ramage consulted the little booklet given him by Admiral Cameron showing the challenge and reply for every day during the next three months, and he gave both to Aitken as soon as he came on deck. The brig—if she was British—would have a copy too, and it was the tradition that the challenge was the first signal hoisted, and if the correct reply was made then each ship hoisted the flags corresponding to her number in the *List of the Navy*. Thus, almost instantaneously, ships could discover a friend and know her identity.

The booklet containing the challenges and replies was the most secret on board: the penalty for letting it fall into enemy hands was at best a court martial, and in a bad case a captain could expect to be dismissed from the service. By contrast, letting the signal book fall into enemy hands, although a court martial offence, was less important: in the signal book every signal had its own number, and it was tedious but not impossible to warn every ship, after the signal book was known to be in enemy hands, to add a certain number—three, or seven, or nine, usually a single figure—to the numbers in the book and once again secrecy was restored. Most signal books had the original printed numbers crossed out and new numbers written in by hand.

Paolo shouted down that the brig had answered the challenge correctly and had hoisted her pendant numbers, which he called out. Ramage took the signal book out of the drawer in the binnacle and turned to the back. There she was: number 613, the *Scourge*, of 22 guns.

"Have the captain come on board: heave-to when she is closer," Ramage told Aitken.

The signal for captain, with the *Scourge*'s number, was hoisted, and in a few minutes the *Dido* was hove-to under backed maintopsail and the *Scourge* was hove-to to windward and hoisting out a boat.

And there was Diamond Rock fine on the starboard bow, sticking up like a jagged tooth. The Rock with a sprinkling of green. Yes, it was a long time ago, Ramage thought, but capturing the Rock and attacking the next French convoy to pass had been exciting; afterwards there was a feeling of achievement—apart from having captured a French frigate, which he was given to command, and which became the *Calypso,* one of the fastest frigates in the king's service.

The captain of the *Scourge* was a nervous young lieutenant who introduced himself to Ramage as James Bennett. He was tall and thin with sandy hair, and very impressed when he found he was talking to Captain Lord Ramage. It was obvious, Ramage thought, that the capture of Diamond Rock made a story still told in the Windward and Leeward Islands.

Ramage took Bennett down to his cabin. "What's going on up at Fort Royal?"

"It's very quiet, sir. The French 74 is still anchored in the Baie du Carénage, under the guns of Fort St Louis, with a frigate close by her. There are the usual collection of droghers anchored off the mouth of the Salée River, along with a few trading vessels. Otherwise there is nothing going on. The last time I saw her, yesterday afternoon, the 74 had her topsail yards sent down, probably doing repairs."

"How close do you go in to look at her?"

"About a mile, sir. Fort St Louis opens fire, and then I usually turn away. It's easy to lose the wind in the bay, and I'm always a bit nervous about lying there becalmed while the fort gives us a pounding."

"Yes, the bay is surrounded by mountains to the north and east: they act like curtains and keep the wind out."

"And they've put in some new batteries covering the town to the west of the fort. Before that, I used to sneak in from the west, but now the batteries keep me well out into the bay."

As Bennett talked, Ramage got the impression of a nervous young man afraid of risking his ship, but nevertheless carrying out his orders to keep a watch on the French 74. But he was not the man to startle anyone by sending a boarding party in one night to try to cut out the frigate, or make a surprise raid on the droghers, and sink or burn a few. Not a man, in other words, who made his presence felt, discomforting the French from time to time. If he ever achieved post rank it would be by luck, being the only man around when the opening occurred, rather than the reward for a particular episode.

It was a pity, Ramage thought, that someone like Aitken or George Hill did not command the *Scourge;* they could make the ship live up to her name. He made a guess at how Bennett had obtained the command of the brig: her previous captain had died suddenly from yellow fever and Bennett, a lieutenant in the flagship and a favourite of the admiral, had been given the command. If that was so, and he suspected it was, then Bennett had been lucky. It was a very familiar story, though of no particular credit to the Navy, because it meant that some spirited and competent lieutenants failed to get promotion because they did not catch an admiral's eyes, never serving in the flagship. Which only emphasized that all too often luck was the most important factor in getting promotion: being around and under the admiral's eye when a vacancy occurred.

Yet if he was fair he would have to admit that was how he got his start: he was at hand in the Mediterranean when Lord Nelson—then a less distinguished rear-admiral—was looking for a lieutenant to command the *Kathleen* cutter and attempt to carry out what he now realized were thought to be impossible orders, although at the time he had been so young and keen that nothing seemed impossible. Nor, in this case, were they.

As he examined the great kidney-shaped bay, memories came flooding back to Ramage. Nothing had changed at Fort Royal, up in the north-west corner. The cathedral stood in the centre of the town and Fort St Louis still sat four-square on the peninsula to the east. Further eastward the 74 was at anchor in the Baie du Carénage, with the frigate half a mile to seaward, swinging just clear of the big shoal in front of the fort.

"That 74 seems snug enough," Southwick grunted, putting down his telescope. "Doesn't look as if she goes to sea very often. They need boats to tow her into that berth: she could never sail in, not with the prevailing wind."

"She only needs to sail when a convoy is expected," Ramage reminded him. "The frigate probably does all the routine patrolling—she's anchored well out."

Even as he spoke, an idea was growing in Ramage's mind. The frigate was anchored well clear—what was that channel called? Ah yes, the Passe du Carénage, and to the west of her was the Banc du Fort St Louis.

"I wonder what they're thinking over there," Aitken speculated. "They probably haven't seen a British 74 off here for many months."

"Well, that frigate never sailed to chase off the *Scourge*, so I don't expect they'll get very excited about us," Ramage said.

"A pity," Southwick commented. "I can't see how we'll ever lure her out."

"We might be able to catch her if she sails to escort a convoy," Ramage said.

Southwick gave one of his familiar sniffs, this time indicating doubt. "They probably only get a couple of convoys a year, maybe not even that many, so we might have a long wait."

"Better than blockading Brest in the winter," Aitken commented. "A gale once a week in the winter, with snow as well. Frozen ropes, clothes wet for weeks on end . . . no I'd rather blockade Fort Royal!"

Ramage, who knew he had not the patience to blockade anywhere for long, thought about his original idea. Already the thought of sailing up and down the coast, or waiting off Diamond Rock for the *Scourge* to make a signal that the French were sailing, was beginning to pall.

But for a day or two, he would let the French settle down again: the *Scourge* would continue her watch on Fort Royal while the *Dido* went back to waiting close to Diamond Rock.

He thought of the row of mountains lining the coast down as far as Diamond Rock. It was almost like coming home again, because he could remember the names of most of them. Once past Cap Salomon, there was Morne La Plaine with another one behind it whose name he had forgotten, then Morne Macabou, followed by Morne Jacqueline, jutting out to sea, and then the highest of them all, Morne Larcher, which formed Pointe du Diamant.

Splendid mountains, all of them, but cutting off the Trade Winds as effectively as a door, unless for a change there was a bit of south in them. All of which meant that a ship had to keep five or six miles out to sea, unless the captain wanted to risk losing the wind and getting swept north by the north-going current.

But, as Aitken said, it was worse off Brest!

He told Southwick to fix the frigate's position, using both the compass and horizontal sextant angles, and as soon as the master had done that Ramage gave the order for the *Dido* to turn away to the south-west, to round Cap Salomon three miles off and then turn south to start patrolling west of Diamond Rock, where the wind was steady and the current less strong.

When hands were piped to dinner, and as the *Dido* turned southwards, Stafford said to the four Frenchmen: "Well, now you've seen it, what do you think of Diamond Rock?"

"You must have been goats to capture it," Gilbert said. "Only goats could climb up there. And as for swaying up guns . . ."

Stafford laughed at the memory. "Yes, goats was about it; that rock is even steeper than it looks. As we sailed past this morning, I was amazed that we ever managed to get a gun ashore there—there's only one tiny landing place. We hoisted the guns to the top direct from the deck, o'course, using a block and tackle. Pity those fools who took over from us ever lost it. More than six hundred feet to the top—made you feel dizzy looking down. But the battery we had at the top—I can tell you, that had a good range!"

"What did you do for water?"

"Ah, that was the problem. The island is as dry as—well, a piece o' rock. Every drop of water had to be landed. I fink that's how the French recaptured it—our chaps ran out of water. I can tell you, it's hot up there—the rock holds the heat. Doesn't seem to get any cooler at night, either."

Jackson said: "Staff's main memory of the place is that he didn't get his regular tot. As you know, he's partial to a drop of rum."

"I dunno about a tot," Stafford grumbled. "All I can remember was wishing for a pint of cold water. That's all I could think about. I even dreamed about it."

"It was just off Diamond Rock that we captured the *Calypso*," Jackson told the Frenchmen. "Mr Ramage was given command of her as a sort of recognition of what he had done in capturing the Rock. By the way, did you notice that frigate in Fort Royal?"

"Yes," Rossi said. "Is like the *Calypso*. A sister, I think."

"I think so, too: she has the same sheer, from what I could see of her."

"I wonder what's happened to our *Calypso*," Stafford said. "Probably commissioned again and flogging up and down the Channel. Chasing French privateers. I'm glad we left her: all that cold and wet. That's what I like about the West Indies— it's nice and warm. Even the rain is warm."

"Wait until we get a hurricane: then you'll change your tune."

"You forget we've already been through one hurricane here. I can still hear those masts going by the board in the *Triton* brig. You must admit, Jacko," Stafford said, "that it was a wet and windy few hours."

"I can remember how we drifted afterwards—what was the name o' that island? Oh yes, Culebra. Sad to think of the wreck of the *Triton* still on that reef."

"You can say one thing about serving with Mr Ramage," Stafford said. "At least there's plenty o' variety. Too much, some might say. Not me," he added hastily. "I enjoy it."

CHAPTER THIRTEEN

RAMAGE sat at his desk and swung the chair round so that he was facing the gathered men. "We've been patrolling off Diamond Rock for three days now," he said, "and the French in Fort Royal will have got over their surprise at seeing us off the port. They'll have been reassured to see the *Scourge* resume her patrol. So I think it's time to give them another shock."

He crossed his legs and said quietly: "I don't know how many of you had a good look at that frigate in Fort Royal. Those that did probably noticed that she was a sister ship of the *Calypso*. This would not be important but for the fact that it means all the former Calypsos know their way around her with their eyes shut. That would not be very important either except that I propose cutting her out in two nights' time, a no-moon period."

The frigate, he explained, could slip out any night and overwhelm the *Scourge*, but the brig would almost certainly notice if the 74 was preparing to sail. "As I see it," Ramage said, "the frigate is the 74's eyes: her job is to go out and scout for the convoy—probably four or five days before they guess it is due. Then it reports to the 74, which sails and escorts the convoy in the last fifty or a hundred miles—through the area where the British might try to interfere.

"If we capture the frigate, then the 74 has to sail to look for the convoy—in other words we get her out of Fort Royal and have a chance of capturing or sinking her."

"Most of my marines never served in the *Calypso*, but I hope that doesn't mean you'll be leaving them out, sir?" Rennick asked anxiously.

Ramage laughed and reassured the marine captain. "No, it just means that the former Calypsos will form a good nucleus. I don't know how many former Calypsos you sent off in the prizes, but with a bit of luck nearly a quarter of your men should have served in the *Calypso*."

"I don't know how many are left, sir," Rennick admitted, "but there are enough that I can make them section leaders."

"Good. Now listen, everyone, this is roughly my plan."

Ramage's plan revolved round the *Dido*'s six boats: the number of men they could carry governed his attack on the frigate. The launch was reckoned to carry 24 men for cutting out, while the two pinnaces and three cutters took sixteen men each, a total of 104 seamen and marines. But they were attacking on a moonless night, so the *Dido* could approach closely, and he could put another five men in each boat, without the danger of exhausting the men at the oars. That brought his force up to 134. Well, the frigate would have a ship's company of at least two hundred, although all but a few would be asleep at the time of the attack. Surprise and darkness should double the effectiveness of his force.

Captains of ships of the line perhaps should not lead cutting out expeditions, but he was determined not to be left out of this one. He would command the launch, Aitken the 32-foot pinnace, Kenton the 28-foot pinnace, Martin and Hill the two 25-foot cutters, and Rennick the 18-foot cutter. Southwick would be left in command of the *Dido*—Ramage anticipated, correctly, protests from the older master, who could not bear the thought of being left out of a fight—and Ramage decided to take the gunner along in the launch, to help control 29 eager sailors and marines. He was also curious to see how Higgins would behave in a boat action. So far, in the two actions in which the *Dido* had so far fought, Higgins had been shut up in the magazine. There was, Ramage knew only too well, nothing like a night boat action for testing a man: was he nervous, was he indecisive, did he panic—all would be revealed, and by taking Higgins with him, any failure on the part of the gunner would not affect the handling of a boat.

He had 88 marines remaining, after losing men to prizes. He needed at least 30 seamen. He scribbled a sum on a piece of paper. Yes, he could take all the marines and still have room for the seamen. Well, that would please Rennick, who would be able to bring along his two lieutenants, four sergeants and four corporals and try them out. Not that there was any need to try out Sergeant Ferris and the two corporals who had come from the *Calypso:* they had already been in action several times.

Ramage found he was enjoying planning the details of the raid. For a start the marines would all carry pistols, not the clumsy muskets which would be cumbersome when boarding the enemy. Pistols and cutlasses. The same for the seamen, who would also have boarding pikes, half pikes or tomahawks—they would be allowed the choice.

He did not like the idea of risking all the *Dido*'s topmen, although the men who went aloft in the darkness to let fall the sails would be the most important in the raid, because they might well end up sailing the frigate out of Fort Royal with fighting still going on. Providing, Ramage told himself, that there was an offshore wind. If there was, the frigate would just about sail herself out to sea: it only needed a couple of hands at the wheel.

And that was the next part of his plan: twenty marines had to be told off to secure the quarterdeck, and particularly the wheel, and hold it whatever happened.

Prisoners? Those Frenchmen who could swim would probably jump over the side as soon as they realized their ship had been captured and was being sailed out of Fort Royal, but that would still leave a large number on board who would have to be secured. They could be sent ashore later under a flag of truce—Ramage decided he was unwilling to sacrifice too many more men in a prize. Returning French seamen did not mean very much, since they could not have the ships to put them in—unless they packed them into the 74.

Muffling the oars—Aitken would have to pay special attention to that. A gun to each boat, in case the alarm was given and they had to fight their way on board—and plenty of case shot, not round shot, because they would be trying to kill men, not damage the ship. Water—they should have enough water breakers in each boat to refresh the oarsmen.

But what if the whole attack failed, and the French were lying in wait for them and drove them off? A rocket to signal the *Dido* to sail in as close as possible to take them off, assuming they would be badly mauled.

Ramage soon found he had a small pile of paper on his desk, notes for Aitken, Rennick and the other lieutenants. As he collected up the pages he told himself that it was not possible to plan against all the eventualities: things happened that no man could have anticipated, and by giving too many instructions it was possible to paralyse the officers, making them too rigid to respond to something out of the ordinary.

He leafed through his notes. Yes, that was about right: he was telling them what he wanted to happen, without making the orders too rigid.

He called to the sentry to pass the word for the first lieutenant. When Aitken arrived Ramage told him to alter course for Cap Salomon, and as soon as they were off it to make the signal for the *Scourge*'s captain to come on board. The captain of the brig had to be told what was going on. There was nothing for the brig to do, other than continue her patrol as usual, but she had to be warned to expect fireworks and to take no notice should she see rockets lighting up the sky from the direction of the French frigate.

It took four hours to get up close enough to make a signal to the *Scourge* and get Lieutenant Bennett on board. The brig's captain listened to what Ramage told him without enthusiasm. Ramage had half expected that the young man would want to take part in the expedition, supplying at least a couple of boats, but there was no such suggestion: Bennett heard Ramage out in silence, and then returned to his ship.

By now it was dusk, and Ramage ordered the *Dido* to return

to Diamond Rock and heave-to for the night. As soon as they were back off the Rock, Ramage sent for Aitken, Southwick and Rennick, and when they were seated in his cabin he said: "Tomorrow we go to the westwards, out of sight of land, and practise the cutting out."

"What do we use as a frigate?" asked Rennick.

"The *Dido*. Her lower-deck gun ports are seven feet six inches off the water forward and five feet eight inches amidships. With the gun ports open, they'll be just about right for the men to climb up from the boats. We might fire a few muskets off over their heads, just to get them used to the idea."

"The new men need it," Rennick said. "The men I brought from the *Calypso* have smelled powder many times. They'll steady the new men, if need be."

Ramage told Aitken: "Don't choose only former Calypsos among the seamen; mix in some new men. We've got to get them blooded."

Aitken laughed at Ramage's unexpected use of the hunting term. "You don't have to listen to the Calypsos grumbling at being left out. They will regard the new men as a crowd of Johnnie Comelatelys. I take it you'll want your usual boat's crew in the launch?"

"Of course," Ramage said with a grin. "The captain's boat has the captain's crew. Jackson and the rest of them wield useful cutlasses."

"Seems as though I am the only one being left out," grumbled Southwick. "You all go off on a cutting out expedition and leave me here on board twiddling my thumbs."

"I don't regard being left in command of a 74-gun ship as twiddling your thumbs," Ramage said firmly. "Think back to the *Kathleen* cutter and the *Triton* brig—you never thought that one day you'd be commanding a ship of the line."

"Nor did you!" Southwick retorted. "But the point is I'm not commanding her in action. I'm just acting as a horseholder while you are off enjoying a good fight. Why not leave Kenton or Martin in command?"

"Because they don't have your experience. If something unexpected happens and the *Dido* has to do something—and you know well enough the chances of that—I would sooner rely on you doing the right things than one of those lads. They're keen and willing, but they just haven't your experience."

"Oh, very well," said Southwick slightly mollified. "It's just that I enjoy a fight, too!"

What Ramage knew he could not say was that there were two sides to an action—a lesson he had learned the hard way. There was the fighting, which was usually straightforward, and there was writing the despatch about it afterwards. It looked bad if a captain wrote that he had left command of his ship with, say, the third lieutenant. It was all right to leave it with the first lieutenant (who was in any case second-in-command) or with the master, who though a warrant and not a commission officer, was always experienced in ship handling. An admiral (and Their Lordships) would accept a master where they would not accept a third or fourth lieutenant. And, Ramage had to admit, it was a reasonable enough attitude. It just made it hard on Southwick, who all too often was the one who was left behind.

It was a hot and humid night, cloudless but dark apart from the starlight. The wind was light, tending to fitful. The *Dido* had just passed Cap Salomon about three miles off and Pointe de la Baleine was now broad on the starboard bow. It was, Ramage reflected, a peaceful beginning to what was going to be a bloody night. The *Dido* was gliding along in a calm sea, leaving little more than a hint of a phosphorescent wake.

Ramage still found it hard to believe, on a night such as this, that he commanded a ship of the line, and he still marvelled at the complexity and sheer size of the ship. For instance, it had taken two thousand large trees, each weighing a couple of tons, to build her. Her sails—hardly strained in this wind—totalled 10,700 yards of canvas, and weighed more than six tons. The standing rigging weighed 27 tons and the running rigging 17 tons.

When one started thinking about the weights involved, the figures were startling—260 tons of water, 52 tons of coals and wood, 214 tons of provisions, spirits, and slops. The men and their effects accounted for 65 tons. And he had forgotten all the blocks—which people on shore insisted on calling pulleys— which with the rigging totalled more than 54 tons.

And for fighting there were 335 barrels of powder and 79 tons of shot, while the guns weighed a total of 178 tons, and the powder came to more than 20 tons.

And all of that was gliding along, pushed by the sails which at the moment obscured large rectangles of the star-filled sky. The down-draught from the mainsail was cooling, but the ship still seemed hot, the heat absorbed from the sun during the day. Astern six boats were towing on painters of varying lengths, and at last the grindstone had been stowed again after grind-ing away most of the day as the men sharpened cutlasses, tom-ahawks and boarding pikes.

The guns were loaded and run out. Many of the regular guns' crews had been chosen as boarders or formed part of the boats' crews, so earlier their replacements had been exercised— just in case the *Dido* needed to use her guns. Now the marines were drawn up on deck for the final inspection by Rennick and his lieutenants. On Ramage's direct order the marines were not dressed in their regular uniforms with pipeclayed crossbelts. Instead they wore shirts and trousers: clothing better suited to scrambling aboard an enemy frigate. They were barefooted, too, though Ramage suspected that many of them would be stamping their feet out of sheer habit.

Only Southwick stood by the binnacle with him: the other lieutenants were with their boarding parties, giving them last-minute instructions and making sure that none of them was drunk or had any liquor with him. It only needed a drunken man to laugh or cry out to spoil the surprise.

Southwick put down the night-glass. "We are coming up to Pointe Blanche and the Ile à Ramiers. Not far to go now."

Not far indeed, Ramage thought: from the island to the anchored frigate was about three miles. Another mile and the *Dido* would heave-to and send off the boats. Ramage felt a tightening of his stomach muscles. Boarding was one of the most unpredictable of operations. It was, he always thought from what he had read of other ships' experiences, one or the other: a complete disaster with very heavy casualties, or a complete success with hardly any casualties. There seemed to be no in between: no happy medium. Obviously the more complete the surprise the more the chance of success, but he had no idea whether the frigate had guard-boats out. It would seem an obvious precaution to have a boat full of armed seamen or marines rowing round the ship all the time it was dark; on the other hand the French frigate might feel safe anchored under the protection of the guns of Fort St Louis. Well, if they bumped into a guard-boat they would be in trouble—not because a guard-boat could do much harm to six heavily armed boats but because it would raise the alarm and spoil the surprise. So, he could only hope that the frigate had been anchored in the Passe du Carénage for a long time and had become used to the only threat being a tiny brig sailing back and forth several miles to seaward.

"I reckon we can see about a mile with the night-glass," Southwick said. "So we should be all right if we leave sending off the boats to a couple of miles out. They'll never hear anything, and they certainly won't see anything, even if they're keeping a sharp lookout."

"I've little experience of cutting out expeditions," Ramage admitted, "but a couple of miles seems a nice distance. Not far enough to exhaust the oarsmen but far enough for everyone to get their night vision and settle down."

Southwick said: "Here we are—the Ile à Ramiers bearing due east of us. Now it's up to the men at the wheel." He called out a new course to the quartermaster and then with the speaking-trumpet gave orders for a slight trimming of sheets and braces.

Over to starboard now, hidden in the darkness, were several beautiful beaches with shallow water and rocks off them. The direct course from the island to the frigate was free of all obstructions, and there should not be too much current. At least, Ramage hoped not: it could set the *Dido* well to the north, but the mountains at the back of Fort Royal would help the boats.

The leadsman in the chains sang out the soundings in a monotonous voice: Ramage had to concentrate: there was a shoal beyond the island and when they reached the far side of it and the water started to get deeper they would be two miles from the frigate and it would be time to heave-to.

The soundings showed they were crossing the reef: six, five and then, in one or two places, four and a half fathoms, only just enough for the *Dido* to scrape across—she drew 23 feet aft when fully laden, though less now since she had been eating and drinking the provisions and water.

Suddenly the soundings went up: seven, nine, twelve fathoms.

"Heave-to," Ramage told Southwick. "Back the maintopsail, have the boats hauled round."

Slowly the *Dido* came to a stop, the wind on the backed sail balancing the thrust on the others. As the boats were hauled alongside to where rope ladders had been put over the side, the boats' coxswains called out a description of them so that the boarders would find their way in the darkness. "Launch here! . . . Red pinnace, men for the red pinnace here . . . Green cutter, green cutter here! . . . Blue cutter—any more for the blue cutter?"

Seamen and marines swarmed over the side and scrambled down the ladders. Ramage shook hands with Southwick and went forward, conscious of the two pistols in his belt pressing against his ribs. And, he had to admit, his heart sounded a bit hollow.

Jackson was already in the sternsheets of the launch, gripping the tiller, and round the boat were Stafford, Rossi and the four Frenchmen. They were a reassuring crowd, Ramage thought. It was curious how being in action several times with men established a bond. Not curious really: it meant that you knew you could trust the men who were covering your back.

Down here in the water, with the side of the *Dido* towering up like the side of a cliff, it was quiet except for the slap of water and the low, urgent calls of officers checking over their men. He could just distinguish the voice of Kenton, counting the number in his party: now "Blower" Martin was cursing a man who had fallen into the boat from the bottom of a rope ladder. Now Aitken was giving crisp orders to get his pinnace away from the ship's side.

Ramage finished counting his men, found they were all present along with the gunner, and gave orders to Jackson to shove

off. In a couple of minutes the *Dido* was just a large shadow
and the men were bending their backs at the oars while Jackson
thrust and pulled on the tiller to avoid other boats in the darkness.

And, away from the *Dido,* it seemed darker. It was an illu-
sion, but Ramage was surprised how much the tiny candle in
the binnacle of the boat compass lit up Jackson's face as he
leaned over to check the course.

"Steer fine," Ramage said, and cursed himself for an entirely
unnecessary order: Jackson was about the last man who had to
be told how important it was to steer an accurate course. Ramage
knew—and the thought irritated him—that he had only said it
because he was feeling nervous. Well, sitting among a boat full
of armed men on a pitch-dark night with the butts of a pair of
pistols threatening to stave in your ribs did not leave you relaxed.

Looking at Jackson's face, every wrinkle exaggerated by the
light from the binnacle (it would have to be covered over very
soon), Ramage found himself thinking of the passing years.
Jackson was no longer the young American who had helped
rescue the Marchesa di Volterra from that beach in Italy so
many years ago; nor, for that matter, was he himself that very
young lieutenant who was the sole surviving officer of his ship
. . . Jackson's face was lined and his hair was thinning and the
years were passing . . . that young lieutenant now commanded
a ship of the line, and it took a cutting out expedition to make
him realize that time did not stand still.

He looked astern and could just make out the darker blobs
of the five boats following the launch. He listened carefully but
could not hear any noise except the faint hiss of the water being
sliced away by the stem of the first pinnace. The oars were well
muffled: even here in the launch there was little more than a
faint groan as they rode against the rowlocks, a noise caused

by movement and not the friction of wood against wood.

He opened the night-glass and looked ahead over the heads of the oarsmen. There was nothing, except blackness. Well, perhaps just a hint of land, but nothing he could be sure of. He could imagine the people in the boats astern straining their eyes to keep a watch on the launch—they were following at four-yard intervals, and as soon as the launch stopped—which she would do as soon as she sighted the frigate—the boats, fore-warned, would form up in pairs for the final approach. Then, in the last fifty yards, they would split up to board from opposite sides.

Were there guard-boats, and if so how far were they from the frigate? Half a mile? Two hundred yards? Or were there no boats? Did the French dismiss the brig as of no consequence? Oh, don't start that train of thought again, he told himself; he had already been over it once and come to no conclusion, and now was not the time to fret: just keep a sharp lookout.

This really was the worst part of a cutting out expedition, the long row to the target. It left a man alone with his thoughts and fears for too long: there was just the slopping of oar blades dipping in the water and the creak of the thwarts as the seated men strained at the looms of the oars. Time seemed to stand still; the darkness left one's imagination open to the wildest thoughts.

What would Admiral Cameron think about this cutting out expedition—would he approve or dismiss it as a wild venture? If it was successful he would welcome an extra frigate—but success always brought approval; it was failure that brought condemnation.

Now Jackson was drawing a cloth over most of the binnacle to hide the light.

CHAPTER FOURTEEN

THERE WAS no mistaking it: that blacker shape was the frigate, lying head to wind and slightly to starboard. Ramage whispered to Jackson, who hissed an order to the men to lie on their oars. Out of the darkness a pinnace came and took its place to starboard and, looking aft over Jackson's head, Ramage could see the other boats forming up in pairs.

Jackson gave another order and the men resumed rowing, and the pinnace kept station. If there was a guard-boat out, Ramage had halved the chance of them being sighted by halving the length of the tail of boats. Anyway, the next three or four minutes were the dangerous ones: they could be sighted first by a guard-boat and then by an alert lookout on board the frigate herself.

But would lookouts be alert, after weeks—probably months —of just peering into blackness? It was unlikely. Most sailors could doze off while still standing up, and there was no reason to expect that the men in the frigate were any different. Ramage knew his best allies were dozy lookouts. How many would there be, anyway? Well, since they could see the frigate now, alert lookouts could presumably see the boats.

Jackson stood up, as though he could see better. Jackson knew the responsibility for the boat now rested on him: he would have to put the boat alongside the frigate's larboard quarter. Each boat had been allocated its own position—with the proviso that, in case of confusion, a boat should put its men on board wherever the opportunity presented itself.

Still no shouted challenges. If there was a guard-boat, it

must be on the far side of the frigate. And by now the boats were well inside the field of vision of alert lookouts—and yet there was no shouted challenge. Ramage felt the tension mounting. He hitched at the pistols, which he realized had made his ribs sore. And he was wearing the sword presented to him at Lloyd's. The presentation seemed a long time ago—another lifetime almost.

It was hard to judge distances in the darkness but they were now close enough that Ramage could see the frigate's rigging obscuring stars. They were down to under three hundred yards. The pinnace to larboard was turning slightly, increasing the distance between them: that pinnace was due to attack from the starboard side. Ramage glanced astern and saw two more boats were hauling out to starboard. Good—that meant that so far the plan was working. But now was the really dangerous time—when the men became excited. Then they were likely to start rowing faster, increasing the chances of catching a crab and making a splashing noise with an oar. Or start shouting when they boarded—although every man had been warned to keep quiet, so that the French would not know the extent of the attack.

Now he could clearly distinguish the rigging and knew they must be within a hundred yards of the frigate. There was no need to give orders since the boarders, crouching in the boat, could see as well as he could that they were approaching their target.

Now they were in the wind shadow cast by the frigate: the sea was calmer and there was practically no wind. Fifty yards. No shout from a lookout: no sign of a guard-boat. Now the ship's transom was looming up high overhead. He could not quite make out the name. Yes he could—the *Alerte,* the letters just distinguishable in the starlight.

Twenty-five yards—and Jackson was leaning on the tiller,

and a minute or two later was hissing orders to the men on the starboard side: he knew the risk of them clattering their oars against the frigate's side.

Suddenly there was a cry in French from the deck above: a hasty, almost uncertain challenge. Immediately Ramage called in French that they had come from the town—not a convincing answer but sufficiently unexpected, he hoped, to baffle the sentry for a valuable couple of minutes.

"From the town?"

"Yes, from the town, with urgent despatches."

"At this time of night?"

"Yes, you fool, the Republic's business cannot wait."

By then Ramage and several of the boarders had leapt up, clawing for the projecting edges of gun ports, or anything that gave a handhold. The sentry was still hesitating, then apparently he looked over the side and decided that the nocturnal visitors were boarding in a strange way, and started shouting. But his uncertainty robbed his voice of its strength.

Ramage found a foothold and levered himself upwards, hauling with his fingertips and pushing with his feet as soon as he found a foothold. He was conscious of a writhing mass of men close to him as the other boarders scrambled up the side of the *Alerte*. With a final heave he managed to grasp the lower edge of the hammock nettings and quickly climbed up them and on to the bulwark. By now the lookout had made up his mind and was shouting at the top of his voice only three or four yards from where Ramage landed on the deck, unsheathing his sword at the same time. He lunged at the shadowy figure and the shouting stopped as the man pitched forward and fell gurgling to the deck.

By now more boarders were jumping down from the nettings. Following their orders, they went after Ramage as he headed for the gunroom. Half a dozen marines headed for the captain's cabin, and Ramage almost breathed a sigh of relief: the *Alerte* was just like the *Calypso*, even to the siting of the binnacle.

By now the two men who had been entrusted with shaded lanterns had climbed on board and were lighting up a few yards of deck. Ramage snatched one of the lanterns before plunging below, realizing he was a good target for any Frenchman who had a pistol.

There had been only one lookout: that was obvious. Had his shouts been heard below, where men would be sleeping in their hammocks? Or in the gunroom, where the officers would be in their cots? No one had answered the sentry, at any rate, and as he made his way down to the gunroom Ramage coughed when the smoke from the guttering candle in the lantern caught the back of his throat.

Now he was standing at the gunroom door, holding the lantern high. There was no movement: the officers were snoring in their cabins, and Ramage was sure that the shouting would not be heard down here. He put the lantern down on the table, sheathed his sword and pulled out the two pistols. Then, with more boarders crowding into the gunroom behind him, he banged on the table with the butt of a pistol until he heard two or three sleepy voices asking in French what was the matter.

As soon as he was sure the officers could hear him, he shouted out a peremptory command in French: everyone was to fall in outside their doors. A few voices, still sleepy, asked who he was. He repeated the order, and told them to hurry.

At that moment he heard muffled shots from forward: boarders were having trouble with men sleeping forward on the lower-deck. It would not take those men more than a few moments to roll out of their hammocks, though they would have to grope their way to find where cutlasses were stowed.

The first of the officers stumbled out of his cabin and stood by the door, blinking in the light of the lantern. More followed until all the officers, looking comical in their nightshirts, were standing uncertainly in their doorways. Ramage looked round at the boarders and recognized a corporal of marines. "Keep all these men standing where they are: shoot anyone that tries to move!"

With that he ran up on deck to find out that the captain had been taken in his bunk and was at present standing by the binnacle in his nightshirt, guarded by two marines. But there were sounds of fighting coming from below, and at that moment he found Aitken standing beside him.

"Some Frenchmen have got hold of swords, sir: quite a number of them, in fact."

"All right, where's your party?"

"Right here, sir: we've just boarded."

"Very well: let's join the fight!"

He heard more shots as he and Aitken hurried below, and he found the lower-deck in chaos: men crouching because of the low headroom, crowded by all the hammocks slung from the deckhead, were slashing and parrying with cutlasses and by now shouting at the tops of their voices in English and French.

There was hardly any light: here and there a lantern glowed dimly on the deck, casting weird shadows. The heat made the air seem almost solid and the lanterns were smoking.

A man appearing apparently from nowhere suddenly hurled himself at Ramage, slashing with a cutlass. Ramage parried the first blow, having stuffed the pistols back in his belt and drawn his sword when he left the gunroom. Ramage was hard put to see the next slash because of the heavy shadows and parried instinctively. Then he caught sight of the assailant's face, which was partly hidden as he crouched down to avoid the deck-beams, and slashed at the throat. The man gurgled and collapsed.

The problem was distinguishing Didos from Alertes, and Ramage cursed himself for not telling his men to wear white headbands. Still, most of the Alertes were either naked or just wearing trousers, as they had tumbled from their hammocks, while the Didos were wearing shirts and trousers, and many of them did have bands round their foreheads to keep their hair and perspiration out of their eyes. But the bands were not white, Ramage noted; they were grubby strips of cloth often obscured by hair.

There was only one way of sorting out the Didos from the Alertes and he took a deep breath and then bellowed out: "To me, Didos! To me!"

The crowd of men gave a convulsive heave and Ramage found himself surrounded by men wielding cutlasses and chattering with excitement. He waited a minute or two and then shouted: "Right, follow me—charge them!"

He was conscious of Jackson on one side and Rossi on the other, with Aitken very close, as he ran crouching towards the waiting Frenchmen, who were obviously bewildered at suddenly finding themselves standing alone. As Ramage lunged at the nearest Frenchman he heard a solid thudding above him: he recognized the noise of axes slamming away at the anchor cable. That meant the topsails had been let fall, which in turn meant that any moment now the *Alerte* would be gathering way.

And that meant his place was up on deck, starting to sail the frigate out of the anchorage, not fighting hand to hand below decks.

"Come on!" he shouted at Jackson and, careful not to turn his back on the French, he made his way up on deck.

"Take the wheel," he told Jackson, and in the darkness he could make out the topsails hanging down from the yards. Even as he watched they began taking up their shapes as men obeyed their orders and sheeted home the sails and braced up the yards.

Now was the time to let Southwick know that the frigate was under way, so that he would light a couple of lanterns to guide them. "Where's the rocket?" he asked Jackson and the American said apologetically: "Still in the boat, sir."

"Hurry up and get it—I'll take the wheel," Ramage said crossly, and seized the spokes as he looked aloft again at the sails.

The wooden spokes felt smooth with wear as he turned the wheel slightly and thought to himself ironically: here is a captain of a ship of the line trying to steer a frigate on a straight course. He could feel a faint breeze on the back of his neck and was thankful because he could not see the sails very clearly and there was no light in the binnacle.

He could just make out the two marines guarding the French captain and he called to them: "One of you come and light the candle in the binnacle from your lantern."

That was something else he had forgotten: to detail a man to see to the binnacle light. Well, he was learning; if he ever cut out a frigate again things would be different.

Still, some things had gone right: the topsails were set, men had cut the anchor cable at the right time, and the sails had been trimmed and the yards braced round. Soon the rocket would be sent off and then he would have to look out for the two lights, one above the other, which the *Dido* would hoist.

Then Jackson was back with the rocket and launcher tube just as the marine shut the binnacle door, having lit the candle. Ramage quickly looked at the compass card, squinting as he focused his eyes. He was steering west-north-west. As far as he could estimate, the *Dido* would be a couple of points over on the larboard hand. Anyway, west-north-west kept them clear of any obstacles and for the moment he was more worried about coral reefs and shoals of sand than he was about the French.

Just as he was thinking that, Hill suddenly appeared. "Mr Aitken sent me, sir: the French have surrendered! At first just a few of them cried for quarter, and the next moment all of them did. Many of them were unarmed and realized they didn't stand a chance."

"What's Aitken doing now?"

"Sorting out the prisoners with Rennick, sir: we've taken twenty as hostages—I told the rest of them that the hostages would be run through if they didn't behave."

"Very well. Go back and tell Mr Aitken to come up here and leave the prisoners to Rennick and Kenton. You had better stay down there where your French will be useful."

By now Jackson had set up the rocket and Ramage said: "Right, fire it. Use the candle in the sentry's lantern."

The rocket went soaring up into the sky and burst into white stars. "Take the wheel," Ramage told Jackson, "she seems quite happy on west-north-west, so steer that until we sight the *Dido*'s lights."

With that he went to the larboard side and stared into the darkness. Sailing the *Alerte* was just like sailing the *Calypso*—except that the gunroom was full of French officers being guarded by marines, and below there was a whole French ship's company being held prisoner by the boarders, while just behind him the French captain stood miserably between two marine guards, his only movement that Ramage had seen being desultory slaps at mosquitoes.

And not a shot from Fort St Louis: the sentries there had

heard nothing of the shots—the *Alerte* was well to leeward—
and either had not seen or had taken no notice of the lanterns
moving around on the deck of the frigate.

Then he saw two pinpoints of light: Southwick had hoisted
the two lanterns in the *Dido*, and they seemed closer than he
expected. He suspected Southwick had been working his way
into the bay, ready to come to their help if the rocket had burst
in a red star.

Now he had to decide what to do with all the prisoners. He
did not fancy losing any more of his men in a prize-crew, and
he was sure that Admiral Cameron would not welcome more
than two hundred Frenchmen as prisoners. Why not send them
back to their comrades under a white flag and an agreement
that they would not serve until they had been regularly
exchanged?

And an exchange would take ages: the French would need
months to capture more than two hundred Britons as a counter-
weight. But Ramage found he did not care; as far as he was
concerned, the important task was to get rid of the prisoners
and then send the *Alerte* to Barbados with the minimum prize-
crew that could handle her.

C H A P T E R   F I F T E E N

HIS instructions to Hill had been very exact: he was to
take a boat to Fort St Louis with a flag of truce flying
from the bow and stern, and he was to offer an exchange of
233 prisoners—the number of Frenchmen in the *Alerte* for the
same number of Britons—thus establishing a credit, but with
the firm agreement that none of the Frenchmen would serve

again until regularly exchanged. No other terms would be acceptable, Ramage had emphasized, and the French acceptance had to be in writing.

Now three hours had elapsed since Hill left the ship in a cutter. The lookouts had seen his boat arrive at the fort but since then there had been no sign of movement. Ramage had suggested, if the French accepted the terms, that they should send out a couple of droghers, and the prisoners would be transferred to them: this would save the tedious task of rowing the prisoners ashore.

Finally, soon after noon, when the ship's company had been piped to dinner, a lookout hailed that the cutter was now leaving the fort. Twenty minutes later an angry Hill arrived on board.

"Not surprisingly, the French are furious at losing the *Alerte*," he reported to Ramage, "and they were determined to take it out on me. First of all I was marched on shore under armed guard and taken to the commandant of the fort. He kept me waiting half an hour and then took two minutes to say it was a matter for the governor, whose residence is in the middle of Fort Royal. He seemed to think it was up to me to walk there, but I reminded him that we were discussing the fate of 233 of his own people. He then provided a carriage and escort.

"The governor was not too delighted at seeing me, but at least he did listen carefully to my proposals. He said he wanted fifteen minutes to think about them, but he kept me waiting half an hour in an anteroom."

Ramage interrupted impatiently. "Get to the point, Hill!"

"Well, sir, he agreed to everything! He's going to send three droghers out later this afternoon—I suggested two, but he insisted on three—under a flag of truce. And I have his agreement to the terms in writing, complete with the stamp of the Republic, 'One and Indivisible.'"

"Good work," Ramage said. "What were your impressions of Fort Royal?"

"The blockade is bothering them. For instance, a wheel came off the carriage before we were a couple of hundred yards from the fort, and from what the driver said when he went off to get another carriage, everything was just wearing out. The fort is in a poor state, and the governor's residence needs the attention of carpenters, and a few coats of paint. The people in the street look starved and unkempt, though there's enough fruit growing on the trees."

Ramage saw Aitken coming on to the quarterdeck and waved to him. "Hill's foray was successful: the French accept our terms. They are sending out three droghers this afternoon, so we'll be able to get rid of our prisoners."

"Are you keeping the captain, sir?"

"No. He's a pathetic specimen, anyway: he's a martyr to stomach ulcers, so he tells me, and I suspect he thinks he's going to die."

"Perhaps he is," Aitken said unsympathetically. "Ulcers can kill you just as surely as yellow fever, only they take a lot longer."

"I'll tell him what you said: he needs cheering up."

Aitken pointed to the frigate anchored a hundred yards to leeward of the *Dido*, all her boats hoisted out and lying astern on long painters. "I can't get over how like the *Calypso* she is. Except for the paint. I don't know when she last saw a pot of paint."

"That's a fair indication of how our blockade is bothering them: the Tropics are no place to neglect a ship's paintwork."

"No. But the *Alerte* really looks sad, as though no one loves her."

"Admiral Cameron will love her!" Ramage said. "He'll soon

have her painted up and fitted out with new standing and running rigging. I noticed most of her running rigging was stretched,
and the standing rigging is more tar than rope. I had no idea
our blockade was hurting them so much."

"I wonder if that 74 is in any better condition," Aitken speculated. "Not that I'm suggesting we try to cut her out," he
added hastily.

"I have been trying to make up my mind who to send to
Barbados with the *Alerte*. We seem to be losing so many officers and men in prizes—men, anyway."

Aitken gestured towards the brig, passing southwards two
miles away on one leg of its sweep. "We could always send the
Scourge along as well, and she could bring our people back."

"That's a good idea," Ramage said enthusiastically. "Well,
that settles it: Kenton can command her and he can take Orsini.
It'll be good experience for them. Twenty men should be enough
to handle her. It's only a hundred miles or so, even if they'll
be hard on the wind. Now, if you'll be good enough to pass the
word to the *Alerte* that Kenton should be ready to transfer the
prisoners to the droghers and then take command. He'll need
a chart and his quadrant. Tell him to pick twenty men from
among the guards, and pass the word to Orsini, too: he'll enjoy
the cruise."

He thought a moment and then added: "Our boats will help
transfer the prisoners to the droghers so that we have them all
out of the ship before it's dark."

"Orders for the *Scourge*, sir?"

"Oh yes, hoist her pendant number and the signal for the
captain. Luckhurst will have his orders written out before he
gets here."

The droghers arrived at three o'clock and anchored to leeward of the frigate, whose boats, along with those from the

Dido, quickly transferred the prisoners. Hill had prepared written receipts for the drogher captains to sign, so there was a record of how many prisoners had been handed over to the French.

Soon the droghers were on their way back to Fort Royal, and the *Alerte* and the *Dido* hoisted in their boats. Ramage was thankful that part of the operation was over: little did the governor in Fort Royal realize how accommodating he had been . . .

With the *Alerte* and the *Scourge* on their way to Barbados, the *Dido* began to patrol across the mouth of the great bay, from Cap Salomon in the south to Pointe des Nègres to the north, a distance of six miles.

The French 74—she was called the *Achille,* according to the *Alerte*'s lugubrious captain—stayed in the Carénage, topsail yards sent down on deck and obviously not ready for sea.

"We might just as well be blockading Brest," Southwick grumbled.

"At least we don't get a westerly gale once a week," Ramage commented. "And we don't have an admiral peering over our shoulder."

"He's not that far away. Who knows what orders the *Scourge* might bring back?"

"He can't be very upset with us at the moment: he was grumbling to me that he hasn't enough frigates, and we've sent him two already."

"Wait a week or two and he'll be complaining that we're using up all the stores in Barbados refitting them," Southwick warned. "There's no satisfying admirals: you ought to have learnt that by now."

"You're probably right," Ramage said. "Anyway, there are no more frigates around for us to capture."

"No, but we'll probably build a reef with our own beef bones, sailing up and down here keeping an eye on this fellow. How are we going to winkle him out?"

Ramage shrugged his shoulders. "I don't know about winkles; he's stuck in there like a limpet. We're going to have to wait until he sails to escort a convoy in—whenever that is."

"We're going to be heartily sick of this bit of coast by then."

"As soon as the *Scourge* gets back she can resume this close watch: we'll spread our wings a bit."

Down at mess number seventeen, Stafford was making a similar complaint. "Back and forth, six miles south and then tack, six miles north an' then tack; I tell you, we'll get dizzy afore long."

"Stop grumbling," growled Jackson. "When we're in the Channel you're always complaining it's too cold and wet. Now you've got lovely weather and you're still complaining. What's the matter, tired of the sun?"

"Not the sun," Stafford said defensively, "just the same view: we're going to be lookin' at it for the next six months."

"Why six months?" demanded Rossi.

"S'gonna take six months for that Frenchman to sail."

"Brest," Rossi said laconically. "Don't forget we thought we were going to blockade Brest."

"At least there's variety there!"

"Variety!" Rossi said scornfully. "Yes—a westerly gale alternates with an easterly one, so one day you're close up with the Black Rocks and then you're giving them a good offing. And for a change, it blows hard from the north and maybe there's some snow, and the canvas freezes. I don't notice any snow round here."

"All right, all right," Stafford said placatingly. "But when we're on the Channel station at least we get fresh meat while we're in port."

"Damnation!" exclaimed Jackson. "Out here you get fresh limes, fresh oranges, and fresh bananas, as well as perfect weather—except for a bit of haze, and the occasional squall. You get cold, you put on a shirt: you get wet, and you're dry in ten minutes."

"My oath!" grumbled Stafford, "a chap can't comment on the view without a lot of bullies jumpin' on 'im."

"And judging from the last few days, there's plenty of prize- and head-money around," Gilbert said unexpectedly.

"Don't *you* start," exclaimed Stafford. "I've had enough from Jacko and Rosey."

"Well, you should be ashamed of yourself," Gilbert said. "Here you are, serving in a fine ship with a good captain and officers, we've had plenty of action in the last week, and now we have to wait for this ship of the line. You are too impatient, Staff."

"Well, I may be a bit impatient," Stafford admitted, "and I wouldn't want to swap this for blockading Brest, but when is this Frog going to move?"

Gilbert ignored the "Frog" epithet and said quietly: "If you were him and you saw what happened to the frigate, and you knew the *Dido* is waiting outside and commanded by the famous Captain Ramage, what would *you* do?"

"I s'pose I'd stay where I was," Stafford admitted grudgingly.

Jackson said: "As long as he stays in there, you stay out here. Which would you prefer, being him trapped in there or us out here?"

"All right, all right, you're boarding me in the smoke," Stafford said. "Can't a chap have a grumble now and then?"

Gilbert, to change the subject, said: "How much do you think we're going to get for the frigates?"

"Not so much for the first one;" Jackson said. "She was armed *en flûte*, so she didn't have many guns, nor a very big ship's company. I can't see the admiral or Their Lordships allowing us much for all those plants—after all, no one knows what they are. Whoever heard of a mango? But anyway she wasn't damaged, nor was this last one, the *Alerte*. We should get a fair price for her—apart from a coat of paint and new rigging, she'd pass for new. And a full crew means plenty of head-money."

"Yes, but it's not like the *Calypso* days: we've got a bigger ship's company to share the money. Nearly three times as big." Stafford sounded as though he could burst into tears at the mere thought of sharing with the new men in the *Dido*. "In the old days we were 225 or so in the *Calypso*; now there are 625 of us. I'm not very good at sums, but I reckon that means we get two-thirds less for every ship we capture."

"There's a big 'but,'" Jackson said. "The bigger our ship, the fewer the casualties. And we could never have cut out the *Alerte* so successfully with the *Calypso*—we wouldn't have had enough men. We cut out the *Alerte* so easily because we had enough men to swamp 'em. If we'd been in the *Calypso* we'd have had only half that number of men. And we may not have carried her. Don't forget that. There's an advantage in being in a ship of the line."

"More deck to scrub and more brass to polish," Stafford said sourly. "That's the only difference."

"And you're alive to grumble about it," said Jackson.

"The way you chaps keep nagging at me, I sometimes fink life's not worth living," Stafford said, far from mollified.

"You forget we have three frigates and one ship of the line within a month, and we're still alive to collect our prize-money," Rossi said. "So cheer up, Staff; you'll have us all in tears in a minute!"

"All right, all right; call me 'appy Staff and I'll sit here making funny faces for you all."

"I'm glad we didn't get sent to Barbados as prize-crew in the

184 : **RAMAGE** & *The Dido*

Alerte," Jackson said. "You never know when you're going to get back to your ship."

"But they sent the brig this time," Gilbert pointed out.

"Yes, and if there's another ship short of men lying in Barbados they'll talk the admiral into transferring you," Jackson said darkly. "Prize-crews are anyone's men, mark my words."

"Well, we've all been lucky—three frigates needing prize-crews, and none of us picked," Stafford commented.

"I reckon we can thank Mr Ramage for that," Jackson said. "He knows what I've just been saying. We'll never see those fellows sent off in the first frigate again: someone will snatch them at Plymouth. That's why Mr Ramage sent the brig to Barbados: he's getting worried about the number of men he's losing."

"When do you expect to see the *Scourge* back, sir?" Aitken asked.

"Under a week," Ramage said. "Give her a couple of days to get there—the winds have been light. And a day at the out-side for the *Scourge* to put the prize-crew back on board and sail. Give her a day or two to get back here and that's your week."

"I'll be glad to get those lads back. Rennick is sure someone in Barbados will steal his marines."

"Not this time, I think. We're in good odour with Admiral Cameron—or should be, anyway—and I think he will make sure we get our men back. It's pretty obvious why I sent the *Scourge*—to bring all our men back."

"I hope you're right, sir," Aitken said. "I hate losing a sin-gle man."

"I think the Barbados ships are well manned: they probably send out press-gangs as soon as a convoy comes in from England."

"One can't help feeling sorry for the men in the merchant ships," Aitken said. "Just imagine—arriving in the Chops of the Channel after a year out here and looking forward to seeing your wife and children, when one of our press-gangs comes alongside and whisks you off, to serve in one of the king's ships until this war is over."

"I don't know anyone who likes the press-gang system, but how else are we to man the ships? With no men for the king's ships, who is to defend the merchant ships? And without the merchant ships we'd be in the sort of state Martinique is in— worse, in fact."

Aitken shrugged his shoulders. "One thing about it, the press-gang certainly produces an odd mixture of men!"

"Yes, the oddest sort seem to turn into prime seamen, whether volunteers or pressed men. It doesn't seem to matter whether the man was a footpad or a footman; he's likely to make a good topman, as long as he's sound in wind and limb."

"By the way, sir, what do you intend for the men this afternoon?"

"Gunnery exercises," Ramage said emphatically. "Keep them at it: don't forget that it won't be long before we're tackling that 74 over there, and the one that wins is the one who fires fastest and most accurately: and I want to encourage Higgins, who is proving an excellent gunner."

"We're short of Kenton and Orsini; I'll have to replace them with a couple of older midshipmen."

"Very well: it'll give them some experience."

Ramage picked up his telescope and walked to the ship's side, examining Fort Royal and the 74 in the Carénage.

"I wish I knew why she had her yards sent down. Have they found some rot in them, or are they changing some running rigging?"

"Judging from the condition of the *Alerte*," Aitken said, "it could be both. I've seldom seen so much stretched rigging and bare wood. They must be getting desperately short of all sorts of stores. But sending the yards down doesn't make it seem they expect a convoy within the next few days."

"I wonder what the *Achille* does when a convoy is due. Does she sail and meet the convoy a few hundred miles out in the Atlantic? Or wait ten miles or so offshore and just escort the convoy in for the last part? Or does she wait off Cabrit Island, at the south end of Martinique? It's hard to know—the convoy could be a couple of weeks late: perhaps more."

"Do you propose to sail out and wait, if he shows signs of getting ready for sea?"

"No—we'll follow him and wait. He and the convoy are bound to meet somewhere and some time, and that's where we'll tackle him, I think."

"It all sounds rather hit or miss, as far as the French are concerned."

"They don't have much choice," Ramage said. "That's the trouble with being blockaded. From the French point of view the blockade isn't—or wasn't, before we arrived—being imposed here. Oh no, it is our cruisers off the coast of France that are making it dangerous for that convoy. It has got to escape them to get here, and it might well accidentally meet one of our ships of the line which just happens to be on passage. And now Admiral Cameron has the ship of the line he wanted—us, in other words—he can impose a close blockade of the island."

"Well, we made a good start by taking the *Alerte!*"

"Yes, but we mustn't let the *Achille* slip through our fingers. The French may have another ship of the line escorting the convoy. So we might find we have to tackle two ships of the line before we can get at the merchantmen."

"It doesn't give the *Achille* much time to get under way, unless she has a rendezvous at a certain date."

"Perhaps the convoy will send a frigate ahead, to warn the *Achille* to sail and meet them," Ramage said. "That's quite likely."

Aitken grinned cheerfully and said: "That might give us yet another frigate to snap up!"

"Certainly I doubt if she'll expect to find a British 74 waiting for her. I think we have had just a frigate or a brig keeping an eye on Fort Royal for a long time. I had the impression from Admiral Cameron that he couldn't spare a 74, until we arrived."

"I get the impression, sir," Aitken said, "that we have not been taking the blockade of Martinique very seriously."

Ramage nodded. "I think you're right; but put yourself in the admiral's place. You're very short of all types of ships, and you know a convoy rarely comes to Martinique. Are you going to keep a ship of the line off Fort Royal—if you have a spare one—or are you just going to keep an eye on the place using a frigate or a brig?"

Aitken thought for a few moments and then said: "One forgets he has responsibility for Trinidad, Grenada, St Vincent and St Lucia, quite apart from the Main coast and Martinique."

"Yes. He's lucky that Guadeloupe comes under the Leeward Islands station, otherwise he'd be even more hard pressed."

"We seem to be sympathizing with admirals," Aitken said ruefully. "It must be because we're in a ship of the line now, not a frigate!"

"It's probably old age," Ramage said. "We're getting on in years and we're growing benevolent."

CHAPTER SIXTEEN

THE *Scourge* came in sight just seven days after leaving for Barbados, and in reply to the signal for her captain, Lieutenant Bennett arrived on board the *Dido* just as the men were being piped to dinner.

He brought a letter from Admiral Cameron congratulating Ramage on the capture of the two frigates, and Bennett told him what had happened to the mangoes. It turned out that Cameron had served in India and knew the fruit well, and thought it a good idea to try to plant them in the West Indies. He was therefore planting half the trees in Barbados and sending the other half to Jamaica.

More important, as far as Ramage was concerned, the *Scourge* had brought back every man who had formed the prize-crews for the *Alerte* and the *Volage*. As soon as Bennett told him this, Ramage gave instructions to Aitken to send the *Dido's* boats to collect them.

Ramage then gave Bennett his orders: he was to resume his patrol off Fort Royal, and the *Dido* would move further south, to cruise off Diamond Rock. If the *Scourge* saw any sign that the *Achille* was preparing to sail she should make the signal to the *Dido*, which would immediately move north to see what was happening. If, on the other hand, the *Dido* sighted a convoy coming round the south end of Martinique she would engage immediately.

Bennett had just left to rejoin the *Scourge* when Kenton and Orsini arrived back on board the *Dido*, both excited at being back.

"What sort of trip did you have in the *Alerte?*" Ramage asked.

"Fine, sir: she's a fast ship. Very like the *Calypso*. Her bottom was very foul, so she didn't go to windward too well."

"Did you see Admiral Cameron?"

"Yes, sir. I gave him your despatch. He was delighted. He remembered that he had complained to you about the shortage of frigates, and made some joke about appreciating that you had listened to what he had said. He was very friendly, sir. And he knows about mangoes."

"Yes, Bennett told me. Well, if the trees take well, perhaps we can sample the fruit the next time we go to Barbados."

"We'll have to be out here for a long time, sir; I don't think those trees will fruit for two or three years."

"A pity, mangoes are beginning to intrigue me. I hope they'll make a welcome change from pawpaw and oranges!"

"I'd give anything for a good apple," Kenton said. "You can't get your teeth into any of these West Indian fruits, they're far too soft."

"Yes, it's a pity apples and pears don't grow out here. I've never understood why olives don't thrive, either: they grow in the hottest and driest spots in the Mediterranean, so I don't see why they don't grow here. After all, the Spaniards brought the orange here from Seville, and the banana from the Canary Islands. Who'd have thought they'd flourish in this climate?"

"By the way, sir," Kenton said, "the admiral is going to plant a couple of mangoes in his garden. He says he won't gain much by it but his successors will be grateful—providing the mango likes the West Indies!"

Shortly after dawn four days later Ramage was walking up and down the quarterdeck, soon after the lookouts had been sent aloft, when there was a hail. The *Scourge* was steering down towards them from the north, the lookout reported.

"What the devil does he want?" Kenton muttered, talking to himself.

The *Dido* was two miles to the westwards of Diamond Rock and the brig was off Cap Salomon, about four miles away, when she was sighted coming clear of the land.

Did Bennett have something special to report? Ramage wondered. That seemed the only explanation of why she would leave her cruising station, unless they were short of water, and wanted some casks from the *Dido*.

"We'll steer up to meet her," Ramage told Kenton. The wind was light, from the east, the sea was calm, and it looked as if it was going to be a typical hazy July day, punctuated by showers and weak sunshine. July was almost always a rather depressing month, starting off the hurricane season. It was unusual to have fully fledged hurricanes this early; instead, at three- or four-day intervals, there were these days of plain dull weather, sometimes with a brisk wind but always the dull cloud scudding through from the east. It would be different in August and September, when this sort of weather could quickly turn into a hurricane, or at least a storm, and a ship had to find shelter or make an offing, well clear of land, where she could ride out the hurricane.

In less than half an hour the *Dido* and the *Scourge* were lying hove-to within a cable of each other and Ramage watched as Bennett was rowed over. The lieutenant was either in a great hurry or nervous at keeping the *Dido*'s captain waiting, because the brig had hardly backed her fore-topsail before a boat was being hoisted out.

By now Aitken and Southwick had come up to the quarterdeck, curious at all the activity.

"Water," Southwick declared. "He's short of water and wants us to give him some. He was too lazy to fill up his casks when he was in Barbados, which was the obvious thing to do."

But Ramage was becoming less sure that water was the reason for the visit. Bennett would not have missed the opportunity of taking on water in Barbados—particularly since he could go alongside for it, instead of having to have the casks rowed back and forth.

Ten minutes later Bennett was saluting Ramage, his face troubled. Then he reported, the words tumbling out. "Sir—a French frigate got into Fort Royal during the night! We sighted her there at daylight—in roughly the same position that the *Alerte* was."

Bennett waited, expecting the tongue-lashing for having let the frigate get into port without sighting her. Instead Ramage said grimly: "She got past both of us—more by luck than anything else, I suspect: she probably didn't even know we were here. And it's a good piece of seamanship to round Cabrit Island and then make your way up to Fort Royal in the dark."

Bennett was still uncertain of himself. "I'm sorry sir, she must have nipped in when we were at the northern end. Just chance. We'd have seen her if we were at the southern end."

"You couldn't have done much about it," Ramage said. "Fired off some rockets and hoped we saw them, perhaps, but you'd have been hidden by the land unless we were well out."

"I'm glad you understand our position, sir," Bennett said, his relief obvious.

"What sort of frigate?"

"It was too dark to make out many details. Flush deck, 32 guns—that was about all we could see. I came south to report as soon as we spotted her."

"Very well," Ramage said cheerfully. "Go back to your station—no sign of the *Achille* stirring, I suppose?"

"No, sir, no sign at all."

"Well, keep a sharp lookout: the frigate might have some news that means she puts to sea."

"Aye aye, sir, I'll stay in really close."

"Keep clear of that big reef on the east side of the Passe du Carénage—what do they call it? Oh yes, the Grande Sèche. I always think that Nature put it there specially to protect the eastern side of Fort Royal."

Bennett returned to the *Scourge,* and as soon as the boat was hoisted in the brig let her fore-topsail draw and headed back up to the north.

"So a French frigate sneaked past us during the night," Southwick grumbled. "Well, no moon and a dark night, and our lookouts must have been asleep. Still, give the devils their due: as you said, sir, it was a good piece of seamanship. What's he up to, though?"

Ramage said: "He brought the French the news we've been waiting for: the convoy is near. Anyway, that's my guess. And I think we'll see the *Achille* cross her yards and get ready to sail."

Southwick rubbed his hands together thoughtfully. "Yes, if the *Achille* gets ready for sea we'll know that's why the frigate came in. But she may be bringing despatches. Fresh orders for the governor, perhaps. Might be something as mundane as wanting water."

Ramage nodded and said: "True, it might be only one of those things. But the only reason for the *Achille* to be waiting here in port is to be ready to escort a convoy in, and the only way she would know where to meet the convoy was if a frigate came ahead and warned her—gave her a rendezvous, in fact."

Southwick gave one of his sniffs, this time an approving one. "Yes, that makes sense. But is the frigate going to sail again at once, without waiting for the *Achille?*"

"I should think so."

"What about getting out to sea and intercepting the convoy, sir?" Aitken asked.

"It's hopeless trying to find a convoy out there. The point is it has to come round Cabrit Island to get up to Fort Royal, and that's the obvious place to wait for it. And with a bit of luck the *Achille* will go out that way too, to the rendezvous."

"Ah yes," said Southwick, "if we wait at the eastern side of Cabrit, out of sight, we may catch the *Achille* napping."

"Exactly," Ramage said. "Just as the damned frigate caught us napping. There's no point in waiting off Fort Royal—if the convoy got up that far, some of the merchantmen might be able to bolt in."

Daybreak was a repeat of the previous day: the lookouts had been sent aloft and Ramage and Aitken were on the quarterdeck, talking about the day's work, when there was a hail from aloft. Aitken grabbed the speaking-trumpet and answered, and the shout came back that the brig was approaching them from the north.

Ramage had a sudden sick feeling he knew why. "Send Orsini aloft with a bring-'em-near; she may be flying a signal."

By chance the *Dido* was heading north towards the brig, and they were approaching each other at a combined speed of nine or ten knots. By the time Orsini had grabbed a telescope and made his way up the ratlines, it was getting lighter, and he was soon hailing the quarterdeck.

"She's flying a signal, *Frigate sailed in night.*"

Ramage cursed and told Aitken: "Acknowledge. Tell him to resume his patrol."

Aitken gave the orders and said: "Does that mean we missed him a second time, sir?"

RAMAGE *& The Dido*

Ramage was not sure. The officers of the deck had been given orders to make sure that the men kept a sharp lookout: the *Dido* had moved further north to patrol off Cap Salomon. The brig was patrolling close in off Fort Royal. There seemed to be only one explanation of how the frigate had eluded the *Dido*.

"I don't think he came this way. If he knew we were down here—and they would have warned him—then I think he made a bolt for it to the north: he had the current to help him and it is a far easier passage."

And, Ramage thought to himself, apart from my own feelings, Admiral Cameron is not going to be very pleased that this damned frigate has fooled us twice—made us look silly on successive nights. Now he knew he should have moved further north, doubling up on the brig. *Now* he knew that. But being wise twelve hours too late was the same as not being wise at all. He had to face the fact that the French frigate had hoodwinked him not once but twice. The first time could be put down to the Frenchman being unexpected; the second just showed that Ramage was unprepared.

Southwick arrived on the quarterdeck, and Aitken told him about the brig's signal. Southwick gave a rueful laugh, and said to Ramage: "I can imagine you getting in and out of a port that the French were blockading. But to have them doing it to us . . ."

Ramage laughed as well, though there was little humour in it. "Yes, that Frenchman caught us napping twice running. We've got to make sure that the *Achille* does not make it three times. We can't rely on the brig."

"No, it's hard to know if young Bennett isn't up to the job or just plain unlucky: being in the wrong place at the wrong time."

"He said he was going to get close in with Fort Royal," Ramage said. "Either he was not close enough or he chose the wrong place."

"He couldn't have stopped the frigate actually sailing," Southwick said placatingly. "He could only have raised the alarm."

"Yes, I was just mentioning to Aitken that she may have bolted out to the north."

"Aye, well, the *Achille* might go the same way."

"That brings up the next problem: do we try to intercept her on her way out to meet the convoy, or when she escorts it back?"

"Does it make any difference?" asked Southwick.

"Yes. We have two advantages over him when he is escorting it back. He is tied to the convoy's course and speed, and he has to come in round Cabrit Island."

"Yes, but he will be reinforced by a frigate or two—maybe another ship of the line: who knows, the French might be determined to get this convoy through, and have given it a big escort."

"In that case," Ramage said wryly, "we are going to be bustling about, but whatever the escort, they'll be coming round Cabrit Island."

"You don't think they'd risk coming north-about, guessing we'd be waiting off Cabrit?"

"No, they daren't risk the whole convoy losing the wind and being carried off to the north by the current. It was different for that frigate—the north-going current would help him. But I can't see those merchant ships making a couple of knots to windward in light airs."

"No, sir," Southwick agreed. "They'd be colliding with each other, especially if they were trying to get in at night."

"I can't see them attempting it at night," Aitken said. "The French merchantmen must be as mulish as the British, and we'd never risk it."

"No," said Ramage, "it will be south-about. By the way," he told Aitken, "you can fetch Orsini down now."

If the frigate had brought news of the convoy, Ramage told himself, then the *Achille* must be making ready for sea. And that was a good point that Southwick had made—that the convoy might have another ship of the line with it. To let the *Achille* join the convoy meant making sure of having to tackle two ships of the line at once. If he could deal with the *Achille* before she joined the convoy . . .

What about going north to look at the *Achille* this afternoon, to see if she had swayed up her yards? He could rely on the brig to warn him, but he admitted he would feel happier if he had a look himself. Would the *Dido*'s sudden appearance off Fort Royal alarm the *Achille,* or warn her what she might expect if she ventured out? Ramage doubted it: the French would know, from lookouts on the coast, that the *Dido* was round the corner, so it should not make any difference.

Well, what was he going to do, go for the *Achille* on the way out or on the way back? He needed to make up his mind. The prospect of another ship of the line with the convoy finally decided him.

By late afternoon the *Dido* was heading into Fort Royal with a brisk easterly wind knocking up whitecaps as she beat in towards Fort St Louis and the Carénage.

Southwick, Aitken and Ramage were all watching the *Achille* with their telescopes. Finally Southwick said: "She's as ready for sea as she'll ever be. There's no doubt that frigate brought her the news she's been waiting for."

"I wonder how far out the convoy is?" Aitken said, speculatively. "Probably fairly close."

"Close enough for the frigate to leave it and return, giving enough time for the *Achille* to get out to it."

Southwick said: "Why doesn't she sail now? She knows she's got to fight us, and a night action is always risky."

"These nights are dark: no moon yet. She might think she can dodge us—and she might be lucky!" Ramage said. "If we sit hove-to off Pointe des Nègres she's going to have trouble getting past us—unless it's squally and she manages to dodge us in a patch of poor visibility."

Ramage looked round at the sky: the usual Trade Wind clouds were coming off the island and the weather looked settled enough. "Not much chance of squalls tonight," he said. "It looks as though the *Achille* is going to have to come out in clear visibility."

"We need some luck after missing that damned frigate," Southwick growled.

Ramage finally made up his mind. "We'll wait off Pointe des Nègres and the *Scourge* can watch to the south. Mr Aitken, I'll trouble you to hoist the brig's pendant and the signal for her captain."

After the brig had sailed in and hove-to a hundred yards to windward, hoisting out a boat, Lieutenant Bennett came on board, nervous as though expecting a broadside from Ramage for missing the frigate when she sailed during the night. But Ramage did not mention the episode. Instead he said: "I am fairly sure the *Achille* will sail tonight. I am equally sure that she will try to get out to the northwards. I shall be waiting off Pointe des Nègres and I want you to watch to the south.

"I'll be hove-to between the Banc de la Vierge and the Pointe, somewhere on the sixteen-fathom line. You can be waiting in

198 : R_AMAGE e) The Dido

your normal position. If you sight her under way, fire two white rockets if she is heading north, and three if south. And you shadow her as close as you can without her getting in a broadside. Set off a false fire at five-minute intervals, so we know where you are, and burn two if there's a radical change of course."

"What if she attacks me, sir?" Bennett asked.

"You either dodge her or you get sunk," Ramage said dryly. "But try to shadow her from astern. She might loose off her stern-chase guns, but you won't have much to worry about after the first round: the muzzle flash will blind the French gunners.

"Now don't forget," Ramage said. "Two white rockets mean he's going northwards and three south. False fires at five-minute intervals and two together for a radical change of course. Do you want me to give you that in writing?"

"No, I can remember it, sir," Bennett said, showing a sudden surge of confidence, as though listening to Ramage had made him more sure of himself.

Bennett returned to the brig, which went back to her patrol line, where she would wait until twilight before returning close in to the Passe du Carénage.

Southwick sniffed. "I wish I could make up my mind about that lad," he said. "One minute he seems confident enough and the next he seems too nervous."

"I think he expected trouble over that frigate," Ramage said. "From his point of view it was entirely his fault."

"Aye, and if you weren't the man you are, your report to the admiral would say so."

Ramage shrugged his shoulders and laughed. "Well, it wasn't so long ago I was commanding a brig. Perhaps I feel a bit sorry for him."

Southwick shook his head. "I hope you're not going soft, sir!"

CHAPTER SEVENTEEN

TWILIGHT turned to darkness with the suddenness for which the Tropics are notorious, and the *Dido* hove-to a mile from Pointe des Nègres, her bow heading into the cliffs which lined the shore.

The Pointe itself stuck out to the south-west like a stubby tail, cliffs right to the narrow end. At one mile Ramage could, with the night-glass, just make out the blacker blur of the land, but he was not sure he would be able to distinguish a ship. The *Achille*, coming out of the Baie du Carénage, would have to sail south for more than half a mile before turning north-west so that she avoided the shallow Banc du Fort St Louis. But what would she do after that if she intended making a bolt to the north—follow the land round to Pointe des Nègres, or head out to the west to make an offing before turning north?

If she went out to the west and the *Scourge* was not following her and burning false fires, the *Dido* would miss her: Ramage was betting that she would keep close to the land. The *Achille* had plenty of choices. She could come out to the south-west before turning north-west: an arc of some three miles which the *Dido* could not hope to cover. Did young Bennett realize how much depended on him? It was probably a good thing if he did not: he might get so nervous that his judgement was affected.

"How many lookouts do we have?" Ramage asked Aitken.

"Eight, sir: two extra ones. One on the starboard bow, one aft on the starboard side."

"We'll beat to quarters now. If they sailed as soon as it was dark they could be along here within twenty minutes or so, and it takes us fifteen minutes to get to general quarters."

Aitken gave the order and in a couple of minutes the two marine drummers were striking up. Once again, even though it was dark, Ramage was reminded of an anthill being stirred up as the men hurried to their positions. They would be loading the thirty-two-pounders, which had a range of 2,080 yards, and the twenty-four-pounders, which could fire a shot 1,800 yards, while the twelve-pounders could manage 1,500 yards. Nor were the shot insignificant—the thirty-two-pounders were 6.1 inches in diameter, the twenty-four-pounders 5.6 inches, and the twelve-pounders were a comparatively modest 4.4 inches.

So much for the figures, Ramage thought. The problem in a night action was the muzzle flash: it blinded the gunners and half-blinded and certainly confused the officers on the quarterdeck. In fact night actions were very rare: the problem of judging distances and aiming the guns properly made most captains, British and French, avoid them if they could. In fact the *Achille* was almost certainly sailing at night because her captain thought it was the best way of avoiding an action with the *Dido:* he was relying on the *Dido*'s reluctance to fight as much as the chance of dodging her in the dark.

Ramage heard the rumble of the carronades being run out on their slides and could imagine Orsini's excitement: his first night action in a 74-gun ship. There was, Ramage had to admit, something awe-inspiring about taking such a big ship into action. There was 200 feet of ship from figurehead to taffrail, 24,000 square feet of canvas aloft, and the ship weighed about 2,800 tons . . . yes, the figures were impressive enough, and it was important to realize that they applied to the *Achille* as well. And when they came to fight each other, both the giants could be blinded by the gun flashes . . .

When Aitken reported the starboard side guns loaded with round shot and run out, Ramage told him to do the same thing with the larboard guns. "But tell the guns' crews to stand by the starboard guns when they've finished; I have a feeling that we shall be engaging to starboard."

In the darkness the deck forward of the mainmast looked curiously empty: all the boats had been hoisted out and were towing astern, so that random shot did not shatter them on the booms and send a shower of lethal splinters across the deck.

Guns loaded and run out: the ship ready for battle. Now was the time to strip the ship down to fighting canvas. The *Achille* would probably come into sight with every stitch of canvas set as she hurried to the north, but she would be unhandy, and Ramage was sure he was not going to get caught in the same trap.

"Take in the topgallants, Mr Aitken."

Aitken began shouting orders through the speaking-trumpet. It would mean that topmen would have to leave the guns, but the main thing was that the guns were now loaded and ready to fire.

As soon as the topgallants were furled on the yard Ramage gave the order to furl the courses. With the *Dido* down to topsails she was now reduced to fighting canvas. All she needed, Ramage thought grimly, was someone to fight.

There were now more clouds than usual and they hid the stars, making it a dark night. It was just possible to distinguish the cliffs at Pointe des Nègres, but there was no sign of the horizon to seaward. They would probably—though not certainly—spot the *Achille* if she passed between the *Dido* and the land, but if she passed to seaward, Ramage estimated, they would miss her unless the *Scourge* was shadowing her. Everything was beginning to turn on the brig, and Ramage wished he had more trust in Bennett.

Aitken said: "It seems an especially dark night. We could do with a bit of a moon."

"Yes—new moon tomorrow, although it sets so early it wouldn't be much use."

"This cloud may clear away," Aitken said hopefully. "Then we'd get a bit more help from the starlight."

"There's not much chance of that. If it hasn't gone by sunset it usually means it's here for—"

He broke off as a white rocket curved up from where he knew the *Scourge* was waiting. "One . . . two . . ." he paused for a few seconds, "—he's coming northwards!" Ramage said jubilantly. "Now for the false fires!"

He began to feel guilty for having doubted Bennett: it looked as though the brig was going to do her job successfully. And, three minutes later, as if to emphasize the point, she set off the false fire and in the eerie blue glow Ramage was sure he could distinguish the outline of the *Achille*, showing that the brig was shadowing closely.

"There she is!" Southwick exclaimed excitedly. "I just saw the sails: a couple of hundred yards or so due east of the brig."

"I thought I saw something with the naked eye: you have the night-glass."

"I've lost her now the false fire has gone out. It seems even darker just there. By Jove, that is her; I can just make her out."

"The *Scourge* should be setting off another false fire in five minutes, so don't worry if you lose her. Did you get any impression of where she's heading?"

"Up towards us, sir. She must have come out of the Carénage and the *Scourge* spotted her as she rounded the Banc du Fort St Louis—that was about where the brig was going to wait."

Now for the gamble, Ramage thought to himself: he was gambling that the *Achille* was going to follow the coast round to the Pointe des Nègres, but she could make a bolt seaward. If she did that, would he catch her in time? It would be a close-run thing.

Southwick cursed as he lost sight of the *Achille* and the five-minute wait for the next false fire seemed to last an eternity. Ramage estimated that five minutes had more than elapsed and decided that the brig had lost sight of the *Achille*. He was just about to tell Southwick to resume his search with the night-glass when suddenly the brig appeared, bathed in an eerie blue light, and just to landward of her Ramage could clearly distinguish the bulky shape of the *Achille*.

There was no doubt about it: she was keeping close in with the shore, once having rounded the shoal off Fort St Louis. And, Ramage decided, if there is any justice in this miserable world, she should pass just the right distance off Pointe des Nègres, blissfully unaware that the *Dido* is lying in wait, unseen and—with luck—unexpected.

Now there was another five-minute wait for the next false fire. Five minutes or an hour? It seemed all the same to Ramage, but eventually the blue light appeared again and he could make out the *Achille* in the circle of illumination thrown by the fire. She was on the same course, and Ramage estimated it would bring her round to about three-quarters of a mile off Pointe des Nègres—which would mean in turn that she would pass close to the *Dido*, even if the *Dido* did not move.

"We seem to be in the right position," Aitken said. "There's no obstruction between her and us that would make her alter course."

"Unless her captain decides he wants more westing before he turns north," Southwick said gloomily. "He may be scared of passing Pointe des Nègres too close."

"I doubt it," Ramage said. "We can see it and we are further away. They must be able to make out the cliffs without any trouble."

At that moment there was a flash from the direction of the *Achille* and, a few moments later, the thud of a gun going off.

"They're firing at the *Scourge* with a stern-chaser," Ramage said. "Silly fellows—they'll lose their night vision and there's not much chance of hitting the brig."

"Aye, but let's hope she doesn't suddenly round up and give the brig a broadside," Southwick said.

"I hope Bennett is paying attention to the fall of shot," Ramage said. "He's about a mile away from her, as best I can estimate, and the brig must appear a small target from the *Achille*. But, as you say, she might suddenly round up."

"One thing about it, firing a broadside means the flash would dazzle them for several minutes: they'd find it hard to distinguish the cliffs—and, with a bit of luck," Southwick added, "they'd blunder into us before they can see properly again."

"Don't forget we'd be dazzled too," Ramage said. "Remember to keep one eye shut if she does start firing broadsides: that's the only way you'll keep any sort of night vision. Once she's alongside us it doesn't matter," he added grimly. "Then whoever fires fastest wins!"

There was another flash as the *Achille* fired a second stern-chaser. "Well," Southwick muttered, "as long as she's playing games with her stern-chasers, she's not worrying about firing broadsides."

"No, she doesn't know we're out here and is probably wondering why the *Scourge* keeps on burning false fires. She could understand the rockets, thinking we are somewhere off Cap Salomon," Ramage said, "but her captain must be wondering why there are no more rockets."

Just then another false fire started burning, and Ramage

could see that the *Achille* was still on the same course and less than half a mile away. In the blue light he could see the curve of her sails and the black blur which was her hull. What could they see from the *Achille*? Would they be able to spot the *Dido* against the blacker northern horizon?

Suddenly Southwick exclaimed: "I can see her very well with the night-glass. All plain sail set. She'll pass about a quarter of a mile ahead of us. She's probably making five knots: no more, I can just make out the phosphorescence at the bow."

"Warn them to stand by at the guns," Ramage told Aitken. "It won't be long now."

A night action against another 74: the fact was he did not know what to expect. Apart from the thunder of the guns, there would be a mass of flashes which would make it hard to see anything. But at least the flashes would give the gunners an aiming point: they would not be hampered by darkness.

"She's coming up quite fast," Southwick said, the night-glass to his eye. "I think I can just make out a black speck that is the *Scourge* in the distance. It's damned difficult, what with this night-glass showing everything upside down."

Ramage cursed that there was only one night-glass on board the *Dido,* but it belonged to Southwick and he did not feel he could demand the use of it at this particular moment.

"How far now?"

"Under five hundred yards, sir. I reckon she might spot us any minute."

Then, Ramage mused, what would she do? She could turn to larboard and head out to sea—in which case the *Dido* would follow her—or she could turn slightly to starboard, trying to give the *Dido* a wide berth but getting close to Pointe des Nègres, or else she could stay on her present course and engage the *Dido,* exchanging broadside for broadside.

Just at that moment the *Scourge* set off another false fire, which lit up the *Achille* perfectly: she was large on the starboard beam and Ramage with the naked eye could make out the tracery of her rigging.

"Let the fore-topsail draw, turn to larboard on to the same course," he snapped at Aitken. He should have turned the ship sooner so that she presented a smaller object for the *Achille*'s lookouts to spot.

Slowly the *Dido* began to move ahead and turn so that the cliffs of Pointe des Nègres moved round from being dead ahead to broad on the beam. Before she finished the turn the false fire died down and Ramage, who had closed his right eye, cautiously opened it, and found he had kept his night vision in that eye. Not only that, but he could now just make out the *Achille*'s position as she approached. He had to go to the ship's side and look astern out of a gun port on the starboard side.

"Three hundred yards," Southwick said. "She's holding the same course and making perhaps five knots."

And then Ramage could make out the big black shape of the ship with a ghostly phosphorescent bow wave which flickered a pale green. She was about two or three hundred yards nearer Pointe des Nègres but, as the *Dido* finished her turn, on the same course.

"They must have seen us by now," Southwick commented. "I wonder why they haven't opened up with bow-chasers."

"Probably learned their lesson from using the stern-chasers against the *Scourge:* they found the flashes blinded them," Ramage said.

"Well, he's not trying to dodge us: he's not afraid of engaging us broadside to broadside," said Aitken.

"He hasn't had much time to think about it," Ramage said mildly.

"Well, he hasn't much choice now!"

The *Achille* was approaching fast. She had not increased speed: Ramage knew it was just a trick of the light, or the dark. But he decided to close the range.

"A point to starboard, Mr Aitken."

As the *Dido* turned slightly, the *Achille* seemed to slide closer. As far as Ramage could make out, she had not reduced sail. But even as he watched he saw the courses being clewed up: an indication that she had only just sighted the *Dido*. Now the French were at a slight disadvantage—being forced to fight with too much canvas set.

The range was closing fast now in the darkness: Ramage could see the ship quite clearly: she was two hundred yards away, broad on the *Dido*'s quarter and overhauling her. Another three minutes and she would be abeam, and the fighting would start.

Ramage found himself timing the approach as he watched. Two minutes. He turned to Aitken. "Tell the guns to be ready for the order to fire in about a minute."

The first lieutenant snatched up the speaking-trumpet and Ramage did not take his eyes off the *Achille*. Now the tip of her jib-boom was abreast the *Dido*'s taffrail. Now her foremast, bulbous with the clewed up course, was level with the poop.

"Stand by," Ramage muttered at Aitken, who lifted the speaking-trumpet to his lips.

There were several bright flashes as the *Achille*'s forward guns opened fire, and Ramage was thankful that he had been watching the ship long enough to know exactly where she was: otherwise he would have been dazzled by the muzzle flash.

More of the French ship's guns fired and Ramage heard the tearing calico noise of the shot passing overhead. The French were aiming too high. Was this because the gunners were not

208 : R**AMAGE** & *The Dido*

used to firing in the dark or were they deliberately firing high to disable rigging?

Now, after firing her guns as they bore, the *Achille* was almost abreast the *Dido* and Ramage said: "Fire!"

It was as though there was a huge clap of thunder and a prodigious flash of lightning as the *Dido*'s broadside fired, every gun going off within a second.

Ramage had been a moment too late in closing his eyes and the combined flash of all the *Dido*'s broadsides had dazzled him. He found it hard to see the *Achille*, although she was a bare hundred yards away, with the *Dido* still on a slightly converging course.

"A point to larboard should bring us on to the same course," he told Aitken just as the *Achille*'s forward guns fired again. It was curious how guns firing individually were never so terrifying as a broadside. Ramage just had time to decide that the French, firing a few guns at a time, had dazzled themselves, when a shot whined between him and Southwick after ricocheting off the mainmast.

Suddenly Orsini's carronades on the poop barked out again: they could be loaded quicker than the carriage guns, and Ramage could imagine the youth's excitement as he spurred on his men.

Then the *Dido*'s second broadside crashed out: slightly ragged this time as the men took slightly different times to load their guns. Now the smoke was streaming across the quarterdeck, making them all cough and spreading through the ship like fog. It blurred the flash of the guns firing, softening the harshness until it was like lightning in a thick cloud.

So this is what a night action between ships of the line is like, Ramage thought to himself. The only startling thing was the flash of the guns: it turned night into what seemed to be the entrance to hell. The rigging threw weird shadows on the sails; the sails themselves were lit up spasmodically and threw more shadows, apparently distorting the masts.

The darkness seemed to emphasize the noise. Obviously the guns were making no more noise than usual, but the darkness seemed to concentrate it, as though the thunder could not escape.

He heard Orsini shouting orders to his guns' crews: the lad was excited but controlled, and the guns crashed out yet again. Firing case shot, they would be sweeping the Frenchman's decks, cutting down men and slashing rigging and sails.

"Look at that!" shouted Southwick, pointing aloft. "They're either firing wild or trying to dismast us!"

In the light of the flashes Ramage could see the main-topgallant yard was hanging down at a crazy angle and in two pieces, obviously hit squarely by a round shot. There will be plenty of work for the carpenter and his mates before this night's over, Ramage thought.

Now the thunder of the guns from both ships was continuous, like thunder exaggerated a hundred times, and the flicker of the guns firing was like summer lightning. It seemed to Ramage that there was an air of unreality over the whole scene. He was too used to fighting in bright daylight to feel comfortable in the darkness.

But, he realized, it must be the same for the French. Not only that but they were probably suffering from harbour rot, his phrase for the strange malaise that came over a ship's company when they did not go to sea. Ships and seamen rot in harbour: a glib phrase but a true one. And when had the *Achille* last fired her guns in anger? Probably months, if not years ago, and Ramage could not see the ship sailing from Fort Royal to exercise the guns' crews at sea.

Just then, one of the men at the wheel screamed and

collapsed, and in the darkness Ramage could see a dark stain spreading across the deck. As Aitken shouted for another seaman to take his place, there was a crash and another round shot hit the mainmast and whined aft in ricochet across the gratings to bury itself in the bulkhead on the forward side of Ramage's pantry, at the larboard forward corner of the coach.

Suddenly Ramage realized Southwick was tugging at his arm and pointing over the starboard bow.

"Pointe des Nègres—it's very close: you can just see the cliffs in the flashes of our broadsides."

And there they were, eerily grey and menacing, and their course—the one being steered by both the *Achille* and the *Dido*— was converging on it; in half a mile or less they would be up on the rocks.

But, Ramage realized, the French had not noticed their danger—either the lookouts had been killed or they were below serving at the guns. Anyway, whatever their fate they were not keeping a lookout.

And this was the *Dido*'s chance: Ramage guessed he had only a couple of minutes to seize it. "Quick, slap us alongside! Turn right into her!"

This was the chance of surprising the enemy: surprise was the secret of all success, and it was the hardest thing to achieve. But if the *Achille* suddenly found the *Dido* coming at her out of the darkness, apparently intending to board, her obvious move was to turn away to starboard—a turn which should take her on to the rocks, because by then if the French saw the cliffs they would not have enough room to turn back again.

The men spun the wheel, helped by Jackson, and Ramage heard as if for the first time the popping of the muskets of the marines. "Boarders stand by," he shouted at Aitken, "and warn Rennick that we might be boarding!"

The *Dido's* broadside became more ragged as the ship's turn meant the guns had to be trained round more, but they soon picked up and the ship seemed to tremble as the guns fired and rumbled back in recoil.

"We're firing faster than they are," Southwick said.

"I should hope so, after all that training."

"And the French still seem to be firing high."

"So much the better: they don't seem to be doing much damage and it means we aren't losing so many men."

Just then a grapeshot crashed into the corner of the binnacle and ricocheted into the bulwark after showering both Ramage and Southwick with splinters, none of which wounded them. Southwick brushed them off his coat. "Lucky that didn't hit the compass."

The words were hardly out of his mouth before the calico-tearing sound of another shot seemed to pass between them, close enough for both men to duck involuntarily.

"Hot work," grumbled Southwick. "Too hot to last."

"They seem determined to knock our heads off," Ramage said.

Now he could see that the *Dido* was easing over on to the *Achille* but the flashes of the guns were too dazzling for him to be able to distinguish the cliffs. Was the *Achille* turning to starboard to avoid the *Dido* crashing alongside or were they just getting ready to repel boarders?

The side of the French ship rippled with the flashes of her guns, and Ramage could feel rather than hear the thud as round shot bit into the *Dido's* side. He heard an occasional scream as a man was hit, otherwise there was just the hollow rumble of the guns firing and recoiling and the cork-popping sound of the marines' muskets. The smoke was now thick on the quarterdeck, eddying and twisting as it was caught by random winds.

Ramage stared hard at the *Achille,* trying to decide whether she was turning away. He finally decided she was not. Which would mean the *Dido* must crash alongside in about three minutes—a manoeuvre he had not intended: he did not want to try to take the French ship by boarding, although he was prepared. Apart from anything else, the French ship was probably carrying a hundred or so extra troops—the easiest way they had of reinforcing the ship in anticipation of meeting the *Dido.* There were always soldiers available in Fort Royal.

Orsini was keeping up a high rate of fire with his carronades: the new design of slides certainly speeded up loading. Providing the aiming was as good as the rate of fire, they should be clearing the *Achille's* decks methodically—carronades firing case shot at close range were lethal, and the spread of the shot at this range was just about ideal.

"She's holding her course," Southwick grumbled. "We're going to run aboard her."

"I'm afraid so: I just hope she hasn't taken on a lot of extra troops," Ramage said.

"We can always hold off and keep this range."

"No, our only hope of avoiding a battering match is to get her to run ashore. Maybe they'll take fright after we get alongside."

Southwick hitched his sword round a bit, as if reassuring himself that he was still wearing it. "It'll make a change for me to board someone," he said, intending to forestall Ramage from telling him that he could not join the boarding parties. There was little he enjoyed more than swinging his big two-handed sword as he swept into the midst of a group of Frenchmen. Yet with his flowing white hair and cheery red face he looked like the peaceful parson of a country parish, more used to writing out his sermons than wielding a sword. Southwick was, Ramage considered, the most deceptive-looking man in the *Dido*'s ship's company.

The gap between the two ships was closing faster now: the outline of the *Achille* was becoming more definite, even though she still had a ghostly quality as the flickering from her own guns and the *Dido*'s lit her up, throwing weird shadows across her sails and making her hull seem to tremble.

The range was down to less than a hundred yards when Southwick exclaimed: "She's turning!"

At almost the same moment Ramage noticed that her bowsprit was diverging slightly to starboard. Not much—maybe a point. But no, the swing was continuing. The captain of the *Achille* had suddenly decided to sheer off rather than risk being boarded. But was he watching the *Dido* and not looking to starboard?

Ramage willed his guns to fire faster, so that the French captain concentrated on the *Dido*. He tried to put himself in the Frenchman's place. Yes, he could imagine himself being obsessed with watching the enemy: it was the obvious thing to do, particularly when he seemed to be moving into a position to run alongside and board.

Again he looked forward at the *Achille*'s bowsprit, and in the gun flashes he was sure she had turned another point to starboard. Two points. Three should be enough. Four would make it certain. As he watched, feeling almost dizzy as the flashes nagged at his eyes, he was sure the French ship was still turning. The only reference point was the *Dido*'s own bowsprit, which was also turning to starboard but at a slower rate.

He gave Aitken the order to bring the wheel amidships, to stop the turn. Every yard the *Dido* made to starboard brought her that much nearer to Pointe des Nègres, apart from making it harder to distinguish how much the *Achille* was turning. The

French captain had it in mind that the Dido was trying to come alongside to board, and that was all that mattered: he probably would not notice that she had in fact stopped her turn: the gunfire and darkness would obscure that. Or at least he hoped it would.

With the Dido's helm amidships he could not distinguish for certain that the Achille was continuing the turn to starboard, turning increasingly faster as her rudder got a bite on the water. How long would it be now?

Another round shot ripped overhead, only a couple of feet clear of Ramage and Southwick as they stood together on the quarterdeck. This time neither man moved; both were trying to see beyond the Achille's bow, for a sight of the cliffs. Suddenly a ripple of fire from the Dido's guns made a concentrated flash which showed Ramage the cliffs: not where he had been looking, across the French ship's fo'c'sle, but just ahead of her.

"Larboard your helm!" he bellowed at Aitken. "We'll be on the rocks ourselves in a few moments."

Even as he shouted the Achille seemed to stop in the water and then appeared to draw astern as the Dido forged ahead and began to turn to seaward away from the cliffs and away from the Achille.

Slowly the gunfire died down as the gun captains realized there was no target, and the night became black. Black with blotches of grey as the eyes tried to recover from the dazzling effect of the muzzle flashes.

"We've done it!" Southwick shouted triumphantly. "She's gone up on the rocks!"

"I'm not sure we're going to get clear in time," Ramage said cautiously. "I can't see a damned thing."

"I'm blinded too," Southwick admitted. "All those flashes were too much. But God, how black it is now."

Ramage waited anxiously as the Dido turned and Aitken

shouted orders for trimming the sails and bracing the yards. Would that sickening crunch come as the *Dido*'s bow rode up on the small reef of rocks extending seaward from the Pointe des Nègres or would she turn in time?

Just at that moment cloud cleared away and let starlight down on to the cliff, giving Ramage a sense of direction and letting him see that the *Dido* would pass clear. But as he looked over the *Dido*'s quarter he could see the black hump of the *Achille,* seemingly hunched up at the foot of the cliff, her shape hard to identify.

Suddenly Southwick gave a bellow of alarm, followed up by an apologetic report that the *Scourge* was fine on the larboard bow. "In the darkness she looked bigger than a brig," he said. "I thought we were in for more trouble."

Ramage said, "Stand by to anchor. We want to put a few more broadsides into the *Achille* at first light, apart from making sure she doesn't refloat tonight."

"She must have been making six knots or more when she hit," Southwick said. "I don't think she's going to get off tonight."

"What's the rise and fall of tide here?" Ramage asked.

"It's only a couple of feet at springs, and it's neaps now, so a foot o' water isn't going to do her much good."

"Let's have a cast of the lead and put an anchor down," Ramage said impatiently. "I don't want to move too far away from that Frenchman, just in case he manages to get off."

Southwick bustled off to the fo'c'sle, shouting orders for the anchor party; Aitken called for topmen ready to furl the topsails.

CHAPTER EIGHTEEN

DAWN CAME with painful slowness. The ship's company went to general quarters, to meet the first hint of daybreak with the guns loaded and run out. During the night the cloud had come and gone, so that one minute the starlight showed the cliff and the *Achille* and the next minute they were blotted out by a bank of cloud drifting across the sky from the east. There was no sign of movement from the French ship of the line; Southwick, watching with the night-glass, swore that the French had not rowed round taking soundings.

"That could mean they are holed so badly it doesn't matter what the depths are," Ramage pointed out.

"True," Southwick admitted, but added: "If they're holed that badly, they'll never get off without help."

Now, as the blackness slowly turned to grey, Ramage watched the ship through his telescope. No, she did not seem to be floating low in the water. But yes, perhaps she was up a bit by the bow. It was hard to be sure in the half-light, but Ramage found himself impatient to know.

Where was the convoy—when and where was the *Achille* due to meet it? He could not wait around too long off Fort Royal and Pointe des Nègres because he had to get down to the south to wait off Cabrit Island for the merchant ships to arrive. Why the devil was it that so often one was supposed to be in two places at once?

The *Scourge* passed close and Ramage grasped the speaking-trumpet and shouted to Bennett. "Thanks—that was a good job of shadowing. You can see the result. Now get down to Cabrit Island and keep a watch there."

Bennett waved an acknowledgement and the brig turned away to head southwards.

With almost startling suddenness it was daylight and Ramage could see the *Achille* clearly. She had run up on the landward end of the short reef running seaward from the cliff. The cliff itself was a good fifty yards away.

"If she'd been twenty yards further out she'd have passed clear," Southwick said, and snapped his telescope shut. "Her captain is an unlucky fellow."

"He's going to have a hard time at his court martial explaining why he was so close inshore," Ramage said dryly. "Gun flashes or no gun flashes, he was passing the Pointe much too close."

"He was probably rattled by the *Scourge's* false fires," Aitken said. "He never thought of us waiting here for him."

"And that's why he's on the rocks," Ramage said unsympathetically. "It should have been obvious that the *Scourge* was shadowing him, and she would only have been burning false fires to warn us."

"Let's be thankful that French captain is unimaginative," Southwick said. "It makes our job easier."

"Well," Ramage said, "now we are at general quarters we may as well go across and give our French friend a few broadsides. Let's weigh anchor, Mr Southwick. We'll do it under topsails, Mr Aitken."

By now it was light enough to see the *Achille* clearly, and Ramage noticed that she had the same faded appearance as the *Alerte:* her paintwork was bleached by the hot sun and she looked as though she had been neglected for months. The effect of the blockade? Ramage suspected it was: paint (and probably rope) was not getting into Martinique. How were the French off for powder and shot? They might be getting short of wine but the island grew enough vegetables, and there were plenty of cattle, so no one would be starving.

There was no doubt that the *Achille* was stranded: she was close up under the cliffs and slightly up by the bow. But, Ramage noted, she was not noticeably down by the stern, so she was not making a lot of water. Just then he saw that there was a stream of water running down her side: her pump was working hard, so she definitely had a leak.

But she sat on the end of the reef like a huge black animal which had been cast up in a hurricane: helpless and at the mercy of the sea. What surprised Ramage was that there was no flurry of boats round her: he would have expected the French to be carrying out anchors, ready for an attempt to heave her off. Had the French captain decided that she was too firmly wedged on the rocks to be hove off? Or were they waiting for a flotilla of boats to come out from Fort Royal?

As if echoing his thoughts, Aitken said to him: "They don't seem very excited over there. I'd have expected to see boats laying out anchors."

"They might be waiting for boats to come round from Fort Royal. Or she might be too firmly lodged on the reef."

"I doubt if she hit that hard—her foremast didn't go by the board."

In the distance Ramage could hear the clanking of the pawls on the *Dido*'s capstan as the anchor came home. Then came a message from Southwick: the seaman announced that the cable was at long stay, and he had hardly left the quarterdeck before another arrived to report it at short stay, followed by another to tell Ramage that the cable was up and down. Then a seaman announced that the anchor was aweigh. Immediately

Aitken picked up the speaking-trumpet and began shouting orders which trimmed the topsails and got the *Dido* under way.

Ramage gave orders which turned the ship to starboard, up towards the *Achille*. The Frenchman was lying with her bows into the reef and her stern to the south. The best way of attacking her without spending too long in the arc of her guns was to sail in towards the cliffs, crossing her stern and raking her. Then immediately the *Dido* had fired a broadside she would have to tack round, to avoid running aground, and head back in the opposite direction, firing her other broadside into the *Achille*'s stern.

A few raking broadsides, Ramage thought grimly, should produce results, although the *Dido* was going to have to tack round smartly, or she too would go aground, right under the cliffs and at right angles to the *Achille*. He explained to Aitken what he intended to do. "There's not much room for us to tack," he added, "so let's not waste any time."

The sun was just beginning to rise over the land and the cliffs looked less menacing, long shadows replacing the harsh blackness of the night. The waves were small and not breaking along the foot of the cliffs. If one was going to go aground, Ramage thought, these were the ideal conditions. The French were lucky, although they did not seem to be doing anything to take advantage of it.

The *Achille* was now less than half a mile away on the *Dido*'s larboard bow, and Ramage told Aitken: "Warn the gunners that they will be engaging on the larboard side, and after we've tacked we'll be loosing off the starboard broadside."

He thought how easy the forthcoming manoeuvre would have been in the *Calypso* frigate: just sail in, rake the Frenchman with the larboard broadside, tack smartly and then sail back along the reciprocal course, raking the *Achille* with the starboard broadside. The frigate spun like a top when she tacked. In the *Dido* tacking was a more stately business: the great ship needed plenty of room to turn, and this was the first time Ramage had handled her in such a confined space. Well, one mistake and the *Dido* would end up like the *Achille*.

Southwick came bustling back to the quarterdeck. "Nothing like a good raking broadside," he said cheerfully, much as one might comment on the beneficial effect of a tot of rum. "Not much room, though."

Ramage watched as the *Dido* approached. Passing thirty yards off the *Achille*'s stern would be just the right range. Probably the aftermost ten French guns would be able to fire at the *Dido* as she went by, and they would be able to rake her bow as she approached and her stern as she tacked, but it was a chance that had to be taken: it would be more than balanced by the 37 guns of the *Dido*'s broadside.

He gave a helm order to Jackson, who once again was the quartermaster, and looked at the *Achille*. He could just make out a group of French officers standing on the quarterdeck. One or two of them were pointing at the *Dido* in a way that reminded Ramage of the Italian gesture for warding off the Evil Eye.

The range was closing fast and Ramage could make out the details of the French ship's rigging. He saw them holding a Tricolour, a gesture which made him glance astern to make sure that the *Dido* was flying her ensign.

Just then he saw puffs of smoke spurting out from the *Achille*'s side as several of her aftermost guns opened fire, and a moment later he heard the thud of the explosions. But he did not feel any thump as shot hit home. Strange: the range was short enough.

"Warn the gunners they'll be opening fire in a couple of minutes," Ramage told Aitken, who snatched up the speaking-trumpet. Just then a French shot tore overhead, missing Ramage by a foot or two, and crashed into the mizen-mast. A moment later a second shot passed overhead with the usual noise of calico ripping and also buried itself in the mizen-mast, which was almost 22 inches in diameter.

Southwick sniffed. "I get the feeling that they are aiming at us, sir."

"They must be poor shots, then, at this range!"

The *Dido* surged ahead, caught by a random puff of wind funnelling off the cliffs, and the range closed rapidly: the *Achille* seemed to be sliding along the larboard side. Suddenly the first of the *Dido's* broadside guns fired and Ramage swung his telescope to watch the *Achille's* transom for shot-holes. Yes, one had smashed in the stern-lights of the captain's cabin, and then he saw several more shot-holes as the broadside continued to thunder out. A section of the transom in way of the wardroom seemed to be beaten in by the weight of shot, and then he glanced forward. The cliffs were advancing rapidly and Ramage turned to the first lieutenant, who was watching him anxiously.

"Very well, tack Mr Aitken!"

Aitken first called to Jackson and then, with the speaking-trumpet, shouted to the men at the sheets and braces. Slowly—agonizingly slowly, it seemed to Ramage—the *Dido* began to turn amid the flapping of the topsails, which seemed to want to flog the masts out of the ship.

"The breeze is freshening," Southwick commented as the ship began to swing, before starting to sail out the way she had come in. Ramage could imagine the gunners, crouched down because of the low headroom, running over to the other side of the ship to man the starboard broadside guns.

Aitken was still busy with the trim of the sails when Ramage gave Jackson a new helm order and the men at the wheel grabbed at the spokes. The ship had only just settled down on her new course with the sails trimmed when the first of the starboard broadside guns started firing, and once again the smoke drifted aft over the quarterdeck, starting them coughing again. Ramage watched the *Achille*'s stern with his telescope and once again saw the shot hitting home. He could imagine the shot smashing their way through the comparatively thin wood of the transom and then tearing their way along the length of the ship below decks, killing men and sending up swathes of splinters.

He realized the *Achille* had not fired, even though the aftermost guns would bear. Had that first raking broadside driven the men from the guns, or even overturned the guns as they rested on their carriages?

Finally the last of the *Dido*'s broadside guns and Orsini's carronades on the poop had fired and Ramage repeated his order to the first lieutenant: "We'll wear, if you please, Mr Aitken."

Again there was a thunderous slapping of the topsails as the *Dido* wore round, and Ramage knew the guns' crews would be frantically reloading, ready for the next run across the *Achille*'s stern. But, below decks, crouching in the half darkness, they would not know what was going on. The gun captains would see the target flashing past the gun ports and would pull the triggerline, but the rest of the men would be too busy to see anything, unless they managed to snatch a glance in the instant before the gun fired. Then they would be like men trapped in a thick fog as the gunsmoke drifted back in through the port, half blinding them and setting them coughing. They would swab out and load the guns by instinct rather than being able to see what they were doing, and no sooner had they got their gun reloaded than it would be time to dash across the deck to the guns on the other side.

Ramage watched the *Achille* again as the *Dido* stretched across towards her. This time there were spurts of smoke as the guns on her quarter opened fire, and Ramage felt rather than heard the thud of some of her shots hitting the *Dido*. It gave one a particularly helpless feeling to sail along being shot at without being able to reply, but the *Dido* was now sailing fast enough that only a lucky shot from the French ship would do much damage.

Ramage was just considering that when a shot tore past him and again thudded into the mizen-mast.

"Our mizen seems to be the favourite target," Southwick commented, but as if to contradict him another shot ripped along the inside of the bulwark on the starboard side, spraying out a shower of splinters which cut down a seaman who was standing just forward of the quarterdeck.

Once again the range was down to a few yards and once again Ramage lifted his telescope to watch the French ship's transom. Yes, it looked battered, but even as he noted that the first of the *Dido*'s broadside guns opened fire, smoke spurting out and the carriages rumbling back in recoil. There were several puffs of dust, showing where shot had smashed their way through the planking, and Ramage could see several rust-ringed holes where shot had penetrated. Then, as more guns fired, another section of the transom was beaten in, and the stern-lights disappeared from the captain's cabin, the frames and windows completely smashed by round shot.

Then the *Dido* had shot past and Aitken was bellowing orders for the ship to tack, with the cliffs looming up ahead, as if inviting the ship to run aground. Once the sails were trimmed and the yards braced round, Ramage watched as the ship sailed back along her own wake, and the starboard broadside was fired, gun by gun, each shot smashing into the *Achille*'s transom.

"I don't know how much more of this she can take," Aitken said. "It must be like a butcher's shop down below there."

"She's had enough," Ramage said, pointing to the Tricolour, which was now being hauled down. "I wonder how many ships have surrendered while being aground on their own soil!"

"What do we do now?" asked Southwick. "We can hardly take possession of her."

"No. We just stop firing," Ramage said. "She's in a terrible position, hard aground and being smashed by our guns. The only thing she can do to stop her crew being slaughtered is sur-render. In fact her captain knows we can hardly take posses-sion of her and he must be worrying about whether we'll take any notice of the fact he's surrendered. I wouldn't like to be him."

"Well, he's a lucky fellow, because not everyone could resist the temptation to take a few more passes across his stern and reduce him to a complete wreck."

"We haven't done too badly as it is," Aitken commented. "The captain's cabin and the wardroom must be completely wrecked, and no doubt the rudder and tiller have been smashed. It'll take months to repair her—that's if they ever get her to float again, which I doubt."

"We'll wear round, Mr Aitken," Ramage said. "Tell the gun-ners we won't be firing again."

"And we never got round to boarding her," Southwick said regretfully, patting his sword. "Well, now we have to find that damned convoy."

CHAPTER NINETEEN

WITH THE *Dido* hove-to close to leeward of the *Achille*, Ramage was able to examine her closely through the glass and decide that she was securely wedged on the ledge of rocks running from the foot of the cliffs of Pointe des Nègres, and he was certain that the French did not have the means to get her off.

He thought about his orders. His main concern was to prevent the convoy getting into Fort Royal, and if he spent too much time on the *Achille*—setting fire to her after getting the crew off—he risked missing that quarry. Far better, he decided, to deal with the convoy and return to destroy the *Achille* in a few days' time. Certainly she would not be going anywhere . . .

He gave orders for the *Dido* to let fall the courses and topgallants and then turn southwards for Cabrit Island, passing Cap Salomon and Diamond Rock. The wind was brisk enough to let the ship make six knots over the north-going current, but it was noon before they were off Cap Salomon.

As the land slipped by to the eastward Ramage felt cheerful. It was a bright sunny day, with the sun almost overhead and the big awning stretched above the quarterdeck, providing some welcome shade. The flying fish were darting out of the sea on either side of the *Dido,* and the occasional tropic bird flew overhead with its urgent wing beats. There was very little sea in the lee of the land and the *Dido* was hardly rolling. The sea was startlingly blue close in with the coast, shading into a bluish purple further out, where the water was deeper. Close along the shore it was a very light green where it broke on sandy beaches shaded by palm trees. Occasionally Ramage could see tiny villages, a dozen huts or so, nestling among the trees.

It was not only the scenery that made Ramage feel cheerful. He was pleased because two of the French ships of war that had been in Fort Royal, waiting for the convoy, had been accounted for. The *Alerte* frigate was in Barbados, by now probably bought into the king's service, and the *Achille* was hard aground on Pointe des Nègres, helpless as far as the convoy was concerned. Which left?

Well, two or three frigates escorting the convoy. There would be the one that had sneaked into Fort Royal that night and got out again without the *Scourge* or the *Dido* seeing her, and probably two more making up the escort. Three frigates to deal with before seizing the merchantmen. Unless . . . unless the French had sent a ship of the line along as well, knowing that the British were blockading Martinique (though unaware that for much of the time it was with a tiny brig).

That would make an enormous difference: the *Dido* would be heavily outnumbered with a ship of the line and three frigates to deal with, especially if the frigates were skilfully handled. In that case three frigates would almost equal another ship of the line. Well, Ramage decided grimly, if that was the escort then Ramage would go at them like a wolf attacking a flock of sheep—he would try and evade the escorts and go for the merchantmen, sinking any that came within range. It would cut down on the prize-money they could expect to collect, but the object was to stop the convoy getting into Fort Royal.

By now the *Dido* was abreast of Diamond Rock. The day when he had captured Diamond Rock and swayed up guns to the top seemed a lifetime ago. He still remembered the excitement, though—and the wild day which had ended up with the capture of a French frigate which had been renamed the *Calypso*. He had been very lucky: there were few young captains who managed to capture frigates and be given command of them, and certainly he had had an exciting life while commanding the *Calypso*. Exciting enough for him to wonder what life would be like in the comparatively enormous *Dido*. Well, so far it had not been too bad. But chasing a convoy was not really a job for a ship of the line, because she was big and comparatively unhandy. Yet, he realized, if there were three frigates escorting the convoy, he would have little or no success with only the *Calypso*.

His reverie was broken as the hands were piped to dinner and the bosun's mates went through the ship blowing their calls, which sounded like piercing bird songs.

"They'll never get her off those rocks, I don't care what anyone says," Stafford announced, sawing away at a piece of salt beef. "You saw how she was up by the bow, and she must have stove in several planks. Probably set back her stem a couple of feet, too.

"Even if they do get her orf," he added, "she'll spend a long time in the dockyard. Her stern was completely smashed in. We were going past her so slowly it was no problem aiming. Every one of my shots 'it her fair and square in the capting's stern-lights."

"It's a wonder we didn't bring her mizen down," Jackson said. "It must have been peppered with shot."

"That's a very exposed reef," Rossi said. "A good blow making her roll might bring it down. Her mainmast too, because those shot must have torn her insides out."

Gilbert, pushing his plate away, leaving some gristle on the side, said: "I wonder how many men we killed."

Jackson shook his head. "A hundred, I shouldn't wonder.

I've never seen a ship so thoroughly raked since we attacked that frigate at Capraia Island. But that was with the *Calypso,* and we didn't have anything like the *Dido*'s broadside. One thing about a big ship—her broadside is something to respect."

"It's the thirty-two-pounders that do the damage," Stafford said solemnly.

"You don't say," Jackson said sarcastically. "I thought it'd be Mr Orsini's carronades."

"Don't underestimate those carronades: they slaughter 'em on deck: cut 'em down like 'ay before a scythe."

Well," said Louis, "we must find the convoy."

"Ah, that might be a needle in a 'aystack," Stafford said.

"But it has to come round the south of the island," Gilbert protested. "If we just wait, it will come to us."

"It's something over twenty miles from Cabrit Island to Fort Royal," Jackson said. "If the convoy arrived at night, it doesn't give us much time to hunt it down."

"Arrive at night?" exclaimed Rossi. "They'd never dare make a landfall at night. *Mamma mia,* they might all end up on the beach!"

"Don't forget they've got frigates that can scout ahead," Jackson pointed out. "They might use them as pilots."

"I bet they won't stop one of them French mules running slap into Diamond Rock!" commented Stafford. "It's just put there for 'em to 'it—specially on a dark night, and we've only got the new moon for an hour."

"This salt beef is even tougher than usual," Jackson grumbled. "They must've had it in pickle since the last war."

"Antique, that's wot it is," pronounced Stafford. "Every piece a genuine antique. You can carve it or polish it. Just don't try to chew it: it'll stave in your gnashers."

"Those dockyard johnnies at Portsmouth knew we were going to the West Indies, so they got rid of some of their old stuff," Jackson said. "It's their favourite trick. They don't issue it to any ship of the Channel Fleet because they know they'd soon hear about it. But the West Indies are far enough away."

"There ain't many currants in this duff, either," exclaimed Stafford. "Who's the cook this week? You, Louis? What happened?"

"You can't have a lot of currants all the time," Louis said defensively. "I put plenty of currants in the last one. There weren't many left. Stop grumbling!"

"Not much to be cheerful about," Stafford said. "Tough meat, no guts in the duff, and where the 'ell's the convoy? I ask yer!"

"The trouble with you is you worry too much," Jackson said ironically. "What with the meat and the duff and the convoy, you've got too heavy a load on your head."

"Yus," Stafford agreed seriously, "that's my problem: I worry too much. Mind you, I 'ave to. You lot don't give tuppence about the meat and the duff, and the convoy might as well not exist. So I worry."

"Very kind of you," Jackson said, keeping a straight face. "We appreciate it, don't we lads?

The others murmured their agreement, and Stafford was satisfied that he was appreciated.

Later in the day there were the funerals. The Reverend Benjamin Brewster read the funeral service over eight men who had been killed by the shot from the *Achille*. Bowen reported to Ramage that the ten men wounded were making good progress and six of them would be able to return to duty within the week.

When Bowen paused on the quarterdeck for a few minutes, Southwick teased him about his chess. Bowen was a keen and expert player who had sometimes managed to trap an unenthusiastic Southwick into playing a game with him. Now the master was relieved to find that the chaplain was a chess player

230 : RAMAGE e) The Dido

and, although not as good as Bowen, only too happy to play him.

Ramage watched as the carpenter and his mates worked hard to finish the main-topgallant yard, splintered by a shot from the *Achille*. The wreckage had been lowered to the deck and the men were working fast on the repair.

Aitken had reported that it would take them five hours: the yard would be swayed up again before darkness fell, and the sail—fortunately not badly torn and already repaired—bent on again.

On the quarterdeck Martin, who was officer of the deck, was having a very serious conversation with Paolo Orsini about playing the flute, the skill which had earned Martin his nickname of "Blower."

"Could you teach me how to play?" Orsini asked.

"I think so," Martin said carefully. "It depends on many things. How musical are you? Are your fingers nimble? And you'll have to learn to read music."

"That won't be any harder than navigation," Orsini said ruefully. "Anyway, 1 hope not. As for being musical—well, I like it when you play Telemann. I thoroughly enjoy it. The Bach, too."

"Very well, I'll lend you my second-best flute. First you have to learn just to blow it. That means controlling your breath. And that means controlling your breathing: you can't run out of breath in the middle of a complicated piece of music."

"I can practise breathing on watch," Orsini said eagerly.

"As long as Mr Aitken doesn't notice: I don't think he would approve. He'd say you aren't concentrating on your job."

"Oh, but I would be. After all, you've got to breathe anyway."

Martin laughed. "Well, just be careful."

The wind fluked round to the north-east and Martin hailed the watch to trim the sheets and brace round the yards. "It would be nice if we sighted the convoy coming round Cabrit Point," he said conversationally. "I can't wait to get into the middle of them."

"I can't get used to being in a ship of the line," Orsini admitted. "I still think in terms of the *Calypso*, then I suddenly realize the size of our broadside. The way we smashed in the stern of the *Achille*, for instance. Those thirty-two-pounders throw a powerful shot."

"Your carronades seem to be quite effective at clearing the deck. They certainly swept the *Achille* clean."

"They have their uses," Orsini admitted modestly. "Having them so high means their shot get over the enemy's bulwarks. There's nothing between us and the target."

"I wonder what would happen if you fitted out a ship of the line entirely with carronades. She'd be fearsome at close range."

"They did try it—at the Battle of Copenhagen the *Dictator* had only carronades. Commanded by Captain William Bligh—'Breadfruit' Bligh. From what I heard she was quite a success, but because of the short range of the carronades she had to keep close."

"They were short enough at Copenhagen," Martin commented. "Any closer and they would have been throwing pikes at each other."

"Ah," Orsini said sadly, "I'm sorry we missed Copenhagen and the Nile, too, for that matter, since Nelson used the same tactics. I suppose we were lucky to have been at Trafalgar. Mr Ramage was at the Battle of Cape St Vincent—and so was Southwick and several of the ship's company—so they have been in two of his Lordship's great victories."

"Earl St Vincent got the credit for that last battle," said

Martin, who had read the description of it several times—in fact David Steel's *Naval Chronologist* had been one of his purchases just before they left Portsmouth. He had eagerly read the description of the battles, including Trafalgar, in which he had taken part.

Admiral Duncan's victory at Camperdown was another battle he would like to have been in—it was, like the Nile and Trafalgar, clear cut.

"St Vincent may have got the title but it was Nelson's victory, no doubt about it," Orsini said contemptuously. "Mr Ramage was there and he saw it all. In fact he lost the *Kathleen* cutter in the battle."

"I heard about that," Martin said. "Well, he would know!"

"To hear Jackson tell the story, it was quite a battle. Mr Ramage stopped a Spanish ship of the line by letting it ram the *Kathleen*. This slowed the Spanish up and gave Lord Nelson— Commodore as he then was—time to catch up. His Lordship never forgot that."

"Yes, we lost a good friend when he was killed. It doesn't do to think what the Navy lost. There'll never be another admiral like him," Martin said.

"Let's hope we don't have another battle like Trafalgar to fight, because I don't think we have an admiral capable of fighting it: they're all so old or inexperienced. Look what Calder did—he was court-martialled, and quite rightly so."

Martin nodded and said: "Yes, but it will be quite a day when Mr Ramage gets his flag. The war may be over by the time he has enough seniority—that's the curse of the Navy, seniority. Why they don't promote on merit alone I'll never understand."

Orsini held his hands out in a typical Italian gesture. "It would never work. It might start off with promotion by merit, but soon the politicians would get their fingers into it, and it would turn into favouritism, influence and patronage. Politicians foul everything they touch. So maybe it is safer to rely on seniority."

Martin was startled by Orsini's matter-of-fact wisdom. "Yes, I suppose you're right, but in the meantime we have to put up with the Calders and the like, promoted on seniority, not merit."

"It's the price we pay. Sometimes merit and seniority combine and we get a Lord Nelson."

"Don't forget," Martin said, "that it was Lord St Vincent that picked him for Copenhagen."

"And put that old fool Sir Hyde Parker in command!" retorted Orsini. "It nearly caused a disaster—in fact if it had not been for Lord Nelson it would have been a complete disaster: the command and the battle."

"Well, Lord Nelson won, in spite of the confusion."

"Yes, Mr Ramage says the Danes never studied the Battle of the Nile. Had they done so, they would never have fought the battle like they did because they let Nelson fight the same sort of battle—with the same sort of results."

At that moment Ramage came on to the quarterdeck and, overhearing Orsini's last few words, asked: "What are you two naval strategists discussing?"

"Lord Nelson and Sir Hyde Parker at Copenhagen, sir," Martin said. "The divided command."

"You can talk about that for a month without reaching any conclusions," Ramage said, deciding not to enter into any conversation criticizing senior flag officers. He had talked about Copenhagen with his father and Paolo at Palace Street, but they were family conversations, not exactly private but not the sort of talks he would have with his junior officers, since he had been very critical of Sir Hyde Parker, who was unsuited to

234 : R AMAGE

Danish waters after several years of comparative luxury in the West Indies, where the only enemies were mosquitoes, yellow fever and occasional enemy cruisers.

"Well, can you two strategists tell me how far we are from Cabrit?"

"Five miles, sir," Martin said with a promptness that told Ramage he was making a guess. Martin, he decided, had learned the old trick of always giving a prompt reply, relying on its promptness to assure the listener of its accuracy.

Not, Ramage admitted, that it mattered on this occasion: they were on course for Cabrit and were about halfway between Diamond Rock and the island itself, so five miles was a good guess. From this angle, Cabrit Island still seemed to be part of the southern tip of Martinique, not yet outlined against the sea horizon.

Which side of the headland should he wait on? He had already decided not to go hunting for the convoy; instead he would wait and tackle it somewhere between Cabrit and Diamond Rock. That gave him a distance of ten miles. In that distance he had to deal with two or three frigates, perhaps a ship of the line, and a dozen or so merchant ships (maybe more).

It was not a great distance, but he could always chase them the last few miles up to Fort Royal, and there was nowhere there for them to hide—they could not all huddle under the protection of Fort St Louis. But how many merchant ships would there be? It was hard to guess. A British convoy to England from somewhere like Barbados could amount to fifty ships, sometimes a hundred, and those coming back were as big. But the French were only supplying Martinique, they were not sending out ships to bring back molasses and sugar and hides and spices: no, they were just breaking the blockade, so the ships would probably be carrying supplies for the Navy (rope, powder, canvas and salt tack) and the army (guns, powder and shot, muskets, clothing) and, if they were lucky, some cargo for the civil population. The French were fortunate to have been able to assemble and sail a convoy from Europe— there were plenty of British squadrons cruising off the French coast, ready to intercept such ships.

Yet the French would be prepared to take risks to supply Martinique. It was one of their more important colonies and, to the authorities in Paris, it must seem to be one of the keys to French power in the West Indies. But at the moment it was a dog without teeth: the *Alerte* frigate was captured and in Barbados, the *Achille* was on the rocks. The army in Martinique was helpless without the French Navy to carry it anywhere.

Anyway, the convoy would have a large escort, and some of the ships might stay behind, to reinforce the French in Martinique. Or at least that would be the intention of the Ministry of Marine in Paris, unaware just what had been happening in the past few days. All of which boiled down to one thing—that the *Dido* might be in for a surprise when the French hove in sight; a surprise and a bitter fight against heavy odds. Well, as usual, the *Dido*'s only ally would be surprise: the French would be expecting to be met by the *Achille* and the *Alerte;* in their place they would find the *Dido.*

As soon as the *Dido* reached Cabrit Point she tacked and began retracing her course up to the north-west. Ramage told Southwick: "We'll hold this course for an hour and then wear round and steer back for Cabrit. We'll continue doing that until we sight the convoy."

"What'll the French do when they don't see the *Achille* and the *Alerte?*" the master asked.

Ramage shrugged his shoulders. "I hope they'll assume there's been some mix-up and that both ships have gone to a different rendezvous. It wouldn't be the first time that something like that has happened. They wouldn't have sent that frigate very far ahead: just to give the *Achille* time to get ready for sea. Perhaps 24 hours, and another day to reach the rendezvous."

"Yes, they wouldn't be sure enough of their navigation to set a time and place too far ahead."

"I doubt if they did much more than give a latitude," Ramage said. "They probably aren't very sure of their longitude after an Atlantic crossing. Most likely they said 'Rendezvous in 14°40' North,' or something like that. I can't see them being more exact. Nor is there any need."

"I'd give a lot to know whether they are going to try to get into Fort Royal in the dark," Southwick said.

"The easiest way of answering that is to ask yourself what you would do if you were the French."

"I'd have a go," Southwick declared. "The frigate did it once, and there's no reason why he shouldn't try it again, and pilot the convoy in."

"Exactly. He will be very confident of himself. And quite rightly so: that was a very creditable piece of seamanship. He fooled us!"

"He did that," Southwick said ruefully. "But perhaps we'll get our own back by fooling him."

"I hope so," Ramage said. "Though we haven't a lot of room to tackle both escorts and convoy."

"But if we manage to destroy the pilot, perhaps a lot of the French merchantmen will run aground through not weathering Pointe du Diamant. It's a big gulf, and a lot of them might go aground on the north shore."

"Not too many," Ramage said jokingly. "I want to send most of them into Barbados as prizes."

"Well, the former Calypsos don't need the money, but the new Didos will be thankful. The prize- and head-money from the *Alerte* will have just whetted their appetites!"

At that moment Aitken came on to the quarterdeck, and Ramage asked: "How did the gunnery exercise go? I was busy writing the *Achille* report for the admiral, otherwise I would have been down there with my watch, timing them."

"I gave my watch an airing," Aitken said, "and their times are much better. That action against the *Achille* seems to have woken them up."

"Well, they'd better be wide awake when we meet the convoy: they're going to have to do a lot of shooting in a very short time."

Ramage thought a moment. "If we're likely to meet the convoy at night it might be a good idea to train the men to work in darkness. Blindfold them, so that they get used to moving round the guns instinctively."

Aitken looked doubtful and Ramage said: "You don't seem very keen on the idea."

"No, sir, to be quite honest I'm not. It's never quite that dark: the flashes of the guns going off—except for the first broadside they never fire at the same time—gives light enough for the men to move about."

"Maybe you're right," Ramage agreed. "All right, let them exercise in daylight, but tell the officers to remind them what it's like at night, with smoke as well as the darkness."

C H A P T E R   T W E N T Y

ALL THAT night and the following day the *Dido* tacked and wore to the north-west of Cabrit Island, but there was no sign of the convoy. Ramage would have worried that the ships had come in round the north of the island but for the fact that the *Scourge* was still off Fort Royal and would come south immediately to warn if any ships arrived.

The fine weather continued but the wind fell light. The sea was almost flat calm, with just a slight swell from the east, and overhead there was the scattering of balls of cotton as Trade Wind clouds made their way westward in even lines, like marching soldiers. Flying fish flashed up from the depths, skimmed above the waves and then vanished as effortlessly as they came. Gulls mewed pitifully in the *Dido*'s wake, as if pleading to be thrown scraps, and the black and menacing frigate birds curved and dived gracefully, swooping down almost faster than the eye could follow to pursue a flying fish or snatch up a piece of rubbish from the sea, careful never to get their feathers wet.

The ship's company had spent the morning exercising at the guns. It was tedious for the former Calypsos, Ramage realized, but the new Didos had to reach their standard, and only constant exercise would do that. And all the time Ramage was waiting for a hail from the lookout aloft, reporting sail rounding Cabrit. There were times when it was as much as he could do not to seize the speaking-trumpet and hail the lookouts. He cursed the fact that he had been born impatient: he wanted the action to start.

Southwick took his hat off and ran his fingers through his flowing white hair. "This light wind must be delaying them," he said. "I can just imagine the trouble those French frigates are having with the mules. I'll bet they're the same as our merchantmen—reefing right down at night, falling astern, and not getting back into position until noon."

"You sound as though you have unhappy memories of convoys," Ramage said jokingly.

Southwick sighed. "Is there any naval officer alive, British or French, that remembers convoy work with affection? D'you remember that convoy we took to England from Barbados, when we met that frigate commanded by a madman?"

"I'm not likely to forget it, since it led to me being court-martialled. I remember it because of the trial; I suppose you remember it for other reasons."

"Well, of course I remember the trial, sir, but it was the last time those mules had a chance of driving me mad!"

"You'll recover in time," Ramage said consolingly. "Just think of other things—like flogging to windward down the Channel with snow flurries and leaking oilskins . . ."

"That's done it," Southwick said, laughing. "I could just feel the cold water trickling down my neck, and my eyebrows begin to freeze up."

"It's amazing how thinking about that can cheer you up," Ramage said. "It's one of the worst experiences I can think of."

"It's worse for the topmen having to handle frozen ropes and sails. I get sorry for them, too!"

"Well, don't waste sympathy on Frenchmen jogging along comfortably in the Trades with reefed sails at night," Ramage said. "They're not only upsetting the French frigates, but they're annoying me!"

The rest of the afternoon passed quickly, with the men aloft exercising at sail handling, this time sending down a topsail and hoisting it again, all against Ramage's watch. It was hot work in the tropical sun but the men, naked to the waist and now well tanned, enjoyed it.

"Next time we'll send down the yard as well," Ramage told Aitken. "If these Frenchmen don't arrive soon, we'll have them sending down the yard at night. I want the men as used to doing things in darkness as in daylight. We were lucky in the action against the *Achille*. Next time we might not be so lucky."

At dusk the lookouts were brought down from aloft and, with more men, stationed round the ship. At the same time the drums beat to quarters, so that the *Dido* met the night ready for action.

When the time came to stand down, Ramage gave orders that the guns were to be left loaded and run out. The big disadvantage of a 74, he reckoned, was that it took a quarter of an hour for the men to get to quarters and be ready for action, against the five minutes it took a frigate. If the French suddenly turned up in the darkness he could ill afford to waste fifteen minutes while the men went to quarters. They would have to sleep by their guns.

A new moon cast a watery light, and it was setting fast. The sky was clear and Ramage knew he could look for some starlight. The wind was still light—the *Dido* was making a bare five knots off the wind—and there was very little sea, the earlier swell having subsided. It was, he thought bitterly, a night more suited to lovers than war.

As the *Dido* headed north-west, the wind on her starboard quarter, there was a down-draught from her mainsail which made the night almost chilly as Ramage stood on the quarter-deck. The sails gave an occasional desultory flap as the wind faltered and then picked up again. The masts occasionally creaked as the ship gave a lazy roll, and the beams groaned in sympathy. Apart from the down-draught, the air was warm and damp and several of the men on watch were not wearing shirts.

Kenton was the officer of the deck and every fifteen minutes he called to the lookouts to make sure they were still wide awake. As a midshipman he had learned to doze off standing up, and he knew it was a skill that most seamen possessed. Thinking of dozing reminded him of the seaman's slang for having a sleep, "taking a caulk." Sleeping on the bare deck in a warm climate, when the caulking in the seams between the planks was soft, usually meant that the sleeper woke with lines of pitch marking his shirt and trousers—a sure sign that he had been "taking a caulk." Indeed, the expression for "Do you want to talk or sleep" was "Yarn or caulk?" On a night like this the pitch was warm enough to mark a man's shirt; indeed it was warm enough to settle in the seams and make sure they did not leak if there was a sudden downpour. And downpour was the right word, Kenton thought. Frequently the tropical rain was so heavy that it was impossible to see the fo'c'sle from the quarterdeck, and it would stop as suddenly as it started, and in a few minutes the sun would be shining, hot enough to send the water back up again as steam. Men out on deck during the rain did not bother to change their clothes: the sun and breeze dried them in minutes.

How unlike the Channel, he thought. Such a downpour usually came after hours of heavy cloud and cold winds: men soaked to the skin would be shivering uncontrollably—and the officer of the deck would give them permission to go below and change into dry clothes, if they had any left. Usually they had not, and they just shivered for the rest of their watch.

Yes, the Tropics had many advantages, including—in some ships—quick promotion, as officers died off from yellow fever, or some other vile disease. Mr Ramage's ships stayed healthy, so there was no promotion—and, Kenton thought, no risk of getting the black vomit, which killed as surely as a round shot knocking your head off. Kenton knew of frigates that had been hit so badly by the black vomit that there were barely enough men left alive to bring the ship back to port.

What caused it? When a ship was first hit it was usual, if possible, to sail: there was some talk that the fresh sea air helped stop the disease spreading. What truth there was in that Kenton did not know; about the only advantage that he could see was that the mosquitoes would not bite as hard.

That, as well as the disease, was another thing he did not like about the Tropics: in port—especially in unhealthy and swampy spots like English Harbour, Antigua—the mosquitoes swarmed on board and bit, turning one's wrists and ankles into itching masses. And at night it was hard to sleep as they buzzed round one's head, ready to swoop and bite.

Mosquitoes, and the things the local people called sandflies, which were hard to see and which bit like red-hot needles at dusk and dawn, were the curse of the Caribbean. There were no poisonous snakes, except in St Lucia, and only a few scorpions and centipedes, which would give a nasty bite if you were not careful. But they usually lived under rocks or in dark places; they were not (like mosquitoes and sandflies) a problem in a ship.

Kenton's eyes swept the coastline: he could just make out the black line of the land. Then he glanced up at the sails, which seemed almost luminous in the last of the moonlight. In fifteen minutes the new moon would have set, leaving the stars bright and the Milky Way a thick swathe across the sky.

There were many stars that could not be seen from more northern latitudes. The Southern Cross would not be rising yet,

and he had to admit that his first sight of the Southern Cross
had been one of the disappointments of his life. He had expected
stars which were very bright in the sky, stars that one would
know at once, as bright as Mars or Sirius. Instead, the Southern
Cross had to be pointed out, a diamond shape of four stars—
well, five, but it was hard to see the fifth in this latitude—low
on the southern horizon. Perhaps they became more startling
if one sailed into the southern hemisphere, but from the latitude of the West Indies they were a sad disappointment.

His thoughts were interrupted by the thudding of feet, and
a moment later a breathless sailor stood in front of him. "Brewer,
sir: lookout on the larboard quarter. Me and Jarvis—he's on the
starboard side—can see a ship just rounded the island, and there
may be more: hard to see at the moment."

"Very well, go back to your post and keep a sharp lookout."
Kenton looked round for a midshipman and told him: "Quickly,
go down to the captain and report a ship in sight near Cabrit."

He looked for another midshipman and ordered him: "Find
the drummer of the watch and tell him to beat to quarters."

What else? Kenton could think of nothing: helm orders
would await the captain's arrival on deck. With only the topsails set they were already down to fighting canvas; the guns
were already loaded and run out, and any moment the drummer would be striking up. Why did he feel more excited when
the *Dido* went to quarters than he ever did in the *Calypso?*
Perhaps the sheer vastness of the ship. Perhaps the knowledge
that there were so many more guns—37 on a broadside.

He picked up the night-glass and went to the ship's side to
peer astern. The night-glass was a mixed blessing because it
gave an upside-down picture. He could see the land of
Martinique running down to the south but it was inverted,
looking like dark clouds. And yes, floating upside down, there

244 : RAMAGE & *The Dido*

was the vague blur of a ship. Damnation, those lookouts had sharp eyes. He moved the glass a fraction and thought he could distinguish other vague blurs astern of it, but he could not be certain.

The captain arrived on the quarterdeck just as the drum started chattering out its urgent order, and Kenton made his report, handing over the night-glass. Ramage snatched it up and went to the ship's side for a clear look astern. It took only a few moments for him to distinguish the ship and be almost certain that others were following her.

"Wear ship and head for her, if you please, Mr Kenton," he snapped. The outline was familiar enough: the ship was a frigate, and as he had expected, she was leading the convoy round to Fort Royal. She would be burning two or three stern-lights and the convoy would be following like ducklings after their mother. Where were the other frigates? Was there a ship of the line? How many merchantmen were there? What did the French make of the non-arrival of the *Achille* and the *Alerte?* It obviously had not affected their plans.

Slowly, with sails flogging until they were sheeted in and the yards braced, the *Dido* turned, with Kenton calling helm orders to the quartermaster. By now Ramage had been joined by Aitken and Southwick, both buckling on swords.

Ramage asked Aitken: "Are you sure that plan for boarders is going to work?"

"Rennick was confident, sir, and our seamen seemed to understand."

Ramage was worried about the prize-crews they had selected during the afternoon. In anticipation of capturing several merchant ships, Ramage had selected a midshipman, five marines and ten seamen for each of ten prizes he hoped they would capture: the midshipmen had orders to make for Barbados, and all the parties were numbered. Although in theory the cry of a particular boarding party should bring the men running, in the excitement and the darkness Ramage had his doubts, but he knew speed was important.

Southwick, who had the night-glass, said: "That's a frigate all right, and I can make out four ships astern of her, but there may be more rounding the island."

A midshipman came up and reported something to Aitken, who turned to Ramage and said: "The ship's at general quarters, sir: all the guns are manned, the gunner's at the magazine, and the fire engine is manned."

The fire engine was the result of Ramage's last orders of the afternoon: he was determined to set fire to any merchantmen he could not take as prizes, and he did not want the risk of flying sparks causing a fire on board the *Dido*. Seamen feared fire more than leaks, which was hardly surprising when one realized how much gunpowder was stowed in the magazine—more than twenty tons of it, enough to blow half a dozen Didos to pieces.

"Five ships," Southwick said suddenly. "I can see five ships as well as the frigate. Can't make out what they are, though."

Well, Ramage thought to himself, there's no doubt that this is the convoy, the only question mark is how big is the escort. They would most likely be following astern, which suited him very well. But how long would it be before the frigate spotted him against the dark outline of the land to the north? More to the point, the frigate would probably assume the *Dido* was the *Achille*. She was expecting the *Achille,* and what more likely than to find her coming down from the north, admittedly late but arriving at last. Very well, that would all help the *Dido* achieve surprise. In the darkness both ships would look similar. The Frenchmen would be very relieved to see the *Achille* and, no doubt, only too willing to hand over the job of piloting the merchantmen to her, since she would know these waters well.

The wind was freshening, and a few small clouds were coming off the land. The *Dido* was rolling slightly and occasionally a startled gull flew by, screaming as though protesting at being disturbed. By now the moon had set and they had to rely on the starlight.

Now he could just distinguish the frigate with the naked eye: not a ship but a small dark blob on the southern horizon, dead ahead, and only visible to one side of the jib-boom and bowsprit when the *Dido* yawed. Ramage waited for the group of lights hoisted in the frigate which would be the challenge—probably a pattern of three lights, lanterns hoisted on a triangular frame. But for the moment there was nothing; the two ships were approaching each other darkly and anonymously. Every minute, Ramage knew, was to his advantage: it increased the margin of surprise.

But time was passing quickly. The *Dido* was making five to six knots in this light breeze, so the two ships were approaching each other at a combined speed of ten to twelve knots. The frigate's bottom was probably foul—not probably but certainly—after the Atlantic crossing, encumbered with goose barnacles and weed, but no more than the *Dido*'s, so the fouling just about evened out. Weed and barnacles wait for no man, he thought grimly, slowing up the best of ships, despite the copper sheathing on the bottom.

Southwick was still searching the southern horizon with the night-glass. "The frigate and six ships so far," he announced. "I reckon all seven are merchantmen, but I can't be sure yet. It's a pity we haven't got a moon."

Ramage looked again at the frigate and found he could now

distinguish her outline. Still no challenge, still no sign—since she must have spotted them by now—that the frigate suspected she was anything but the *Achille* sailing down to help shepherd them all in to Fort Royal.

"They seem to be playing follow-my-leader," Southwick reported. "One following the frigate—she'll be burning a stern lantern—and the rest strung out astern. Like fruit on a bough, ready for plucking. The only trouble is they'll disperse the moment we start firing at the frigate."

"They won't get very far," Aitken said. "The wind is too light to move these mules very far. And they're probably reefed down, too; you know what merchantmen are like at night."

"We'll soon see," Ramage said. "We're approaching the frigate quite fast now. This breeze is slowly strengthening."

"What I'd give for a bit o' moonlight," repeated an exasperated Southwick. "Trying to judge with the upside-down image in this glass makes my eyes go funny."

"We'll attack the frigate to starboard, so we don't get blinded by our own smoke. Warn the guns, Mr Aitken."

The first lieutenant sent one of the midshipmen below while he shouted up to Orsini on the poop.

Ramage saw the frigate dead ahead again as the *Dido* yawed slightly. By now Jackson had taken over as quartermaster, and Ramage gave him a helm order which brought the frigate round to fine on the starboard bow: on this new course they would pass her about fifty yards off. Just the right range for the gunners, Ramage thought, but far enough not to alarm the frigate if she was in fact still under the impression that the *Achille* was approaching.

He could imagine the clicking as the second captains cocked the locks on the guns: the captains would be standing behind them, firing lanyards held in their right hands, ready to drop on one knee as the frigate loomed up close. Well, they had some experience of a night action; he only hoped that what they had learned attacking the *Achille* was going to stand them in good stead tonight.

The range was closing fast now and, after another look at the frigate, Ramage told Aitken: "Tell the gunners they'll be opening fire in about three minutes."

Still no challenge from the frigate: well, that bit of carelessness on their part was going to cost them dearly: had they challenged, the lack of a correct reply would at least have warned them.

"There's another merchantman rounding the island," said Southwick. "But maybe she's a frigate."

"Eight ships," mused Ramage. "Quite a good-sized convoy, and there may be more escorts."

Ramage gave another helm order to Jackson and the men at the wheel turned it a couple of spokes. The frigate was barely two hundred yards away and Ramage could see that she had everything set to the topgallants. Her rigging now stood out spidery against the stars; there was just a hint of phosphorescence at her stem as she butted her way through the water.

It seemed almost unsporting, Ramage told himself, to come out of the darkness and fire a broadside into the unsuspecting frigate; but this was war, and if one was careless the price was usually heavy.

Ramage moved a few steps on the quarterdeck so that he could see the frigate clear of the *Dido*'s jib-boom and bowsprit. A hundred yards. Fifty yards. Still the frigate ploughed on, obviously thinking that the 74 approaching on her starboard bow was the *Achille*. Twenty-five yards. A ship's length. Ramage imagined the *Dido*'s gunners taking the strain on their trigger lines.

The crash of the first guns of the broadside came as a shock even though he was expecting it: a series of blinding flashes and muffled explosions and the rumble of the guns flinging back in recoil. Finally the last guns in the broadside thundered out as Orsini's carronades swept the frigate's decks, spraying them with a deadly hail of case shot. Ramage thought of the unsuspecting Frenchmen standing about on the frigate's deck; then he reminded himself that if the position had been reversed the French would have shown no mercy.

There had been plenty of hits on the frigate: it was almost impossible to miss at this range, and he had imagined he had heard the shot crashing into the hull. Now, in response to his hurried order to Aitken, the *Dido* wore under the frigate's stern and prepared to come alongside, firing another broadside. The sails slatted and cracked, the yards creaked as they were braced round and the sheets trimmed. Ramage could hear Orsini's gunners shouting with excitement as they crossed the poop to man the larboard carronades.

For once Ramage felt remote from the action. Perhaps it was a bit too cold-blooded, perhaps there had been little excitement before opening fire, but there was something lacking. He found himself thinking of the frigate now about to receive another broadside when she had just had one smash into her. Well, he thought grimly, if it was a French 74 attacking the *Calypso* the French would not be feeling squeamish.

Once again the *Dido*'s broadside crashed out, the flashes destroying his night vision but lighting up the frigate perfectly so that he could see every detail of her rigging and sails and observe that her hull was painted black with a wide red strake.

Suddenly amid the gunfire he could hear a French voice shouting through a speaking-trumpet. He thought for a minute that it was hurling defiance, but as the last half of the broadside crashed out he realized that the man was surrendering. He called to Aitken to stop the guns firing and shouted a helm order to Jackson so that the wheel was put over and the *Dido* turned into the frigate, crashing alongside her.

At last the guns stopped firing as the two midshipmen sent below by the first lieutenant managed to pass the word to the officers at their quarters. Ramage himself shouted up to Orsini to stop the carronades firing again, but only made himself understood after several of them had gone off. By now the two ships were grinding against each other and Ramage told Aitken: "Get the first boarding party over: tell Rennick to add ten marines."

Even with the extra marines it was not a very large prize-crew to take command of a captured frigate, but if the French tried any tricks, he thought grimly, the threat of another broadside would probably bring them to their senses.

He watched as the boarding party scrambled down to the frigate—whose name he had noticed was the *Sirène*—and he wished he could have sent Hill along as well, so that his French would make sure that orders were obeyed quickly, but felt he could not spare an officer from his quarters with a lot more shooting still to be done.

He suddenly remembered the stern lanterns and snatched up the speaking-trumpet. He then realized that leading a prize-crew taking command of a frigate was too much for a midshipman, and decided that after all Hill would have to go.

"Send Hill over to take command of the frigate," he told Aitken, "and tell him to douse the stern lanterns. Then put the frigate's wheel over otherwise we'll never get free of her."

Another midshipman was sent below to fetch Hill, who suddenly appeared on the quarterdeck. Ramage repeated his orders and added: "If we don't see you again make for Barbados. I'll send the *Scourge* to collect you. If you see any merchantmen they'll be the ones we've captured, so escort them."

Hill, delighted at once again commanding a prize-frigate, eagerly scrambled over the side of the *Dido* and down on to the frigate's deck. Ramage could just make out movement on board the frigate as fighting lanterns were brought up from below. In the starlight he could see that most of the boats on the booms had been smashed and a thirty-foot length of bulwark beaten in, making an unsightly kink in the frigate's sheer. But it was too dark to see other damage and anyway Ramage knew that most of it would be below decks, because the *Dido*'s gunners had orders to fire into the hull. The boats had probably been smashed by the carronades, whose task was to sweep the decks, killing men and cutting rigging.

Ramage looked astern and could just make out the first of the merchantmen faithfully following in the frigate's wake. Their masters must now be in something of a panic: they had suddenly seen their pilot attacked by an unknown ship, and Ramage thought it very unlikely that they had charts for the voyage up to Fort Royal—charts on a large enough scale, anyway.

By now Hill should be putting the frigate's wheel over, turning her to larboard so that she came clear of the *Dido*, which in turn would be turning to larboard as she wore round to tackle the first of the merchant ships.

"That was a wise move sending over Hill as prize-master," Southwick said. "He'll be quick to spot if the French try any tricks. You never can tell with these Frenchmen: once they haven't got us alongside pouring broadsides into them, they might get their courage back . . ."

"That's just what I thought," Ramage agreed. "That's why I sent over some extra marines."

By now Aitken was giving the orders which wore the ship, and once again the sails slatted as she turned. Ramage changed his position on the quarterdeck to get a better view of the first merchantman, and Southwick growled: "I shall be very surprised if we have to fire a shot to take this one!"

Ramage had already reached the same conclusion and was conning the *Dido* round to come alongside the ship, within hailing distance. "Pass the word that no guns are to fire without receiving orders," he told Aitken, "and make sure Orsini's carronades understand."

Quickly the sheets were trimmed and the yards braced, and the *Dido* turned on to the same course as the merchantman and started to overhaul her.

"She's reefed down—can you believe that?" Southwick exclaimed. "These mules are all the same, whether French or British."

As the *Dido* began to overhaul the merchantman, Ramage picked up the speaking-trumpet and went to the ship's side. As the bowsprit drew level with the merchantman, Ramage bellowed in French: "Surrender—or I'll fire a broadside into you!"

He quickly reversed the trumpet and put it to his ear, and almost immediately heard an agitated yell: "We surrender . . . we surrender!"

"Heave-to—I'm coming alongside," Ramage shouted back, and gave a quick helm order so that the *Dido* turned slightly, her big hull with its pronounced tumblehome crashing into the side of the merchant ship.

"Get that second boarding party over," Ramage snapped at Aitken, and while the two ships pressed together a midshipman led his mixed party of seamen and marines, jumping down several feet on to the deck of the merchant ship. Ramage waited to see that they were in control and then ordered the *Dido* to wear.

Once again the *Dido* repeated the manoeuvre which had

separated her from the frigate, and Southwick said: "Six more merchantmen and another frigate." With that he snapped the night-glass shut.

"Let's hope these merchantmen give no more trouble than that one," Ramage said.

"Yes, leave the frigate until last," Southwick said. "No chance of taking *him* by surprise!"

Ramage looked round for the next merchantman and pointed her out to Aitken, who conned the ship round until she was overtaking her from astern. Ramage picked up the speaking-trumpet as the *Dido*'s bowsprit drew level with the ship and then began to pass it.

"Surrender and heave-to!" Ramage shouted in French, but when he reversed the speaking-trumpet to hear the reply he was startled by the stream of defiance and French obscenities.

He recognized the Gascon accent and the voice seemed very determined. He reversed the speaking-trumpet and shouted: "If you do not surrender I will fire a broadside into you."

This threat brought more cursing and it was obvious the French master did not intend either to surrender or heave-to.

Ramage thought for a moment. A broadside would almost certainly destroy the ship. He decided to give him one more chance. "Heave-to or I'll blow you out of the water!"

More curses and shouts of defiance showed that the Gascon master was determined to take no notice of the British ship of the line almost alongside him and Ramage told Aitken: "He refuses to surrender or heave-to. Give him a whiff of the car-ronades!"

Aitken called up to Orsini on the poop and a few moments later the carronades barked out, sweeping the merchantman's decks with case shot. Again Ramage hailed through the speaking-trumpet and received a shower of abuse in reply.

Very well, he thought to himself, you've brought it on your-self: the carronades gave you a taste of what to expect. "Fire a broadside into him, Mr Aitken," he said. "I've given him four chances to surrender."

The flash and crash of the broadside caught him unawares, before he could close an eye, and he was blinded for several seconds. He had just heard Southwick exclaim: "Look, she's afire," when he saw flames coming up her forehatch. The hatch cover had obviously ripped off and the flames were lighting up the foot of the sails.

He shouted to Jackson to turn two points to starboard and then ordered Aitken: "Man the fire engine!"

As he quickly looked round the flames began spreading and lighting up the night sky. He caught a glimpse of the surren-dered frigate and merchantman ahead, and saw the string of merchantmen astern, their sails lit up.

The *Dido* seemed to be turning very slowly and already the flames were licking up the sails of the merchantman. Ramage could hear the crackling of burning wood and as, horrified, he watched the flames, the ship's foremast slowly, almost lazily, leaned over forward and crashed down on to the bowsprit.

This stopped the ship as if she had run into a wall, and the *Dido* continued sailing, passing her as she began her turn away.

"I hope she isn't carrying powder," Southwick said.

"We're too close if she is," Aitken commented.

"If she's carrying powder, her master is a fool," Ramage said. "You don't invite a broadside from a ship of the line if you've got powder in the hold. Even if you're a Gascon," he added, half to himself, remembering the reputation that Gascons had for boasting—indeed, giving their name to the word *gasconnade*.

At that moment the ship blew up. One moment she was dead in the water, flames leaping up from her forehatch; the next moment she was a livid red flash.

Now the darkness seemed more intense.

Ramage suddenly felt sick. The Gascon master's stubborn behaviour, in spite of four warnings, had left him no alternative to opening fire, and he had no particular qualms about the ship being set on fire—the men could always escape in their boats—but blowing up like that, killing those who agreed with their master and those who, given the option, would have surrendered . . .

But there was no time for regrets: he gave orders for the *Dido* to tack and make her way to the next ship in the convoy. As soon as they were almost alongside her, Ramage called on her to surrender and heave-to. This time the master, having just seen what had happened to his next ahead, shouted his agreement and the *Dido* went alongside to put a prize-crew on board.

As the *Dido* tacked to get clear and headed for the next merchantman, Ramage looked ahead carefully for the second frigate, but could not see her. "Where's the other frigate?" he asked Southwick.

"I haven't looked for several minutes, sir, what with that ship catching fire and blowing up." He opened the night-glass and put it to his eye. After a minute or two he said: "That's strange, there's no sign of her. Just three more merchantmen, but not a sign of the frigate. D'you think she's bolted?"

Ramage shrugged his shoulders in the darkness. "Couldn't blame him if he has. There's nothing much he can do to save this convoy."

Southwick gave one of his famous sniffs but made no comment. The last three merchantmen surrendered without any fuss, all three obviously intimidated by the fate of their countryman. With the last of the prize-crews put on board, Ramage said to Aitken: "We'll go and see how Hill is getting on with the *Sirène*."

It took fifteen minutes to get back up to the *Sirène*, the *Dido* having to thread her way between merchant ships which were anyway clumsy sailers but were now being handled by inexperienced midshipmen with very few seamen.

Ramage hailed Hill, who had the frigate hove-to under a backed fore-topsail. With the whole convoy now dealt with, Hill might as well carry a despatch to the admiral.

Ramage went to his cabin to write a rough draft of the despatch so that Luckhurst could make a fair copy. The report to the admiral was brief, describing how he had found the convoy, attacked it and captured one frigate and all the merchant ships. He regretted, he said, that a second frigate forming the escort had escaped in the darkness, and a merchantman refusing to surrender and apparently carrying powder had been fired at, catching fire and blowing up. He finished his draft with all the usual formalities and then called Luckhurst to make the fair copy.

He then went out on to the quarterdeck and told Aitken: "I have a despatch for the admiral which must be taken across to Hill. Also, give him a hail and see if he has enough people. Send Orsini over with the despatch—tell him to make sure Hill is satisfied that he has everything under control."

Paolo was soon back from the *Sirène,* reporting that Hill and his marines had now secured all the prisoners and would be getting under way in about ten minutes, that he did not need more men and that the French were very cowed. "Most of them saw the merchantman blow up," Paolo said, "and that knocked the stuffing out of them."

Ramage waited with the *Dido* hove-to until he saw the *Sirène*'s fore-topsail sheeted home and braced sharp up as she bore up for Barbados. Then he said to Aitken: "Set a course for Fort Royal: we still have some unfinished business there."

CHAPTER TWENTY-ONE

EARLY IN the forenoon with the sun hot and the wind still light the *Dido* hove-to off Pointe des Nègres half a mile from the stranded *Achille*. Through his glass Ramage could see that the French ship's boats were busy ferrying the crew to the one small beach at the end of the Pointe, leaving them an arduous climb up the cliff before they could make their way back to Fort Royal. More important she was again flying a Tricolour: the surrender was being ignored.

He told Southwick about the colours and added: "They've given up any hope of getting her off, for the time being anyway. Perhaps they're going to bring in shipwrights to patch her up, and then pump her out until she floats clear."

"They'll probably make an effort," Southwick said. "After all, she's the only ship of the line they've got out here."

"She's the only ship of any kind they have," Ramage corrected. "So they're bound to make every effort to repair her. They haven't a ship to send to France asking for reinforcements!"

"The Navy is short of everything, but I wonder how badly off the Army is."

"Well . . . they haven't had the losses that the Navy has had, so perhaps they are not in such a bad way," Ramage said.

"Let's hope they don't bring out any guns and set them up on the cliff to cover the *Achille*."

Ramage shook his head. "We'll attack the *Achille* tonight. We'd lose too many men if we attacked in daylight."

The rest of the day was spent planning the attack on the *Achille*. All the officers were assembled in Ramage's cabin, and he opened the proceedings by saying: "Tonight we set fire to the *Achille*. We can only guess how many men they've left on board. Nor do we know whether they're expecting an attack. We must assume they are—they've seen the *Dido* come back and anchor close by. So we have to plan the boarding on the basis that it will be opposed.

"We'll attack with as many men as we can get in our boats. Three boats will attack over the bow, and three on the quarters: that way we can keep out of the arcs of their guns. Once we have boarded, then we set fire to her. We don't have to capture the whole ship to do that. But what is important is that the fires—I want them set at several places—take hold, and once you can see they can't be put out, then quit the ship as quickly as possible: I don't want any men on board when the magazine goes up!"

Ramage then outlined his plan, giving each of the officers their orders: telling them how many men they were to take in which boat, where they were to board the *Achille*, and where they were to start a fire. The men were to carry combustibles—cloths soaked in grease, jars of inflammable paint, light battens that would catch fire quickly—as well as lanterns, which would be hidden from sight until they were on board.

The point of the lanterns, Ramage explained, was that they would let the men see what they were doing, once they were on board the *Achille*, and the candles then could be used to set light to things, helped on by liberal applications of candlewax.

The men could choose whether they had cutlasses or boarding pikes. No one would carry a musket—they were too clumsy for boarders—but all the men would be issued with pistols. At least, he amended, they would be issued with as many pistols as were available.

Oars would obviously be muffled—it was up to the first lieutenant to see that all the oars were bound with keckling—but
it was impossible to say whether the boarders would achieve
surprise. They must assume they would be opposed, but only
with small-arms fire.

"The important thing is setting the fires," Ramage emphasized. "I don't want men getting carried away with fighting the
French: any fighting should be only to protect the parties as
they start the fires. Our job is done once she's burning; we are
not trying to carry her by boarding."

"Should the men carry slowmatch, just in case the lanterns
blow out?" asked the gunner.

"Slowmatches, and they might as well have a few false
fires—they will light the place up as well as setting fire to things.
A few topmen getting aloft and setting off false fires in the
courses should help: the canvas is so dry it will burn easily. So
remember, you who are carrying topmen in your boats should
have false fires and slowmatches, and make sure the topmen
know what is expected of them. Any more ideas?"

"Shall we try and set fire to the magazine, sir?" asked Kenton.

"Most certainly not!" Ramage exclaimed. "You will only
blow yourselves up. No, the magazine goes up as the ship
burns."

"How do we judge when a fire is well set, sir?" asked Martin.

"As soon as it's bigger than you could put out with buckets," Ramage said. "There'll probably be a good breeze blowing,
so flames should spread quickly. Bear that in mind: where you
can, always set a fire to windward of something that is obviously combustible."

"Scattering some powder around would help, sir," the gunner said.

"No," Ramage said decidedly, "no powder. Too much scope
for accidents. We don't want to blow ourselves up."

"Shall I go with the boarders or stay here?" asked Bowen, the surgeon.

"You stay here," said a startled Ramage. "What good could you do on board the *Achille?*"

"I was thinking that I could attend to casualties on the spot," Bowen said lamely. His suggestion had been an attempt to join in the excitement, and he had the uncomfortable feeling that Ramage had realized that immediately.

"Very well," said Ramage, looking round at all the officers. "If there are no more questions, we may as well get started."

The moon set soon after eleven and one hundred fifty seamen and marines were formed up on deck in groups, ready to board the boats, which had been hauled round alongside. In addition to cutlasses, pikes, tomahawks and pistols, many of the men carried the greasy cloths with which they would start fires. Others had shaded lanterns and some carried lighted slowmatch.

The officers were drawn up ready to take command of the boats and their own parties of men. But it was slow work in the darkness preparing for the expedition. The starlight was spasmodic, interrupted by high blankets of cloud, and although the wind was still light from the east and the sea almost calm, it was hot and humid, and any effort soaked a man in perspiration.

Southwick, cheerfully striding round the deck with his great double-edged sword strapped to his waist, was looking forward to the operation because all too often lately—and in the *Calypso's* last actions in the Mediterranean—he had been left on board while others went off to do the fighting. This time Mr Ramage was leaving the first lieutenant in command of the *Dido,* Southwick had noted happily, and had put him in command of one of the pinnaces. So now he had 25 men in his party, ready to fight or burn the enemy. Although Southwick appreciated the main task was to set fire to the ship he hoped that the French would put up a fight. It was a long time since he had been able to use his sword, and the thought of soon unsheathing it was exciting.

Martin said to Kenton: "I hope this is going to make up for George Hill getting command of that frigate. That's the second time. It doesn't seem fair, just because he speaks French."

"If he didn't speak French one of us would get the job," Kenton said soothingly. "It's our fault, really, I didn't pay much attention at school—whoever would have thought that speaking French would come in useful? It seemed to be the last thing you'd need at sea. Mathematics and geography, yes: but French and Latin . . ."

Orsini, who had been listening to the conversation, said: "Well, I speak French and Italian, but I don't get command of the prizes!"

"You're only a master's mate," Martin said unsympathetically, "and anyway, your navigation is a bit suspect."

"It was but it isn't now," Orsini said defensively. "I've been working hard at it since we joined the *Dido*. Mr Southwick is very pleased with the progress I've made."

"Maybe so," said Kenton, "but do you feel confident enough to take command of a frigate?"

"Give me a few good men and let me have the chance," Orsini said impulsively. "The trouble is there don't seem to be any frigates left!"

"Be patient," Martin said, "the French may send out some more. Or we might find the one that got away."

"If he's got any sense he's already on his way back to France," Kenton said. "That merchantman blowing up probably persuaded him."

"More likely he saw us in the flash and realized that the

convoy was being attacked by a ship of the line."

At that moment Aitken's voice came out of the darkness: "I hope you have inspected your men and are all ready to embark."

The three of them assured him they were, and he added: "Don't be misled by the French landing some of their men: there may be a couple of hundred—maybe a lot more—still left on board. Don't forget, we're not trying to capture the ship; we just want to set fire to it."

After Aitken had gone, Kenton said: "If the French have a couple of hundred men still left on board, we've got a fight on our hands. Boarding a ship of the line isn't like boarding a frigate: her freeboard is so much higher. Still, since she's bigger the French have more to defend."

"And we have more to attack," Martin said ruefully. "On the other hand, it hasn't rained for days, so her woodwork is nice and dry. It should be easy enough to start fires."

"Wood that's been soaked hundreds of times in salt water won't burn too easily," Kenton warned. "I'm going to go for sails, if I can."

"Even rigging should burn well," Orsini said. "After all, it's coated in tar, so it won't have soaked up much salt. If you set fire to a few shrouds the flames should run up the masts and set fire to the courses."

"What we need is a thunderstorm so that lightning strikes her," Martin grumbled. "That'd save us a lot of bother."

It was after midnight when Ramage gave the order to start and led the way down to the boats, boarding the launch and settling himself down in the sternsheets, telling Jackson: "Shove off. And no talking. You know where to make for, and make sure you don't get in the field of fire of those guns—just in case they spot us."

"Aye aye, sir," Jackson said. "We'll be like ghosts."

Ramage sat alone with his thoughts. He was still not sure that he was doing the right thing. For the task of destroying the *Achille* he had two choices: he could bring the *Dido* in and, as he had done when he attacked her in the first place, sail back and forth across her stern, raking her. That would take hours—destroying a ship by gunfire alone could be very difficult. Silencing her was one thing; destroying her was something quite different. Which left him with boarding her and setting her on fire. That was certain but was far riskier. As far as the *Achille* was concerned, it was riskier because he had no idea how many Frenchmen had been landed, and therefore how many were left on board. When the *Dido* had arrived and anchored, the *Achille* was landing men on the beach. Were they abandoning the ship? Were they the first fifty or were they the last? There was no way of knowing. So they were boarding her not knowing whether there were five hundred men on board or twenty.

That was why he had emphasized to his officers that all they were concerned with was getting on board the ship, setting a few fires, and then getting off as quickly as possible: they were not trying to capture the Frenchman; this was not a regular boarding—as when they had taken the *Alerte*. They were, he thought wryly, concerned only with arson.

He could make out the black shape of the *Achille*—she seemed enormous in the darkness. To anyone who loved ships for themselves, it was a sad thought that this handsome ship—for she had a pleasing sheer—was not only wedged on the rocks, but if all went well within half an hour would be only so much charred wreckage floating on the sea. Two thousand large trees, each piece carefully shaped by skilled men, had been used to build her . . . his imagination roamed, helped by the darkness.

The men were rowing easily and silently: Aitken had done

a good job of making sure that each oar was bound with keckling to stop it squeaking against the thole pins. The men were
being careful to dip their oars deeply so they did not "catch a
crab" and make a splash.

He looked astern and could just make out the other boats
following in the launch's wake. In a few minutes three of the
boats would turn to starboard to make their way to the *Achille*'s
stern, still keeping out of the field of fire. What sort of lookout
were they keeping in the French ship? For the moment they
would not be able to see very far because of the darkness, but
would they spot the boats in the starlight during those last few
yards?

Ramage decided they would not be keeping a special lookout because they would not expect the *Dido* to board them: they
knew that the English realized they were stuck on the rocks,
and helpless. They might expect a further attack in daylight,
with the *Dido* raking her and doing more damage by gunfire.
Indeed, that might have been the reason for them landing
men—to save casualties.

Casualties! The word made him shiver. If the French had
not landed many men, then he was likely to suffer a lot of casualties tonight. He did not doubt that his own men would be
able to start a few fires, but at what cost?

Some captains, he knew, could send their men off on operations where the number of casualties would be enormous, and
the fact did not make them lose any sleep. But he was not one
of these captains. He did not know whether to call them lucky
or not—in war men did get killed or maimed. But the fact was
that he shied away from operations where the casualties would
be heavy. He had shied away from this one until he persuaded
himself that if he did not destroy the *Achille* now, the admiral
would send him back to do it.

So now he was setting off with more than one hundred fifty seamen and marines not knowing whether there were five hundred or fifty Frenchmen on board the *Achille*. The more he thought about it, the more it seemed the most absurdly risky operation he had ever undertaken: it was, literally and figuratively, a leap into the dark.

He stared ahead and could just make out the black shape of the *Achille* outlined against the stars. Judging from the height of the masts they were closer than he had realized. He glanced astern and saw that the last three boats had already left to make for the French ship's stern. There was just the faint hiss as the launch's bow cut through the water and the muffled gasping as the men strained at the oars. The launch, carrying thirty men plus the oarsmen, was a heavy boat to row.

Yes, it was a hot and humid night: already he could feel the perspiration soaking through his clothes. But he was thankful there was little wind. Wind meant waves and waves meant a slop at the bow which could be spotted by the French lookouts. Thank goodness there was almost no phosphorescence tonight. It was extraordinary how one night it would be bright and another night there would be almost none at all. One thing was certain—had there been much of it then it would give away the positions of all six boats, warning the French long before they could actually see the outline of the raiders.

Forty yards, perhaps less. Jackson had brought the launch round—with the two pinnaces following—in a half-circle, so that he stayed out of the arcs of fire of the *Achille*'s guns and approached from dead ahead, the direction it would be hard for the French lookouts to see, because of the network of rigging supporting the jib-boom and bowsprit.

Ramage loosened the two pistols stuck in his belt: they were digging into his ribs, and they would jab him when he climbed.

He hitched at his sword, making sure it was free in the sheath, ready to be drawn instantly. He was, he realized ruefully, behaving just like a nervous man, but damnation, he _was_ nervous: not at the thought of boarding the Frenchman, but at what they might find. Fifty or five hundred—they were not the sort of odds to attract a gambler . . .

Thirty yards—no more. Jackson was hissing an order at the nearest oarsmen and they were passing it forward, from man to man. The rate of rowing slowed. The _Achille_ was huge now, looming over them—and there was no challenge. No shooting from aft, either, so that the other boarding party had not arrived yet. He had thought of trying to synchronize the two attacks, but finally decided against it: the trouble involved increased the risk that they would be discovered if one or other party had to wait in the darkness.

Twenty yards—and Jackson was beginning to put the tiller over and hissing another order to the oarsmen nearest him. The _Achille_ was now like the side of a huge cliff; her rigging was outlined against the star-filled sky like a fishnet, and the masts stood up like enormous trees, reaching up into the blackness.

Ten yards, and the men on the starboard side tossed their oars. Ramage poised himself, ready to leap upwards at whatever projection would give him a foothold. Still no challenge and, mercifully, still no shooting from astern. In the few seconds before the launch came alongside the French ship he thought how extraordinary it was that she was keeping such a poor lookout.

Then he smelled the stench of rotting seaweed and realized that it had been growing beneath the waterline but had been exposed when the bow had lifted as the ship had run on to the reef. He noticed that the French had not let go an anchor—an indication of how firmly she was wedged. Probably firmly enough to make this boarding quite unnecessary, but one could not be sure.

Then, in a frantic rush, the launch was alongside and he was leaping up, grasping at a loop of rigging and kicking out with his feet to find a foothold. The wood was slippery from the weed but his feet found the edge of a plank that was standing proud. He levered himself upwards, kicking and grasping, until he found he had reached the headrails. He ducked through them and worked his way up to the beak-head bulkhead, conscious just as he reached it that a French voice was shouting a challenge.

Several more men from the launch had managed to scramble up, and were almost alongside him. In fact as he looked below, the whole bow of the ship seemed to be a wriggling mass of men. He stretched up again and got a grip on the marine's walk, the short strip of gangway leading from the fo'c'sle to the bowsprit. Then he swung himself up, kicking and struggling, until he was sprawled on the walk, and a few moments later found himself on the fo'c'sle, only a few feet from the foremast.

By now the French voice was shouting hysterically: it had stopped challenging and was calling out an alarm. Obviously there had been a single lookout forward, and he must have been dozing. Ramage heard a voice answer in the distance and knew it would be only a matter of moments before the men boarding aft would be spotted. The shooting would start any second now, and as he stood upright on the fo'c'sle he wrenched out the pistols from his belt.

He suddenly realized that Jackson, Stafford and Rossi, all puffing from their exertions, were standing beside him at the forebitts, beside the foremast. More men were climbing up the beak-head bulkhead while others were scrambling up on to the marine's walk.

Suddenly there was the rattle of musket fire from aft and shot ricocheted off the mast. "Start those fires!" shouted Ramage, knowing that any moment a barrage of musketry fire could sweep the deck.

Lanterns suddenly appeared and he saw several slowmatches sparkling in the darkness. There was a glow as someone took a candle from a lantern and used it to light a piece of cloth.

Now the musketry fire from aft was closer: the French were advancing along the deck towards them. What had happened to the boarders aft? Just as he wondered, Ramage noticed that some of the muskets and pistols were now aimed aft: at last the rest of the Didos had appeared. They had a far more difficult task than the men boarding over the bow: there was much less to hold on to.

"Come on," Ramage called, "let's get some fires started amidships." He noticed that one of his men was crumpled up on the deck, obviously hit by a musket ball, and then Jackson shouted: "Here they come!"

Ramage just had time to see a group of Frenchmen running along the gangway each side, heading towards them, cutlass blades reflecting in the flash of muskets and pistols. By now many more men, including Gilbert, Louis, Auguste and Albert, had joined him and Ramage led them along the starboard gangway, to meet the French halfway.

The fire from the muskets and pistols had stopped: obviously the French were not going to stop and reload, so now it would be a fight with cutlasses and boarding pikes—except that the Didos had not yet fired their pistols. How many Frenchmen were there? It was difficult to distinguish in the darkness. How many were trying to drive off the Didos attacking from aft? Impossible to say. Perhaps fifty, maybe more. The Didos had the slight temporary advantage that the French would be sleepy, just roused out of their hammocks, but they would soon be wide awake: there was nothing like a few gunshots to get rid of sleepiness.

Ramage cocked the pistols as he ran, cursing as he bumped into various projections which all seemed to have been fitted shin-high. He found himself ahead of the others but heard Jackson shouting at them to hurry.

Then the first of the French were only a few feet away, running towards him, shouting at the tops of their voices. Ramage stopped and raised his pistols, aiming into the midst of the mass. He squeezed the triggers and the twin flash of them firing blinded him momentarily.

And then the French were on him. He threw away the pistols and wrenched his sword from its sheath and at the same time Jackson was alongside him, shouting defiance and slashing with his cutlass. Ramage sliced at a boarding pike jabbing at him and then ducked backwards to avoid a swinging cutlass. There was only the starlight now, apart from the occasional flash of a pistol or musket, and he found himself fighting shadows.

He felt rather than saw a cutlass blade rip his right sleeve and immediately stabbed into the darkness with his sword. He felt the blade entering flesh and heard a shriek of pain. Then behind him he heard a roar as Southwick joined the fight, and Ramage could imagine him twirling his sword two-handed, his white hair flying.

By now more Didos were running along the gangway to join him and the French were halted. He cut at a shadowy Frenchman and heard a grunt as the man collapsed. He recognized a stream of French curses as coming from Auguste and Gilbert. Then he glanced forward for a moment and saw that a small fire had been started by the forebitts and the wind was fanning it.

It was also throwing a flickering light on the Frenchmen, and Ramage jabbed again at a bearded and wild-eyed man who was slashing away with his cutlass with all the abandon of a frenzied axeman chopping at a tree trunk. The man collapsed like a pricked bladder, and Ramage guessed he had been drunk.

There was now a lot of shouting from aft, and Ramage guessed that the Didos who had boarded from aft had now sorted themselves out and were driving the French back so that they could start some fires. Another glance forward showed at least two more fires had been started, one against the beak-head bulkhead and another by the knightheads. And out of the corner of his eye he saw men scrambling up the foreshrouds— the topmen whose job was to start fires aloft among the sails.

All at once the French rallied and fought their way a few feet along the gangway, shouting and slashing with cutlasses. For a minute or two Jackson and his men were driven back, and Ramage and Southwick found themselves fighting side by side, surrounded by Frenchmen. Cutlass clanged against cutlass, men grunted and shouted, and for a moment Ramage thought he and the old master would be overwhelmed, but suddenly Jackson appeared out of the darkness with Rossi, and Stafford, all of them shouting "Dido" at the tops of their voices, to distinguish themselves in the darkness.

By now the flickering of fires forward was lighting up the Frenchmen and Ramage was able to see that there were several bodies lying on the gangway. There was a spurt of pistol fire from aft as the other Didos fired and then attacked with cutlasses and boarding pikes.

How many men were there fighting on the gangways? Ramage estimated about 25 French and the same number of British were fighting on this side, and guessed an equal number were fighting it out on the larboard gangway. But the important thing was that fires were being started: as the French were being held on the gangways, the men were able to set fire to the greased cloths and, any moment now, the sails.

The fire by the forebitts was now big enough to start a glow which lit the underside of the rigging and forecourse; Ramage could make out the belfry and the galley chimney. The fire, he thought grimly, had taken a good hold and beneath it—admittedly many feet away in the bowels of the ship—was the magazine.

Ramage parried a sudden attack from a Frenchman wielding a cutlass like a scythe and slashed him across the throat. Out of the corner of his eye he saw Southwick launch himself at a group of Frenchmen, his great sword jerking in front of him like a flail.

He could again distinguish Jackson, Rossi and Stafford: they had been joined by Gilbert, Louis, Albert, and Auguste, and they were making concentrated attacks where the Frenchmen seemed thickest, keeping up a constant cry of "Dido."

Just then Ramage saw that the great forecourse above his head was now ablaze: the wind was spreading the flames and it was burning like the wick of a gigantic lantern, beginning to throw strong shadows the length of the ship. He watched a burning piece of the sail float down and land on the deck, still aflame. While that was happening flames were running up the rigging from the deck as they got a grip on the tarred rope, and Ramage hoped the topmen would find a way down without burning themselves.

How long would it take the French to realize they were in greater danger from the fires than the boarders? What would they do? Anyone trying to put out fires would be attacked by boarders, yet their attempt to deal with the boarders was failing.

As if to emphasize that, Ramage found the Frenchmen in front of him were being driven back along the gangway: step by step they were going back aft, although soon they would back into their comrades fighting off the Didos who had boarded aft. A quick glance showed at least half a dozen fires were now burning on the fo'c'sle, and the blaze by the forebitts had really taken hold, spreading along the deck-planking. The forebitts themselves were now burning, looking like tree stumps.

If only they could drive the Frenchmen away from the main rigging, so that topmen could get up to set the main course alight. Just as the thought occurred, Ramage saw flames spreading along the mizen topsail—men must have got aloft there as soon as anyone got on board, and with the wind acting as a bellows the flames were spreading rapidly.

Gradually it was getting light on board the *Achille* as flames spread forward and aloft: the wind was freshening, as if allying itself with the British, and Ramage could smell the burning and could see smoke wreathing itself in the flames.

With a desperate howl a group of Frenchmen tried to break through to the fo'c'sle, obviously intent on getting at the fire round the forebitts, but the Didos beat them back, driving them even further aft. By now they were abaft the mainshrouds, and Ramage saw some of his men run from forward, weave their way through the group of men fighting, and scramble hand over hand up the ratlines.

He was just plunging back into the fight when he was startled to see both Jackson and Stafford break away and run forward. Ramage paused a moment to watch them and then saw that they had run to a large piece of blazing foresail, which had just fallen to the deck. Slashing at it with their cutlasses, they sliced away burning sections and spread them out over the deck to start more fires.

By the time Ramage looked aft again to the main course, he saw it was now ablaze and the topmen were scrambling back along the foot-ropes to safety. The wind was spreading the fire and Ramage guessed that the flames would run up the rigging and set the topmast alight.

Both the forecourse and the main course were now well ablaze and the mizen topsail was now burning. He could see the topmen who had set that sail alight now scrambling down the mizen ratlines. The three blazing sails looked like fiery crosses and Ramage imagined what a fine sight they must make from the *Dido:* Aitken and his men would have no doubt about the success of the operation so far.

He could hear the crackling of flames above the shouting and clanging of cutlasses, and wind eddies were now bringing smoke from the burning sails down to deck level. He just had time to ward off a boarding pike wielded by a huge Frenchman and was about to lunge at him with his sword when the man collapsed and a jubilant Orsini, waving a bloodstained cutlass, shouted: "Not many left now!"

Nor were there: the Didos were forcing the Frenchmen aft, past the mainshrouds and into the arms of the men who had boarded from aft: the French were caught in between. And, almost more important, Ramage saw that other Didos following up the boarders were crouching down, setting new fires.

For a moment he thought of the French captain: the man would be in agony, seeing his ship slowly begin to blaze, set on fire by an enemy he could not dislodge. And he must be cursing at having put ashore some of his men: he would now be glad of anyone who could wield a cutlass or stab with a pike.

Southwick was gesticulating aloft and Ramage looked up to see that the great foreyard itself was now on fire, the dry wood obviously set ablaze by the burning canvas. Then he noticed that flames or sparks had set fire to the next sail: the fore-topsail was now beginning to burn.

There were now twenty or more fires burning on the fo'c'sle: the burning sail spread about by Jackson and Stafford had started three or four others, and the original one round the forebitts had spread across twelve feet or more of deck, lapping at the foot of the foremast like flaming waves at a mangrove root.

The fires, Ramage realized, were more than the French could put out without using a fire engine: no buckets would douse the flames. And the fire engine was not on deck: it would take them ten minutes to manhandle it up from below.

Just at that moment the whole main course dropped to the deck as the rope bands burned through along with the gaskets. The blazing mass of canvas blanketed almost the whole width of the ship, and at that moment Ramage knew the ship was doomed: the canvas was a massive torch. The flames lit up the whole ship, and nothing now could save her.

The time had come to save the Didos. Already the French were breaking off the fight and dashing to the blazing sail, wrenching at the unburned parts in a hopeless attempt to pull them clear. But the sail was enormous: it lay across the deck like a sinuous fiery dragon, spurting flame and sparks.

The fires were now crackling like burning bracken, and the *Achille* was lit up as though by a dozen small suns. The Frenchmen who had been fighting on the gangway were now all struggling with the burning sail, and the Didos were watching them.

"Why don't we attack 'em?" bawled Southwick.

"It's time for us to go," Ramage shouted back. "The fires have taken a good hold."

With that he shouted: "Didos—to the boats!"

The nearest men heard him and began to make their way

forward, ready to climb down into the boats. What about the
boarding parties aft—would they be able to see that the forward parties were withdrawing? He could not risk it, and looked
round for Orsini.

"Can you get through to the after parties and tell them to
withdraw? At once!"

"Aye aye, sir," said Orsini, delighted at being given a special
task. There was so much movement amidships that he saw no
difficulty getting through in the confusion.

As he walked forward Ramage was surprised at how successful his men had been in setting fires. Apart from the big
blazes where the foresail had dropped down and round the
forebitts, there were many more smaller ones where flames had
got a firm grip on woodwork. A six-foot section of the bulwark
was now burning fiercely in one place and a twelve-foot section in another. The whole deck was burning at the foot of the
belfry and the galley chimney stood up amid a sea of flames.

The boarders were now climbing down into the boats, and
Ramage reflected on how he had imagined this episode might
have ended: that the French would drive them back into the
boats amid a withering fire of musketry. Instead the men were
boarding with as little concern as they had shown when they
first boarded the boats from the *Dido.*

He and Southwick had looked at the bodies left on the gangway. Five Didos were dead, and he saw that four wounded
were being helped down into the boats. There were many
French dead on the section of the gangway where they had
been fighting. There were more aft. How many of the after
boarding parties had lost their lives?

Finally the last of the men had scrambled off the marine's
walk and the beak-head, and Ramage said to Southwick: "It's
our turn now."

"Not as agile as I was," grunted the old master as he clambered through the headrails, "and this blasted scabbard hooks in everything."

"At least we can see this time," Ramage said. When they had climbed up it had been by the light of the stars, which were often hidden by clouds. Now every detail showed up in the light of the flames. In fact, Ramage thought, they add an urgency to everything: the flames must now be spreading down below, making an octopus-like progress towards the magazine.

And when they reached the magazine, he thought grimly, we all want to be at least half a mile away: the explosion will tear the *Achille* apart and scatter the wreckage like chaff before the wind.

And, as he scrambled into the launch, Jackson giving him a helping hand, he realized the wind had freshened: the boats were pitching and rolling as the waves hit the *Achille* and swirled back. A wind . . . the bellows that would spread all those fires. He glanced up and was startled at the view from this angle: the burning sails were making great crosses of fire, and the fore-yard was well ablaze. Any moment the slings and jeers would burn through and it would come crashing down, like the gates of hell opening.

The gates of hell . . . he had thought of that because the whole scene was unreal. Now the *Achille* was mottled with so many fires that even if they had a couple of fire engines working, as well as all the deckwash pumps, they could never control half of them.

"Shove off," Ramage ordered Jackson, and he commented to Southwick, who was alongside him in the pinnace: "It's a terrible sight."

"Aye, it is that. The French captain must be going mad—he hasn't even got the fire engine on deck."

"He never expected an attack like this. He didn't even expect boarders, judging from the lack of sentries."

"What did he expect us to do—stay on board playing cards and drinking gin?"

"Apparently," Ramage said with a grin. "I think he made the mistake of thinking that because he was stuck on a rock then we wouldn't make a move, either. Or else—more than likely— he knows his ship is finished and assumed we knew, so that we wouldn't try anything."

"You mean we might have done all this—" Southwick waved towards the burning ship, "—for nothing?"

"It's a possibility," Ramage said. "But it wasn't a risk I could take. It seemed to me that fetching shipwrights from Fort Royal, apart from using their own carpenters, could put the ship to rights and she could be towed off. And that's what the admiral would think."

"Well, we've made a thorough job of it. Ah, there are some boats—one, two, three. The after boarding party has got away. Just look how those flames are lighting up the *Dido!*"

By now, as the launch and pinnace were rowed back, the 74 showed up in the darkness as though someone was shining a huge lantern on her: the sails seemed luminous and the rigging showed up like netting, the bowsprit and jib-boom jutting out like a vast fishing rod.

Jackson steered the launch back to the *Dido,* with the other boats following, and soon Ramage was climbing back on board. Once on deck he turned to look at the *Achille* and she was a terrible sight: most striking were the yards, all of which had now caught fire, and all the rigging staying the masts was burning as thin red lines pointing up into the sky. The whole of the fo'c'sle now seemed ablaze and there was a big fire amidships, where the main course had fallen.

278 : RAMAGE

In the light of the flames he could just distinguish the other three boats approaching the *Dido,* the blades of the oars flashing as they were lifted out of the water. How many casualties had there been among the after boarding parties? He only hoped Orsini was safe.

"A terrible sight, sir," said Aitken, who had been waiting at the entry port. "You made a perfect job of it."

"Yes, they can't save her now. The wind freshened at just the right moment—it was as though we had a thousand bellows at work."

"Many casualties, sir?"

"Five dead in our party and four wounded. We left the dead on board. I'll give you their names presently."

The other three boats were soon alongside and the excited Kenton was the first on board, his face twisting into a delighted smile as he greeted Ramage. "Well, you got your end burning first, sir, but we soon caught up!"

"How many men did you lose?" Ramage asked soberly.

"Seven dead and five wounded, sir."

"Is Orsini with you?"

"Yes, sir, he's helping get the wounded on board."

At that moment Kenton turned and looked at the *Achille,* seeing her clearly for the first time from the height of the *Dido's* deck. "Ye Gods, just look at her. Those masts and yards, they look like great crosses—burning on her grave."

The four officers stood and watched, silenced by the sheer horror of what they were seeing. Finally Southwick said: "Her magazine will go up any minute now."

The words were hardly out of his mouth before the flaming mass of ship suddenly disintegrated and there was a gigantic thunderclap which almost stunned them. Blazing yards, burning beams, deck-planks and futtocks were hurled up into the sky, curving down in precise parabolas. The flash of the explosion had blinded them all for several moments, and then the night seemed blacker than ever, with just the memory of what they had seen burned deeply into their minds. It was a sight, Ramage realized, that he would never forget.

CHAPTER   TWENTY - TWO

THE *Scourge* met them off Diamond Rock soon after noon and both ships hove-to while Hill came on board to report on his trip to Barbados. First of all he handed over a sealed packet from the admiral, then he said delightedly: "The admiral is buying the *Sirène* and all the merchant ships have been condemned in the prize-court in Bridgetown: they held a special hearing so that I could give evidence. By the way, what happened to the *Achille,* sir?"

"We blew her up during the night," Ramage said shortly.

"Thank goodness for that," Hill exclaimed. "The admiral was very worried about her: he thought the French might repair her and get her off. He wouldn't be persuaded, even though I did my best to tell him how firmly she was wedged on that reef."

"Well, now she's floating in tiny pieces off Pointe des Nègres and the French have no ships-of-war in Fort Royal."

"That'll cheer up the admiral even more, sir," Hill said. "He was delighted about the convoy—but he'll be telling you all about that in his letter, I expect."

"Yes, I'll go below and read it. Now, you had better start getting your prize-crews back on board here. You must have been crowded in the *Scourge.*"

"It's not far from Barbados, and most of the men have been sleeping on deck. I think they've enjoyed their cruise!"

In his cabin Ramage sat down at his desk and slit open the letter from the admiral. It was a long letter and started off, after the usual preliminaries, with congratulating Ramage on capturing the *Sirène* and the convoy. He was buying in the *Sirène* and the prize-court had condemned all the merchantmen. But he was worried, he wrote, about the *Achille*. Ramage was to take immediate steps to make her unseaworthy, either by gunfire or some other means. The important thing was that the French should not have the use of a ship of the line at Fort Royal. Having accomplished that, Cameron continued, Ramage should return to Barbados without loss of time to take part in another operation of considerable importance.

An operation of "considerable importance"—what could that be? Stopping the convoy getting into Martinique was, he would have thought, just such an operation. What else was there going on in the Windward Islands that needed a ship of the line? At least the admiral was not still short of frigates—he had just received the *Alerte* and the *Sirène,* and the *Volage* with her mango plants, which should have cheered him up, apart from allowing him to promote a lot of his favourite young officers. A commander-in-chief, he thought, was in a happy position. First of all, he could send his favourite frigate captains out cruising in the best areas for capturing prizes. Then he collected his share of the prize-money from every capture. After that he could promote favourites into the prizes, if he bought them into the king's service. If you were a young lieutenant, Ramage thought cynically, the way to rapid promotion lay in becoming a commander-in-chief's favourite . . .

He folded up the letter and called for Luckhurst to copy it into the letter book. He then walked through to the sick bay to talk to Bowen and see the men wounded the previous night. Bowen was his usual cheerful self and reported: "All the patients are doing well. Four of them will be back on duty in a week. The rest I'll have to keep a bit longer."

"The first time you have had any work to do for days," Ramage said teasingly.

"You'd be the first to complain if I had many on the sick list," Bowen said. "So far we've been lucky. Only gunshot wounds. Let's be thankful we haven't had a visit from the black vomit."

"I say a prayer of thanks every day," Ramage said soberly.

He went on deck to find that the last of the Didos were coming back on board from the *Scourge,* and he told Orsini: "Give Mr Bennett a hail and tell him to come on board."

The brig would have to be left behind, continuing her lonely patrol off Fort Royal, but it was necessary to give Lieutenant Bennett his orders. The next few weeks were going to be dull for him, compared to the past week or so that the *Dido* had been around, but the young lieutenant had seen one of his former enemies, the *Alerte,* captured, and had arrived back just too late to see the other one blown up.

Ramage turned to find the chaplain, Brewster, gossiping with the purser. Jeremiah Clapton was also a tubby man, with spectacles and a large, bulbous nose, that made him look like a heavy drinker, which was unfair because he did not drink at all.

"I was just remarking to Mr Clapton that we have left our mark on Martinique," Brewster said.

"Yes, and we've been lucky that Martinique has not left its mark on us, apart from a few men in the sick bay."

"I've never heard of a ship of the line being boarded with so few casualties, sir," Brewster said admiringly. "And that frigate, too."

"I've never judged the success of anything by the size of the butcher's bill," Ramage said shortly. "On the contrary. The more one can achieve with the minimum of casualties, the happier I am."

"I'm afraid Their Lordships don't always see it that way," Brewster said. "They seem to honour those captains who lose half their ships' companies in some enterprise."

This was not a subject that a captain of a ship of the line should be discussing with the chaplain and purser, Ramage decided, and waved to Aitken, who was just crossing the quarterdeck. "As soon as I've given Bennett his orders we shall be leaving for Barbados," he said. "Have the boats hoisted in."

Bennett seemed to have mixed feelings about his orders. Ramage felt that the young lieutenant had enjoyed working with the *Dido*, and saw the immediate future patrolling off Fort Royal as a time of boredom, since there were no enemy ships-of-war to watch. His job now would be catching the odd drogher making her way up and down the coast, with cargoes no more exciting than barrels of molasses, and occasionally a bale of hides.

Finally the *Scourge* got under way and turned north, and the *Dido* made sail to the southwards, gradually hauling round to stretch south-eastward round Cabrit Island and out into the Atlantic to make for Barbados, which was stationed like a lonely sentinel, guarding the chain of islands.

Rear-Admiral Samuel Cameron was in a cheerful mood when Ramage went on board the *Reliant* in Carlisle Bay, Barbados. At first he was cautious, knowing that Ramage could have only just received his orders, sent in the *Scourge*, to destroy the *Achille*, but he was delighted when he was told that the French 74 had been destroyed even before the orders had arrived.

"Well, Ramage, I must congratulate you: one 74 destroyed, three frigates captured and a veritable fleet of merchantmen taken. By the way, I have bought in the frigates—they are being valued at this minute."

"I am fortunate in having a good ship's company, sir. Many of them have been serving with me for years."

"Yes, well, I am looking for someone to command one of the frigates—the *Sirène*. The only suitable man I had, I've given the *Alerte*. What about your first lieutenant?"

"Aitken. He would be an excellent choice, sir."

But Ramage's heart sank. Under Aitken, the *Dido* was run like a ticking clock. Years ago Aitken had refused promotion to post captain because he said he wanted to continue serving longer with Ramage. But now, if one was honest about it, the time had come when Aitken deserved to be made post, whatever his feelings might be. Yet the loss to the *Dido* would be considerable: he was cheerful and thoughtful, hardworking and reliable. He was, Ramage knew, as good a first lieutenant as a captain could hope to find. But a good first lieutenant deserved a good captain, and a good captain did not stand in the way of promotion which was both deserved and overdue.

"Aitken, eh? A Scot? And you recommend him?"

"Most highly, sir, although I'll be very sorry to lose him."

"Well, that's settled then: I'll make him post and give him the ship. It'll all have to be confirmed by the Admiralty, but that'll only be a formality. How does that leave you in the *Dido*?"

"I'll just move everyone up a place, sir. My second lieutenant, Kenton will make a good first lieutenant. My third, Martin, will be a good second. My fourth lieutenant, Hill, whom you met when he brought in the prizes, will make a good third. I'd like to make a master's mate the acting fourth lieutenant,

sir. Indeed, will you be assembling a board for examining lieutenants? This master's mate, by the name of Orsini, is about
ready to take the examination."

Cameron grunted and made a note on a sheet of paper. "Yes,
I have three or four midshipmen ready for the examination too:
your youngster can take it with them. I'll call the Board for
next Wednesday—you won't be sailing before then."

The admiral leaned forward and handed Ramage a folded
sheet of paper which was covered in neat, copperplate handwriting. "Read this. My clerk has just finished copying it out.
It is my letter to Their Lordships about your Martinique operation."

Ramage took the letter and read it quickly, conscious that
the admiral was watching him keenly. It was very flattering;
quite the most flattering despatch he had ever read, in fact.

"I'll be enclosing your letter as well, of course," the admiral
said, "which means it will be a *Gazette* letter. Not your first, I
know, but it all helps!"

"Thank you, sir: I appreciate it," Ramage said, and thought
to himself, this has been quite an eventful quarter of an hour:
I've lost my first lieutenant, started Paolo off on the first steps
to being a lieutenant, and had my despatch to the admiral
almost certainly made into a *Gazette* letter, which will please
father, who has saved all my *Gazette* letters so far. And it will
please Sarah, too: Father will make sure she gets a copy and
appreciates the significance.

But the fact is, Ramage thought grimly, I still don't know
what the admiral has in store for me.

More Action, More Adventure, More Angst . . .

This is no time to stand down! McBooks Press, the leader in nautical fiction, invites you to embark on more sea adventures and take part in gripping naval action with Douglas Reeman, Dudley Pope, and a host of other nautical writers. Sail to Trafalgar, Grenada, Copenhagen—to famous battles and unknown skirmishes alike—and find out why nautical fiction is the next best thing since sliced bread with weevils.

All the titles below are available at bookstores. For a free catalog, or to order direct, call toll-free 1-888-BOOKS-11 (1-888-266-5711). Or visit the McBooks website, www.mcbooks.com, for special offers and to read excerpts from McBooks titles.

ALEXANDER KENT
The Bolitho Novels

___ 1 Midshipman Bolitho
    0-935526-41-2 • 240 pp., $13.95

___ 2 Stand Into Danger
    0-935526-42-0 • 288 pp., $13.95

___ 3 In Gallant Company
    0-935526-43-9 • 320 pp., $14.95

___ 4 Sloop of War
    0-935526-48-X • 352 pp., $14.95

___ 5 To Glory We Steer
    0-935526-49-8 • 352 pp., $14.95

___ 6 Command a King's Ship
    0-935526-50-1 • 352 pp., $14.95

___ 7 Passage to Mutiny
    0-935526-58-7 • 352 pp., $15.95

___ 8 With All Despatch
    0-935526-61-7 • 320 pp., $14.95

___ 9 Form Line of Battle!
    0-935526-59-5 • 352 pp., $14.95

___ 10 Enemy in Sight!
    0-935526-60-9 • 368 pp., $14.95

___ 11 The Flag Captain
    0-935526-66-8 • 384 pp., $15.95

___ 12 Signal – Close Action!
    0-935526-67-6 • 368 pp., $15.95

___ 13 The Inshore Squadron
    0-935526-68-4 • 288 pp., $13.95

___ 14 A Tradition of Victory
    0-935526-70-6 • 304 pp., $14.95

___ 15 Success to the Brave
    0-935526-71-4 • 288 pp., $13.95

___ 16 Colours Aloft!
    0-935526-72-2 • 304 pp., $14.95

___ 17 Honour This Day
    0-935526-73-0 • 320 pp., $15.95

___ 18 The Only Victor
    0-935526-74-9 • 384 pp., $15.95

___ 19 Beyond the Reef
    0-935526-82-X • 352 pp., $14.95

___ 20 The Darkening Sea
    0-935526-83-8 • 352 pp., $15.95

___ 21 For My Country's Freedom
    0-935526-84-6 • 304 pp., $15.95

___ 22 Cross of St George
    0-935526-92-7 • 320 pp., $16.95

___ 23 Sword of Honour
    0-935526-93-5 • 320 pp., $15.95

___ 24 Second to None
    0-935526-94-3 • 352 pp., $16.95

___ 25 Relentless Pursuit
    1-59013-026-X • 368 pp., $16.95

___ 26 Man of War
    1-59013-091-X • 320 pp., $16.95

___ 26 Man of War
    1-59013-066-9 • 320 pp., $24.95 HC

DOUGLAS REEMAN
Modern Naval Fiction Library

___ Twelve Seconds to Live
    1-59013-044-8 • 368 pp., $15.95

___ Battlecruiser
    1-59013-043-X • 320 pp., $15.95

___ The White Guns
    1-59013-083-9 • 368 pp., $15.95

Royal Marines Saga

___ 1 Badge of Glory
    1-59013-013-8 • 384 pp., $16.95

___ 2 The First to Land
    1-59013-014-6 • 304 pp., $15.95

___ 3 The Horizon
    1-59013-027-8 • 368 pp., $15.95

___ 4 Dust on the Sea
    1-59013-028-6 • 384 pp., $15.95

continues . . .

DUDLEY POPE
The Lord Ramage Novels

___ 1 Ramage
    0-935526-76-5 • 320 pp., $14.95
___ 2 Ramage & the Drumbeat
    0-935526-77-3 • 288 pp., $14.95
___ 3 Ramage & the Freebooters
    0-935526-78-1 • 384 pp., $15.95
___ 4 Governor Ramage R. N.
    0-935526-79-X • 384 pp., $15.95
___ 5 Ramage's Prize
    0-935526-80-3 • 320 pp., $15.95
___ 6 Ramage & the Guillotine
    0-935526-81-1• 320 pp., $14.95
___ 7 Ramage's Diamond
    0-935526-89-7 • 336 pp., $15.95
___ 8 Ramage's Mutiny
    0-935526-90-0 • 280 pp., $14.95
___ 9 Ramage & the Rebels
    0-935526-91-9 • 320 pp., $15.95
___ 10 The Ramage Touch
    1-59013-007-3 • 272 pp., $15.95
___ 11 Ramage's Signal
    1-59013-008-1 • 288 pp., $15.95
___ 12 Ramage & the Renegades
    1-59013-009-X • 320 pp., $15.95
___ 13 Ramage's Devil
    1-59013-010-3 • 320 pp., $15.95
___ 14 Ramage's Trial
    1-59013-011-1 • 320 pp., $15.95
___ 15 Ramage's Challenge
    1-59013-012-X • 352 pp., $15.95
___ 16 Ramage at Trafalgar
    1-59013-022-7 • 256 pp., $14.95
___ 17 Ramage & the Saracens
    1-59013-023-5 • 304 pp., $15.95
___ 18 Ramage & the Dido
    1-59013-024-3 • 272 pp., $15.95

DEWEY LAMBDIN
Alan Lewie Naval Adventures

___ 2 The French Admiral
    1-59013-021-9 • 448 pp., $17.95˙
___ 8 Jester's Fortune
    1-59013-034-0 • 432 pp., $17.95

JAMES L. NELSON
___The Only Life That Mattered
    1-59013-060-X • 416 pp., $16.95

ALEXANDER FULLERTON
The Nicholas Everard WWII Saga

___ 1 Storm Force to Narvik
    1-59013-092-8 • 256 pp., $13.95

PHILIP McCUTCHAN
The Halfhyde Adventures

___1 Halfhyde at the Bight of Benin
    1-59013-078-2 • 224 pp., $13.95
___2 Halfhyde's Island
    1-59013-079-0 • 224 pp., $13.95
___3 Halfhyde and the Guns of Arrest
    1-59013-067-7 • 256 pp., $13.95
___4 Halfhyde to the Narrows
    1-59013-068-5 • 240 pp., $13.95

DAVID DONACHIE
The Privateersman Mysteries

___ 1 The Devil's Own Luck
    1-59013-004-9 • 302 pp., $15.95
    1-59013-003-0 • 320 pp., $23.95 HC
___ 2 The Dying Trade
    1-59013-006-5 • 384 pp., $16.95
    1-59013-005-7 • 400 pp., $24.95 HC
___ 3 A Hanging Matter
    1-59013-016-2 • 416 pp., $16.95
___ 4 An Element of Chance
    1-59013-017-0 • 448 pp., $17.95
___ 5 The Scent of Betrayal
    1-59013-031-6 • 448 pp., $17.95
___ 6 A Game of Bones
    1-59013-032-4 • 352 pp., $15.95

The Nelson & Emma Trilogy

___ 1 On a Making Tide
    1-59013-041-3 • 416 pp., $17.95
___ 2 Tested by Fate
    1-59013-042-1 • 416 pp., $17.95
___ 3 Breaking the Line
    1-59013-090-1 • 384 pp., $16.95

JAN NEEDLE
Sea Officer William Bentley Novels

___ 1 A Fine Boy for Killing
    0-935526-86-2 • 320 pp., $15.95
___ 2 The Wicked Trade
    0-935526-95-1 • 384 pp., $16.95
___ 3 The Spithead Nymph
    1-59013-077-4 • 288 pp., $14.95

C. NORTHCOTE PARKINSON
The Richard Delancey Novels

___ 1 The Guernseyman
 1-59013-001-4 • 208 pp., $13.95

___ 2 Devil to Pay
 1-59013-002-2 • 288 pp., $14.95

___ 3 The Fireship
 1-59013-015-4 • 208 pp., $13.95

___ 4 Touch and Go
 1-59013-025-1 • 224 pp., $13.95

___ 5 So Near So Far
 1-59013-037-5 • 224 pp., $13.95

___ 6 Dead Reckoning
 1-59013-038-3 • 224 pp., $15.95

V.A. STUART
Alexander Sheridan Adventures

___ 1 Victors and Lords
 0-935526-98-6 • 272 pp., $13.95

___ 2 The Sepoy Mutiny
 0-935526-99-4 • 240 pp., $13.95

___ 3 Massacre at Cawnpore
 1-59013-019-7 • 240 pp., $13.95

___ 4 The Cannons of Lucknow
 1-59013-029-4 • 272 pp., $14.95

___ 5 The Heroic Garrison
 1-59013-030-8 • 256 pp., $13.95

The Phillip Hazard Novels

___ 1 The Valiant Sailors
 1-59013-039-1 • 272 pp., $14.95

___ 2 The Brave Captains
 1-59013-040-5 • 272 pp., $14.95

___ 3 Hazard's Command
 1-59013-081-2 • 256 pp., $13.95

___ 4 Hazard of Huntress
 1-59013-082-0 • 256 pp., $13.95

___ 5 Hazard in Circassia
 1-59013-062-6 • 256 pp., $13.95

___ 6 Victory at Sebastopol
 1-59013-061-8 • 224 pp., $13.95

NICHOLAS NICASTRO
The John Paul Jones Trilogy

___ 1 The Eighteenth Captain
 0-935526-54-4 • 312 pp., $16.95

___ 2 Between Two Fires
 1-59013-033-2 • 384 pp., $16.95

Military Fiction Classics

R.F. DELDERFIELD
___ Seven Men of Gascony
 0-935526-97-8 • 368 pp., $16.95

___ Too Few for Drums
 0-935526-96-X • 256 pp., $14.95

Classics of Nautical Fiction

CAPTAIN FREDERICK MARRYAT
___ Frank Mildmay OR
 The Naval Officer
 0-935526-39-0 • 352 pp., $14.95

___ The King's Own
 0-935526-56-0 • 384 pp., $15.95

___ Mr Midshipman Easy
 0-935526-40-4 • 352 pp., $14.95

___ Newton Forster OR
 The Merchant Service
 0-935526-44-7 • 352 pp., $13.95

___ Snarleyyow OR The Dog Fiend
 0-935526-64-1 • 384 pp., $16.95

___ The Phantom Ship
 0-935526-85-4 • 320 pp., $14.95

___ The Privateersman
 0-935526-69-2 • 288 pp., $15.95

RAFAEL SABATINI
___ Captain Blood
 0-935526-45-5 • 288 pp., $15.95

WILLIAM CLARK RUSSELL
___ The Yarn of Old Harbour Town
 0-935526-65-X • 256 pp., $14.95

___ The Wreck of the Grosvenor
 0-935526-52-8 • 320 pp., $13.95

A.D. HOWDEN SMITH
___ Porto Bello Gold
 0-935526-57-9 • 288 pp., $13.95

MICHAEL SCOTT
___ Tom Cringle's Log
 0-935526-51-X • 512 pp., $14.95